D0170140

Praise for
Karen Winters Schwartz's
Where Are the Cocoa Puffs?
A Family's Journey Through Bipolar Disorder

Where Are the Cocoa Puffs? is an engaging family story of what happens when the eighteen-year-old daughter develops bipolar disorder. It is very well written and accurately reflects the effects of this disorder on all members of the family. Strongly recommended.

> – E. Fuller Torrey, M.D., author of *Surviving Schizophrenia* and
> *Surviving Manic Depression*

Where Are the Cocoa Puffs? is a coming of age story. It provides an authentic look at a teenager, her family, and friends who struggle to come to terms with the onset of her mental illness and to find a balance between hope and acceptance. Read it for its own sake. Read it to learn. It speaks to many truths.

> – Michael J. Fitzpatrick, MSW Executive Director, NAMI National

Fasten your seat belt as you're drawn into the Benson family's desperate struggle to manage their eighteen-year-old daughter's terrifying plunge into a world where the line between rationality and madness is often blurred—the world of bipolar disorder. I highly recommend this book. It will challenge, educate, and most importantly, it will inspire you.

> – Dr. Joseph J. Luciani, bestselling author of *Self-Coaching:*
> *The Powerful Program to Beat Anxiety & Depression*

Welcome to the world of mental illness. This emotionally raw novel pulls you into the belly of the beast — in this case, into the chaos of the Benson family, where survival and sanity hang by a thread. There is no escape; it feels like you are part of the family. Ultimately, this is a love story. It's about the love that binds a family together in the midst of dealing with everything that threatens to pull them apart. Very highly recommended!

–Alan Gettis, Ph.D., author of the award-winning book *The Happiness Solution: Finding Joy & Meaning in an Upside Down World*

What would it be like to be part of a family in which the teenage daughter begins to exhibit wild mood swings that are finally diagnosed as bipolar disorder? By entering the interiors of this young woman, her mother, father, sister, and boyfriend, Karen Winters Schwartz's novel *Where Are the Cocoa Puffs?* takes the reader on that roller coaster with insight and sympathy for all. Spending time with this family will be a comfort to those who have had similar experiences and it will deepen the compassion of those who haven't. The novel accurately portrays the complexities and strain of living with someone who has a mental illness, but it also offers hope as a result of the medical world's increasing understanding of biochemical imbalances in the brain.

–Ginnah Howard, author of *Night Navigation*

Where Are the Cocoa Puffs? is a tragic tale of a family besieged by perhaps the most insidious of all diseases. It is one of those rare reads that can teach us something about the trials faced by those attempting to live with or support loved ones with mental illness, while also teaching us something about ourselves. It is a story of betrayal and anguish, of coming to terms with loss and accepting alternatives all of us should pray we never suffer. If you already know how arduous living with mental disorders can be, you owe it to the author to read this book.

She has given your cause a beautiful voice—a fine example of the perseverance and will required to love someone so afflicted. But if you only think you know the trials and tribulations endured by those poor souls, you owe this read to yourself.

    –Donald R. Dempsey, author of *Betty's Child*

where are the cocoa puffs?

a family's journey
through bipolar disorder

a novel by
Karen Winters Schwartz

GB

GOODMAN BECK PUBLISHING

Copyright © 2010 by Karen Winters Schwartz
All rights reserved.

No part of this publication may be reproduced, stored in a retrieval system, or
transmitted, in any form or by any means, electronic, mechanical, photocopying,
recording, or otherwise, without the express written consent of the publisher.

GOODMAN BECK PUBLISHING

PO Box 253
Norwood, NJ 07648
www.goodmanbeck.com

The characters and events in this book are fictitious. Any similarity to real
persons, living or dead, is coincidental and not intended by the author.

ISBN 978-0-9798755-6-4

Library of Congress Control Number: 2010936932

Printed in the United States of America

10 9 8 7 6 5 4 3 2 1

For parents everywhere.
Let go of your preconceived dreams
and allow your children to fly.

1

"I'm getting a tattoo," Amanda announced as if she were referring to her fall wardrobe. Carol's eyes met Jerry's across the dining room, and with a look she deferred to him. He put down his fork and swallowed the beef he'd been chewing sooner than he might have wanted to. "Is that so?" he finally managed to say. His words came out light, almost pleasant. He was impressed with himself. It was best not to overreact.

"Maybe a large dragon across my back." Amanda swung her head so that her back was made free of her long dark hair, making it easy to see the possibility of a steaming nostril, a curved claw. Jerry saw Carol's face whiten just a bit.

"Cool," offered fifteen-year-old Christy.

"Absolutely not!" Carol's voice held no pleasantry.

Amanda's eyes grew dark as they flashed her mother's way, squinting with hatred. Carol met her look, and Jerry felt a shiver creep across his neck.

There was the sharp ping of Amanda's fork as she freed it from her grasp and it fell rudely against her plate. "*You* can't stop me! I'm eighteen now. I do what I want!" She gave her mother a look that equaled a thousand *screw you*s.

"Amanda!" Jerry's voice came out harsh and daunting, his own fork dangling precariously from his fingers. He was about to throw out the as-long-as-you-live-in-this-house cliché, but Amanda's face had crumpled into agony; and before he had the chance to speak, she was fleeing from the room, the imaginary dragon wings beating fast, as if her very life depended on the flight.

The three remaining members of the family glanced glumly at one another. Christy shrugged and went back to her food. Jerry's eyes lingered a bit on his wife and a small sadness crossed between them. Carol set her fork gently on her plate and pushed it slightly away. She was done with food for the night. Jerry closed his eyes and sighed deeply. There was no thought of going after her; they had been trained and finally learned that it always made matters worse.

This was nothing more or nothing less than what a typical meal had become.

~

Amanda slammed her bedroom door and flung herself onto her bed. She hated them! She hated them all! Her heart was beating madly, banging against her chest. She could hear it quite clearly. It was almost a pleasant sensation, her body bursting out from within. But she could not stay on the bed with her body bursting as it was. She grabbed her purse and cranked open her bedroom window as far as it would go. She wiggled her slight body—feet first and stomach against the window jam—through the small vertical opening. Her feet searched blindly through the night air for solidness before finally locating the overhanging roof of the porch below. This was her favorite part of the escape, the flinging motion she had to make to ensure her body landed on the roof and didn't sail toward the earth. And when it was done and she sat securely on the small roof, she smiled as her bursting body calmed. The next step was easier as she walked lightly to the corner, grabbing the rafter of the main roof and using her super-woman forces to lift herself up and onto the roof of the main house.

The air was cool; the sky was clear. These were the soft days of late

September. The smell of autumn mingled with tar as she arranged herself against the slant of the roof, the rough shingles rubbing through her thin tee shirt. Soon the smell of fall was made all the sweeter by the exhale of weed as she blew it gently from her lungs. She closed her eyes briefly as her mind thankfully slowed. Her body withdrew and sailed beyond the autumn leaves that rocked gently from the branches hanging over the house into the amazing stars that danced before her eyes.

~

The ball went zinging past Jerry's head; he had barely escaped collision. He jumped forward and twisted as the racquetball ricocheted off the back wall. An astounding movement for fifty-three, but not astounding enough—he couldn't make the connection and the point went to his brother.

Tom flashed him a smile of victory. "Take that, old man!"

Jerry bent over, resting his hands on his knees. He was breathing too hard to respond. His light brown hair, wet with sweat, was dripping into his eyes. Jerry pushed up his glasses with a finger then wiped at the sweat with the back of his hand. Whose idea had this been? This was a hell of a way to spend a lunch hour. He looked at Tom and was grateful that his brother was also breathing hard, his own stock of thick brown hair wet and his face beet red.

Tom slid to the floor and feebly raised his hands in triumph. Jerry laughed. "We are too old for this shit," Tom said. "It's an invitation to a heart attack."

"I won't argue with that," Jerry managed to get out as he made his way to his water bottle in the corner of the court. He slipped to the floor in relief and rested his back against the wall. Then he reached over and picked up Tom's water bottle and rolled it neatly to him. Tom captured it easily and brought the tip to his lips, closing his eyes in pleasure as the cool liquid soothed his throat.

After a moment of silent hydration, Tom asked hopefully, "We done?" Jerry nodded his head. "Thank God," sighed Tom.

Tom was fifty-one, a couple inches taller than Jerry and in decidedly better shape, but he'd let himself soften a bit this last year. They both had. This was their first attempt at remedying that. Pathetic really; they had the court for an hour and it was barely at the thirty-minute mark. Jesus! How had he let himself get so old? It must stop immediately! "Can you play again Friday?" he demanded.

Jerry, who had been leaning the back of his head lazily against the wall, opened his eyes and looked at Tom a bit desperately. "Really? So soon?"

Tom shrugged; he could be easily dissuaded.

Jerry mimicked his brother's shrug. "I guess so."

Tom nodded with resignation. "Friday then." He left his racquet and scooted to the wall a few feet from Jerry. They sat a minute, catching their breath, the normal color returning to their faces.

Jerry finally broke the silence. "How are things at work?"

"Oh … well, just about as exciting as things can get in an accounting firm."

Jerry rolled his eyes good-naturedly and shook his head slightly. He knew Tom really wasn't all that dissatisfied with his profession. "And the family?"

"Pain in the ass as always," Tom smiled.

Married now for twenty-eight years, he and Sarah had certainly had their problems—most of them Tom's doing—but Jerry knew they were happy. Their three boys, all grown now, were Tom's biggest source of pride. And Tom had every reason to be proud; they were all good boys. Sure there were wrecked cars, drunken parties, brushes with the law, fist fights, and tears, but they were all still alive, not in jail, and fully-functioning citizens—for the most part.

"I just have to get David out of my house and things will be perfect!"

"He's still taking classes at SCCC?"

Tom nodded glumly. "Doesn't know what the hell he wants to do except eat my food and leave his crap all over the house."

"How's Matt like his new job?" Jerry asked. Matt was twenty-five, the oldest and most difficult of Tom's three sons. He was gone now, thankfully, living in New York City and working in advertising. Tom shrugged his shoulders. "Can you believe it? Now he says he may go back to school to study graphic design! As long as it's not on my dollar, I don't care." Tom picked up his water and took another drink.

Jerry considered asking about Casey, who'd just attained his teaching certification and was searching for a permanent teaching position in Binghamton, but changed his mind. He was waiting for Tom to ask him about his family, and when it became clear that it wasn't going to occur, Jerry said, "Amanda's been especially difficult lately."

"Well, she's always been difficult," Tom said in his typical flippant way. Even though Jerry knew he was correct, it wasn't the same as if he had said it. He felt the sting of hurt and a need to defend his daughter. He put aside the need and sighed.

"This is different," Jerry said softly.

Tom looked at Jerry, once again proving he wasn't a total ass. "How so?" There was a hint of concern in his voice.

Jerry shook his head slightly. "I don't know. She's just so ... angry."

Tom nodded his head with understanding. "Teenagers are angry creatures. And this is an especially hard time to be a teenager. Not like when we were growing up—a lot more pressure."

Of course Jerry knew all that and more or less agreed. But if anyone had had a right to be angry teenagers, it would have been the two of them—an abusive drunkard father who left them when they were small, a mentally unstable mother. How many times had he come home from school bursting with some sort of news only to find his mother unavailable? She was always busy at her one and only hobby: TV, the frenzied mania of after-school cartoons blasting through the room. It might have been funny, the sight of a grown woman so totally engrossed in Loony Tune drama, if it weren't just so damn sad. It was no wonder they'd ended up with the names Tom and Jerry—just one more childhood ribbing to endure. (At least Jerry was the smarter of the two.) But really all he could remember was the determination to make something of his life—of their lives. He didn't remember anger. Why was it harder now for his kids? Maybe they had too much—too many choices.

"Senior year was always the worst with all three of the boys," Tom continued. "You remember the three of them wanting to spread their crazy adolescent wings, knocking everything over in the process? About drove Sarah and me crazy. I don't envy you, Jerry."

Yes, adolescent behavior—you could read a hundred books on the subject, watch documentaries, even work directly with other people's kids, but nothing—no nothing—could prepare you for actually living with these creatures. Jerry knew all about adolescent behavior. It had been a major area of study during his residency in psychiatry. In fact, he still dealt with it almost on a daily basis—the departure from norm, the diagnosis slipping to abnormal and then into serious mental illness, falling into his specialty of major mood and thought disorders. He saw these troubled kids and it wasn't often so black and white. But they were talking about Amanda now. Normal adolescent behavior—did it have to be so hard?

"We can't even get her to talk about colleges, much less actually visit one. The deadlines are coming up quickly," Jerry told Tom. "I think Carol may actually put in the general SUNY application online herself."

"She's always been a great student, always succeeded," Tom assured him. "Amanda won't have any problems getting in somewhere, even if it's last-minute." He smiled with nostalgia, "Jesus, even my kids got into colleges and they were as dumb as rocks, especially in high school!"

Jerry laughed, and the laughter felt good. Tom was right. His kids were dumb as rocks and they were doing okay. Amanda was a straight-A student. She had grown into an amazing, beautiful young woman. He felt a rush of love for her. She had tons of friends, her teachers loved her. Hatred of her parents did not equal failure.

"Trust me, Jerry. She'll be fine." Jerry nodded grimly at his brother and couldn't help but laugh again as Tom added, "Just remember, any possibility of easily hiding her body has long passed—there's so much less digging, chopping, whatever, with a baby! Hell, at this point, you'd spend more time in jail than the time it takes her to reach full adulthood."

~

Amanda slipped into the car. "Hurry," she said, slamming the door and looking around with excited nervousness. "Get the fuck out of here!" she shrieked with laughter. With that, Ryan put the car in drive, jerking them forward then back against the seats as they made their getaway in his little beat-up Jetta. Once out of the school zone and safely on the road, Amanda sat back against the car seat, shoving several empty fast food bags and cups out of the way to make more room for her feet. She opened the glove compartment and pulled out the pack of cigarettes she'd hoped would be there. She offered one to Ryan, who shook his head *no* and brushed his crazy dark rocker bangs out of his eyes. She shrugged a bit as she took one for herself and lit it with the lighter tucked into the pack. "Thanks," she said. "I just had to get out of there."

"No problem." He flashed his brilliant smile her way and turned back to the road. "Where to?"

"Don't care," Amanda said.

He turned onto the main drag of Niskayuna, heading toward Albany. Amanda flipped through his collection of CDs and changed the classic rock mix that was playing (something her dad might have liked) to something more to her liking, something from the present century. If Ryan minded he did not let on. The fast upbeat tempo of techno filled the car, and Amanda settled back once again in her seat, closing her eyes as the rhythm banged its way into her head. They drove in silence for awhile. Already the nicotine was magically soothing away the stress of school. The wind from the slightly opened window blew sweet air through her hair. She flung the remainder of her cigarette out the window and turned to him. She admired his ropey arms as he drove, his serpent tattoo twisting to the beat of the music as he drummed his fingers against the steering wheel. She reached out and stroked it gently. She was rewarded again with his smile.

She'd met Ryan a week ago at a party near the campus. They'd talked, danced a bit, exchanged cell numbers. They'd texted each other a few times, but now he was here, helping with her escape. She didn't think he was a student though. Lots of people hung out near the campus. "You taking classes at Albany?" she asked, slowly tracing the length of the snake up his arm with her fingertip.

"Naah, not this semester." His muscles rippled slightly under her touch. He removed his right hand from the steering wheel and gathered her long thick curls around his fingers. "Damn, girl. You look good." She leaned into his hand and licked the inside of his arm, the tiny tip of her tongue a gentle caress. "Damn," he whispered.

Amanda felt her own sexuality swelling up inside her, becoming a force of its own. She was afraid to speak or even to open her mouth for fear it would explode from her and set the car on fire. Yes—set the car on fire!

Ryan turned onto the main road leading toward campus, toward his apartment. He parked on the street in front of his building, not quite getting the gear to shift into park before she was on him. Ryan met her kiss with equal enthusiasm, but when her hands tugged at his shirt with a determination that threatened its very existence, he broke away, leaving the car and pulling her waiting body toward the building. Once in the foyer, he pressed her against the nearest wall, where they explored each other with more than just their hands, using their lips, their legs, their tongues, and their hips. Then, once again, she was ripping at his clothes, and he was forced to break away. It was all they could do to make it up the stairs to his second floor apartment, removing clothing as they progressed, so that by the time they reached his door, there was not much left to do but fling their naked bodies to the mattress.

There, Amanda clung to his body, to his movement, as he beat back the menacing force, dousing the threat of self-combustion and decreasing the possibility of any real damage. And when he was done giving all that he could, she lay panting in relief from the momentary calm that descended upon her, her mind slowing to a soft whirl. He shifted from her body and lay on his back, his face to the ceiling, and gently sighed. It wasn't long before he turned her way and smiled sleepily, his hands lightly brushing her face.

"Where did such a tiny little girl learn to fuck like a mink?"

She offered him a little smile of her own, but did not answer. Instead she stood up and started jumping lightly on the old mattress, not getting much of a bounce as there was no box spring. "Let's go dancing!"

He laughed. "It's two in the afternoon." He brought his hands back behind his head and gazed at her, the smile still on his face.

"We have to do something!" She was bouncing higher now, one foot and then the next, one foot and then the next. Her small breasts moved with the beat of her body, her hair a flying tangle of silken curls.

Ryan was getting dizzy watching her. He leaned forward and gently grasped her foot, pulling her to a stop. "Come here," he said softly, reaching up for her hand and pulling her down. She fought against his pull, not wishing to be stilled. "I have to take you home. I have to work at four." She looked at him with disbelief as her face suddenly turned to horror.

"Home?!" she shook her head vigorously.

He captured her head between his hands and told her, "If you don't go home your parents will know you cut school. You don't want that grief."

"I'll stay here," she said, pushing away from him and settling onto the bed. She looked around the dirty little room. She could learn to love it here.

"No you won't," he said, sliding his shirt over the face of the small dragon that adorned his chest. "*I* don't need that grief. Your old man would kill me."

"You don't even know my dad! He wouldn't step on a cockroach!" Something about her statement hit her funny and she laughed with glee. She stopped suddenly and lightly pointed her finger at him. "My mother however, she might kill you." Before he could reply she was on her feet again and back to bouncing.

"Come on, Mandy. I really need to get going."

She stopped her movement and looked at him. No one had ever called her Mandy. Mandy! She loved it!

"I'd love to ditch work and play with you," he said, "but I just can't."

She breathed in hard, fighting back the urge to scream at him, tear at his throat, and force him to let her stay. With satisfaction, she pictured him bloodied and bruised before saying, "Fine!" with a pretty little pout. He threw her bra at her and she caught it by its strap before it sailed past. She wanted to cry but refused to act like a baby in front of him. She got dressed in silence.

As they walked toward the door, Ryan put his arm around her. "Hey," he said softly. "I don't have to work on Friday. We'll go out somewhere. Dancing if you like."

When they pulled up to her house, she turned to him, "Do you want to come in?" Ryan looked at the large intimidating structure, the beautifully manicured front lawn and gardens. The fall flowers were just reaching their peak, the bushes bright red against the brick house. "What does your dad do?" he asked.

"He's a doctor." Amanda was shocked and then embarrassed by the pride that came through her voice. "A shrink," she added quickly. "Fucked up crazy people."

"Your mom?"

"Dean of Women's Studies at Union."

Ryan whistled vaguely between his teeth. "Smart genes," he said, giving the jeans she was wearing a little pat. She smiled, not able to hide her pleasure from his words. "My parents aren't home yet. You could meet my little sister!"

"Maybe some other time. I gotta get to work." He kissed her softly before she got out of the car. He watched as she sauntered up the walk to her house, swinging her purse as if she owned the world. "Man!" he said aloud. "This girl is a hoot!"

Amanda slammed the door as she entered the house. From the small mudroom off the garage, she could peer into the large kitchen and then into the even larger living room beyond. The sun was getting low in the sky and its rays broke through the huge windows that overlooked the vivid autumn display of the valley below. The windows reached way up, almost to the top of the cathedral ceiling, and the light stretched across the room, giving it an almost magical aura. She breathed in the aroma of home and was immediately hit by a blanket of despair. She could feel the house sucking her very core, draining her life force.

2

Carol Benson sat at her desk, relieved to be back at work. It was Monday morning and hot coffee steamed with a pleasant aroma around her. The gentle sun warmed her back from the window that overlooked the campus quad of Union College. It was another beautiful fall day. She dreaded, however, the forthcoming winter that could not be denied, but before dread took hold she shook her head slightly and left the thought behind. She picked up the stack of department memos and started leafing through them. After a couple minutes of sorting, she reached for her coffee and closed her eyes to the sensation as the liquid caressed her tongue. The weekend had been particularly unpleasant. Amanda had been in rare form—even for Amanda. She was barely home, but when she was, she had a way of blanketing the house in misery; when she wasn't home, shivers of fear and worry ran through Carol.

Amanda hadn't come home until well past two a.m. on Sunday, then slept the rest of the day. Then there was Christy—just feeling the need to fly on her own, testing the waters and her mother's patience. Surely there must have been a full moon—Jerry was on call for the weekend and every nut in Albany was vying for his attention, leaving her alone to deal with their two rotten daughters.

Carol was relieved when her phone rang, putting an end to her pointless musings. What she needed now was a really messy interdepartmental mêlée. She reached for the phone with hope. "Hello?"

"Mrs. Benson?"

Carol closed her eyes in trepidation. A tiny shot of adrenaline pulsed through her. No one at the college called her Mrs. Benson. "Yes?"

"Oh, hi, Mrs. Benson. This is Mrs. Burk, from the high school."

Carol's heart began to beat faster in her chest.

"I'm just calling about Amanda, making sure she's okay. All those doctors' appointments she's had lately and now—I assume she's sick today?"

Carol's mind raced with confusion. *Doctors' appointments?* "She's not there?" Carol asked.

"No. She's not sick?" There was a hint of suspicion and underlying satisfaction in the woman's voice. Carol flashed to the memory of what they'd gone through two weeks ago when Amanda received her first and only school detention for some little transgression. She'd been inconsolably hysterical. Carol could not face that again.

"Well," Carol said. "It's possible she's sick. I left before she did. You know she has late arrival." What kind of mother was she? Not even sure where her daughter was, possibly covering up her deceit. "She wasn't up when I left," Carol continued. "Let me check and I'll get back to you."

Carol hung up the phone and thought she might cry. She wanted to call Jerry and demand that he deal with it, but she knew that was impossible—Monday was his office day; he'd be booked solid seeing patients. She dialed the house number. The machine picked up on the fourth ring. She hung up before the melodic voices of her girls sang, "Hello, you have reached the Bensons..." and giggled with wild music in the background. It was an old message. She picked up her cell phone and hit send. Amanda was the last one she'd called. She was almost always the last one she'd called. It went to voicemail after five rings. Carol snapped the cell phone shut in anger, tapping it hard against her desk before flipping it open again. Cussing silently, it took her several tries before reaching the right screen.

WHERE RU, she finally managed to text and hit the send button. She watched the screen as it read: MESSAGE SENT. She flipped it closed and waited. She got up and paced behind her desk. She stared at the phone crossly. She would have to drive all the way back home. Then she heard the familiar beeps and grabbed the phone. She flipped it open and hit read. HOME, it said on the tiny screen.

She shook her head in relieved frustration. It took her over a minute, fumbling with the tiny keys to text back: WHY?

SICK, was the immediate reply.

Enough with the texting! She hit the call button again. Amanda did not pick up. She almost threw the phone in annoyance. "Damn it!" she said, slapping the phone down on the desk. She sat down, trying to calm herself. Ten deep breaths. Okay then, another ten.

~

Carol cleared her last two meetings and was home by three. She walked in the door and found Christy in her usual after-school position, eating a snack in front of the kitchen TV. She looked up and smiled distractedly, "Oh, hi, Mom. You're home early."

"Yes," she smiled back and flipped through the mail that Christy had deposited on the kitchen counter. "Where's your sister?" Carol tried to make her voice sound casual, but Christy's face tensed just slightly. With a twist of her head, Christy indicated the den as she returned to her TV. Of course. Where else? Carol took off her coat and flung it in the general direction of the mudroom. She stood there a moment, gathering strength, before heading down the large hall that led to the den.

She felt the tension before she even hit the room. Amanda sat in front of the computer screen, the monitor casting an eerie glow on her thin face. Her mouth was set in a tight frown. Her eyes, worst of all, were glassy and far away. Carol had to look somewhere else. "How are you feeling?" she asked lightly. When she got no response, her presence not even acknowledged, her anger gave her strength to say again, this time firmer and louder, "How are you feeling?"

"Fine."

Carol felt slapped by the word and actually stepped back from the sound. How could such a simple word evoke so much hatred?

As if remembering, Amanda added less vilely, her eyes never leaving the screen, "Better."

Carol sighed. "And what was not feeling well this morning?" Carol waited. No response—the computer trance was too powerful. It was absurd.

"Amanda!" She laughed at the absurdity. "Back away from the screen," she said in her best scary movie-star voice and passed her hand across her daughter's line of vision. Amanda blinked and turned toward her mother. She smiled then, and Carol admired her four-thousand-dollar teeth. Or was it five thousand?

"Sorry," she said sweetly. "What did you ask?"

"What did not feel well this morning?"

"Oh! I had a migraine." Amanda had been suffering from migraines since fourteen. She started to turn back toward the screen, but her mother stopped her.

"And you did not call me because ...."

"Oh, sorry. I took an Imitrex and fell asleep. I meant to call you. I'm really sorry."

The dread that had descended upon Carol began to lift. Everything was fine. Just a little failure to communicate, that's all. "You know the school calls me when you don't show up—" Then she remembered. "What's up with these doctors' appointments Mrs. Burk asked me about?"

Amanda looked momentarily confused and then said, "I had that dentist appointment last week."

Carol had forgotten about that. They'd let her drive the winter rat to school. "But she said appointments," Carol persisted, stressing the s.

Amanda didn't even blink. "She must have me confused with someone else."

Carol sighed heavily. "Amanda. Do I look dumb?"

Amanda smiled sweetly. "A little," she teased.

Carol could not stop her laughter and suddenly felt a surge of love for her daughter. She wanted to reach out and pull Amanda to her chest.

"Amanda, you cannot skip school. This is your last year, then you never have to be in high school again." Carol hadn't forgotten her own misery in high school, her own adolescent turmoil and heartache. She'd been known to skip a few classes herself.

"I mean it, Amanda. If you skip class again, you'll lose the car for a week. Do you understand?"

"Yes." She turned back to the screen.

"I mean it!"

"I know!"

~

Carol decided that since she had some extra time, she'd scrap the pasta she'd planned for dinner and make something more substantial. She thawed some chicken breasts and boiled pasta for baked macaroni and cheese. It was Amanda's favorite. While the chicken and macaroni casserole cooked in the oven, Christy made a salad and Carol cut up broccoli to steam. She and her younger daughter talked pleasantly about their day, joking good heartedly about all that was lacking in men. Carol had asked Amanda to help them, but she begged off, claiming she still felt a little sick. It was nice to have Christy all alone; they were having fun.

Carol glanced at the clock. It was a little past five-thirty. Jerry would be home soon. Since this was an office day and his hospital duties were minimal, he could usually leave at five. She turned the water on for the broccoli.

~

Jerry turned off of Troy Schenectady Road and weaved his way through the streets of Niskayuna. His day had been a bit more stressful than his office days usually were. A lot of his week was spent at the hospital, teaching the residents, admitting and diagnosing patients he might never see again, and treating the in-house patients of the psych ward. He spent Mondays and Fridays at his own private office looking at a parade of med checks. He sprinkled a longer session in now and then to break up the day, which was almost always less demanding than the sessions he held at the hospital. The volume of patients that demanded his attention had increased over the years, and with the increased effectiveness of psychopathic drugs, sometimes he felt more like a pharmacist than a doctor. He missed just talking to his patients, helping them through their difficult lives. He could not remember the last time he'd been able to give someone more than a half an hour of his time.

He'd seen Mary Jacobs today. She was a longtime patient with a diagnosis of manic-depression and borderline personality defect—a tricky combination to treat. To say she was a difficult person to be around was an understatement. Today, she was especially angry with him for taking a phone call from her mother. Mary was forty-eight, unable to function on her own, and was still living with her elderly mother. He could only imagine what it would be like for her to deal with her malicious, and sometimes violent, daughter day after day.

Although he never broke *his* definition of confidentiality, he also never refused to talk to the family of his mentally ill patients. He knew, more often than not, that the family ended up as primary care givers; their understanding and help in the diagnosis and treatment of serious mental illness was crucial. Mary had come into his office screaming about HIPAA and threatening to call the police. It would have been funny, if it had not been so terrible. He almost had to call security, but she'd finally calmed down. He only hoped he'd angered her enough that she would seek care elsewhere, but he knew from years of dealing with people, that the more annoying they were, the more likely he had them for life.

He smiled a bit as he made the final turn toward home. After all, it *was* sort of funny. He'd always pictured the HIPAA police in crazy riot gear resembling surgical scrubs and brandishing large hypodermics as guns, rushing some poor sap of a doctor who failed to respect the privacy laws. Jerry chuckled at his little fantasy as he turned into the driveway of his home.

~

Carol removed the casserole and chicken from the oven, and as she turned to get the broccoli, Amanda came strutting into the room, purse on her arm. "Dinner's almost ready. I made mac and cheese," offered Carol, choosing to ignore the purse.

"I'm going out," said Amanda.

Carol looked at her. "No you're not." She tried to make her voice calm yet firm.

Christy glanced from her mother back to her sister and braced herself.

"Why not?"

"You were sick today. Tomorrow's a school day."

"Yeah! A migraine! It's gone now!" Carol was shaking her head *no*. "You can't stop me!" threatened Amanda.

"You may not have a car!"

Amanda screamed in frustration.

Jerry stood in the doorway of the kitchen. No one had noticed his arrival. "What's going on?" he asked with tired caution.

His wife and daughter looked at him with relief—at least someone reasonable had arrived. "Mom won't let me have a car to go out!"

Carol rubbed her forehead and sighed. "She was sick today. She did not go to school."

"No car. You're staying home," Jerry stated. The matter was closed to further discussion.

"Are you fucking kidding me?" Amanda screamed. Both Carol and Jerry looked at her in shock. Christy hid her face in her hands. Then suddenly the crystal vase they'd received for a wedding present sailed through the air toward Carol. She side-stepped to avoid an explosion of glass and the pretty flowers Carol had picked in the garden yesterday. There was a small dent in the woodwork of the kitchen cabinet, and one flower dangled sadly from the drawer-pull, its damaged petals dripping water onto the floor. Amanda was stunned as she stared at the mess she'd made. She screamed and fled to the safety of her room.

Carol and Jerry stared at one another, mouths agape, before Carol closed hers in despair and rested her face in her hands—the counter kept her from joining the broken pieces of glass. Christy slipped off her stool and disappeared. As Jerry bent down to pick up the first of the flowers, the words, "What a lovely homecoming," escaped, almost inaudibly, from his mouth.

~

"Do you thinks it's drugs?"

"I don't know. Maybe…probably," answered Jerry. They were lying side by side, not touching, in the dark. It was late; they were nowhere near sleep. He'd checked on Amanda an hour or so ago and she was fast asleep, but her face seemed troubled even in its slumber.

"What do we do?"

"I don't know," came Jerry's answer in the dark. For a professional who was supposed to know about these sorts of things, he was certainly no help. "Even if we could somehow force her to submit to a drug test—what then?"

"We can't even get her to clean her room. At least we'd know if it were drugs."

"True," agreed Jerry. He was never a fan of forced drug testing or the mandatory administration of medication, but sometimes it was necessary. In his experience, it was always done in a controlled environment—a clinic, hospital setting—but certainly not in a private home. Certainly not with his own child. "I think maybe she's just having an unusually hard time with adolescence," he offered.

"Jerry, she threw that vase right at me. She wanted to hit me with it." Her voiced cracked slightly, but she drew in a breath and made her point, "Plus, she's eighteen. It's not like she's twelve. Shouldn't she be getting better, not worse?"

"Every kid is different." But he could not quite convince himself, much less Carol, which brought them back to the drug theory.

They knew Amanda smoked pot on occasion—they weren't totally clueless—but it was possible there were other drugs. Marijuana use should not cause the behavior they were seeing.

Carol began to cry again and Jerry reached for her in the dark. "Have we been bad parents?" she asked. They'd had this discussion several times over the last few years. "Am I a terrible mother?"

"You're a wonderful mother."

"Did we do something wrong? Should we have been harder on her when she was small?" Amanda had always been stubborn and defiant but not out of control. She'd not been an unhappy child. In fact, she'd been such a lovely baby—calm and soulful. Even as a two-year-old, she'd happily entertained herself. She was sweet and loving. She was a joy. It really wasn't until she was four that she learned the true meaning of the word "no" as a response. "It's not like we ever hit her or abused her in any way," Carol continued. "Our family is together, stable—" She was crying harder now and Jerry tightened his grip on her.

"We did nothing wrong. We dealt with her personality as best we could."

God knows, it had not been easy. With Christy, all you had to say was "no," but with Amanda—well, that was a different matter. The more they tightened control the more out of control she became. They'd tried using softer discipline—withholding privileges and her favorite toys—and for the most part it had worked, until now.

"I'll talk to her about the drug thing. She's obviously not happy with the way things are either."

Surrounded by doubts and trepidation, at some point they finally fell asleep. It was in the wee hours of the morning when Jerry heard the subtle squeak of their bedroom door and the small uncertain voice of his older daughter. "Mom?"

Carol stirred from her sleep, a little panic in her voice, "Amanda, what's wrong?"

"I'm sorry," she was crying. "I don't know what to do. I'm so afraid."

"Come here," Carol said, and Amanda crawled into bed with them as she had done as a child. The three of them made a human sandwich: Amanda, Carol, and Jerry—each one's back against the other's stomach.

"Do you hate me?"

Carol pulled her arm up until her hand rested on Amanda's baby-soft curls. "Never."

"We love you, Amanda," Jerry said, his hand slipping across Carol and finding his daughter in the dark. "We will always love you ... no matter what."

When Jerry and Carol opened their eyes to the first light of dawn, they were on opposite sides of the bed, and Amanda was gone.

3

Jerry and Tom wore their old purple sweatshirts with the large gold and purple *A* splayed across the chest. The words *UALBANY* arched over the *A*. The sleeves were tattered and the collars terribly frayed, but both men believed, somehow, that the game would surely be doomed without this attire. Carol and Sarah chose to wear something from this century—Carol dressed in a subtle gold sweater and Sarah a pretty lavender one with a gold scarf. Sarah's short dark hair was topped with a cute little purple cap. She'd brought one for Carol, but Carol had found it impossible to secure over her unruly auburn curls. It was Saturday and the first official home game of the season. The weather had decidedly turned cooler, but the afternoon sun was shining brightly. Purple and gold banners were flying, coolers were cooling, grills were sizzling, hopes were soaring, and spirits were elevating in the parking lot.

Carol was already feeling the gentle release of tension that only good friends and a cold beer could induce. She'd have to pace herself—it was going to be a long evening. The game wasn't until seven, but the men had insisted they get there at two, because, God forbid, they might miss something. Carol's gaze turned away from whatever Jerry was saying and landed on Bob Radcliff, who was plopping raw chicken on the grill with his bare hands—dipping his fingers into the slimy mass of marinade with one hand and sipping his beer with the other—as he bellowed, "Someone bring me those burgers!" She looked around. The other dozen or so people who stood around the open truck bed were totally ignoring him, with the exception of his wife, Maura, who rolled her eyes. Carol smiled as she heard him mumble, "Oh. Hell with it!" and he took a few steps toward a cooler and pulled out the meat himself. He was the self-appointed grill-man; no one was about to interfere.

Her eyes flickered back to Jerry and she watched him laugh at something his brother was saying. She felt her smile solidify and she savored the . . . what was she feeling? Joy? Yes, that was it. Jerry caught her eye and smiled back. With that smile, they shared a private moment and Carol felt almost giddy with happiness. Ever since Amanda's little explosion on Monday night, things had improved dramatically. Carol hadn't received one hysterical phone call from her daughter nor any allegations from the school. Amanda had gone to school each day. She was reasonably pleasant around the house—well, at least she wasn't angry. The couple of times she'd gone out, she'd come home at a reasonable hour. Carol held on to the hope that the burst of violence was a turning point, that it scared Amanda more than it had the two of them. When they'd left for the game, both girls had yet to emerge from their rooms. She checked her cell phone—four-forty, no messages. She'd call them later, but for now she was just basking in the pure joy of being alive.

Suddenly, as if some bell had gone off, there was activity in the group. The chips were being pushed aside and the women were placing their dishes to share on the table. Bob was yelling something about a platter and being ignored. Men were swigging down the last of their beer, preferring a cold one with dinner. Carol went to her cooler for the salad she'd brought. She pushed a rather nasty looking rice dish toward the back of the table and placed her salad up front. She brushed her hands together with satisfaction and turned from the table. Maura Radcliff was right there; she almost ran into her. "Hi, Carol." Carol glanced quickly back to the table. She hoped that rice-thing had not been Maura's.

"I haven't had a chance to talk to you yet," Maura continued. "How are things?"

Carol smiled. "They're good. How about with you?"

Maura was off, rattling on about her and her husband's work and their children's accomplishments. Carol nodded her head and tried to insert a comment here or there, but was feeling swallowed by chatter. The meat would be cold before she ever got to the table. "Jason is working hard on his college applications," Maura was saying. Jason was in Amanda's graduating class. "He's applying to Brown, Harvard, MIT, Princeton, and Cornell. Cornell's his fall-back school, of course."

"Of course," said Carol. Carol felt dread creeping upon her. She glanced around…was there no escape? Then it came. The question she'd been dreading.

"What about Amanda? Where is she applying?"

Carol felt a deep inward sigh pulse through her body as she exhaled softly. Why did this feel like a competition? Then the surge of irritation. She would simply refuse to compete. "I think she's feeling a little overwhelmed by the whole process. I'm not sure she's decided yet."

With the scrunched up face of disapproval, Maura said, "Really? The deadlines for early action and early decision are coming right up for a lot of the best schools."

Carol waved her hand in dismissal. "Oh, there's still plenty of time." Then finally, like a savior, Sarah appeared.

"Carol, I have to show you something," Sarah was saying as she gently took Carol's arm. "Oh, hi, Maura!" Sarah smiled her best smile at Maura. "Can I borrow Carol for a minute?" And led her to safety.

Jerry took a long cool drink of beer as he watched Carol and Sarah make their way to the food table. As he tilted his head back, his eyes left his wife and rested on Lenny Couch heading toward the group. "Here comes your buddy," Jerry warned Tom with a wicked grin. Lenny Couch rubbed Tom like sand paper. They'd known him since college and no matter how rude Tom was to him, he was always showing up—as far as Tom was concerned—that little *sharksucker* of a man.

Tom glanced up from the food table and quickly looked away. "Is it too late to run?" he asked Jerry.

"Definitely," Jerry said as he looked up and acknowledged Len's approach. "Hi, Len. How are you doing?" Jerry didn't really think Lenny was all that bad. In fact, he found him rather entertaining. And he was having an especially hard time of it lately. He'd somehow managed to find a woman, besides his wife, to have sex with—a fact that Jerry and Tom found astounding. This, of course, had given his wife an out, and now he was at the tail end of a very messy divorce.

Lenny stood close and peered up at Jerry with tragic eyes, the top of his round, bald head glinting in the sun. He shook his head sadly, "I'm okay, Jerry. I'm okay. A survivor." He immediately saddled up to Tom and gave him a rough slap on the arm. "How you doing, buddy?" Tom grunted his reply and Jerry tried not to laugh. Lenny looked like a tiny Michelin Man next to Tom. "Been working out?" He gave Tom a good-natured punch in the gut.

"Some."

"I've been running, you know. Did ten miles this morning. Last weekend, fifteen." Both Jerry and Tom stared at him blankly, their eyes settling on Len's round belly.

"Wow. That's great, Len," said Jerry. Tom rolled his eyes at Jerry over the top of Len's head. Lenny went to the cooler to get a beer and helped himself to some food at the table. Jerry and Tom had their backs to him. Lenny returned with his plate laboring under the weight of his food.

Lenny set his beer down and tapped Jerry lightly on the arm. "Oh, Jerry? I need to ask you a medical question." Tom rolled his eyes again and gave Jerry a look of exasperation. They had discussed the annoyance of friends wanting free accounting or medical advice many times. "I went to the doctor last week and he gave me one of those prostate exams—" Tom raised his eyebrows at Jerry in disbelief. Jerry had to bite his tongue lightly to keep from laughing. "So I'm standing there, you know, all spread out..." Lenny squatted a bit and stuck out his butt, both hands holding his plate before him. Jerry and Tom laughed in spite of themselves. Lenny beamed with pleasure. "...and the doctor sticks his finger in there—"

"Did this cause you psychological distress?" Tom interrupted.

"No. Not really." Lenny looked up at Tom from his squatting position. Jerry took a sip of his beer. "So, anyway, he has his finger in there and—"

"Jerry's a fucking psychiatrist, Len! Why are you talking to him about your ass?"

Jerry almost spit the beer at Lenny as he laughed. Carol and Sarah looked over to see what was up. They both saw Lenny and quickly turned away.

"He went to med school, didn't he?" said Len, just a tad indignant, and Jerry might have felt sorry for him if he wasn't still, by God, in a squat.

"No one cares about your ass," said Tom, and then he was suddenly distracted. Jerry and Lenny followed his gaze. Lenny stood up quickly, sucked in his gut, and stood ever so slightly on his toes. A group of lovely young college girls were walking by. They were dressed in tiny little shorts and halter tops, seemingly oblivious to the cold—except that their luscious nipples betrayed them. "Oh my," whispered Tom. Jerry involuntarily licked his lips.

The three of them stared dumbly for a moment before Lenny set his plate down. "I'll catch you guys later," he said.

"Where do you think you're going?" asked Tom incredulously.

"You're just jealous 'cause you can't," said Lenny as he scurried after them.

"Pathetic," mumbled Tom as they both watched a bit wistfully while Lenny caught up with the girls. He said something to them and they all looked at one another and then laughed merrily. "Pathetic," Tom repeated.

Carol glanced over and watched the three men as the girls walked by. Their tongues were practically lolling out. She was about to point out the pathetic spectacle to Sarah, but stopped herself just in time, remembering Tom's affair that had almost broken up their marriage. Even though it had been—what?—ten years now, it was and would always be a subject without humor.

Sarah saw the men gaping at the girls and her eyes looked away and down at her own breasts, well-secured in her lilac sweater. She sighed and felt somewhat deflated, like her old, sad boobs. But they had all gotten older, a little rounder....

"Dear God," said Carol. Lenny Couch was chasing after those girls like a dog in heat! No, more like a bowling ball rolling feebly toward the pins! The man was totally delusional. Carol caught Sarah's eye and they burst out with laughter. Carol took great joy in verbalizing her bowling ball analogy to Sarah.

They laughed, and Sarah's old, sad boobs didn't seem all that tragic anymore.

~

Amanda looked at herself in the mirror. "Oh my God! I love it!" she exclaimed. She ran her hands down the straight red strands, picking up the black tips with pleasure.

"It's awesome," agreed Christy. (She had chosen a slightly less dramatic change, her naturally straight, light brown hair now laced with red streaks.) But her sister's hair—it was the definition of dramatic. It had taken most of the afternoon—first the bleaching out of Amanda's dark chestnut mane, then the red dye, followed by black tips, and finally the long strenuous task with the flat iron, calming the stubborn curls that cursed Amanda's head. When Amanda had suggested—no, demanded—that Christy help her with this hair venture, Christy had been more than a bit apprehensive. But they'd had a blast. Amanda had only freaked out once, hardly even screamed. And now, the final result—awesome.

"I hope Ryan likes it," said Amanda, still running her hands through her new tresses.

"You're going out with him again tonight?"

"Yeah." There was just a hint of danger in Amanda's voice that Christy failed to pick up on.

Christy shrugged her shoulders good-naturedly. "I don't know; I just thought you liked Jonathan," she said as she combed her own hair with her fingers. Amanda's eyes flashed at her in the mirror and Christy immediately saw her error.

"What! Are you calling me a *whore?*" The words shattered through the bathroom, Amanda's fiery hair taking on an angry life of its own.

"I never said that!" screamed Christy, afraid and angry at the same time.

"You're the fucking whore!"

Amanda was in her face now. Christy could smell the cigarettes on her breath. She raised herself up, not willing to seem vulnerable. Although younger, Christy was bigger-boned. She could take Amanda in a fight. "Whatever! Back off!" she screamed. Amanda laughed and Christy, washed in relief, almost began to cry, but she would not give her sister the satisfaction.

~

They were packing away the food and gathering up the debris. It was six-fifteen and time to head to the stadium. Jerry was amazed, as he hefted the bag of bottles and cans into his car, at the volume of beer the group had consumed. He had limited himself to three, as he did not wish to sleep through the game. The game was, after all, why they were here. Many of his friends were droopy-eyed and staggering slightly as they prepared for the short walk to the stadium. Jerry looked at his brother, who had not been without a beer all afternoon, and was, as always, astounded by his capacity for alcohol.

Tom was alert and as animated as a boy going to an amusement park. "Come on, Jerry. Let's just leave these losers," Tom was saying, bubbling with anticipation. "I don't want to miss the warm-up."

As the four of them made their way through the crowd, Carol called home. No one, of course, answered. She did not know why she always tried—except if someone answered, she knew that person was definitely at home. With a cell phone you never knew. Amanda answered her cell on the second ring. "What," she said.

Carol ignored the impatience of Amanda's voice. She wasn't going to let her surly daughter ruin her one night out. "What are your plans for the night?" she asked lightly.

"Going out with friends."

"I don't want you taking the car."

"I know!"

"Don't stay out all night."

"I know!"

Carol sighed. "Let me talk to Christy."

"Call her cell. I really need to go."

"No, just get her for me, please." But when there was no response, Carol checked her phone. Amanda had hung up. "Jesus Christ!" she complained. When Jerry looked at her, she waved off his concern. She scrolled down to Christy's number and hit SEND.

"Hi, Mom," Christy said in a pleasant voice. "Who's winning?"

"The game doesn't start until seven. What are your plans for the night?"

"Going to Katy's. I'm going to spend the night, okay?"

Katy was a nice girl. Carol knew her parents well. "You have a ride? Parents will be home?"

"Yes and yes."

"Everything okay at home? How's Amanda?"

"Everything's fine, Mom."

"Well, okay then. Call me if you need us." She flipped the phone closed. Why was talking to her children such a chore? Somehow, she just never felt totally satisfied.

"Everything okay?" asked Jerry.

"Apparently."

Jerry nodded his head. "Okay then. Go Danes!" he declared.

Carol laughed. Jerry was right. She put away her doubts as they pushed through the turnstile, allowing herself to get caught up in the excitement of the first home game.

~

29

Ryan pulled up to the curb in front of Mandy's house and sent her a text that he was there. NO RENTS COME IN was the text back. He considered for a moment before leaving his car and making his way to the house. Should he go in the front door or through the garage as he'd seen Mandy do? The front door was large and somewhat daunting. He chose the garage. The door next to the large garage doors was unlocked; he opened it cautiously and stepped inside the three-car garage. It took a moment for his eyes to adjust in the dimness, and then he could make out the two cars nestled in their home. One was a Lexus RX Hybrid, which Ryan glanced at with passing interest, but his eyes settled on, and then grew wide as he took in the cherry-red Porsche 911. *Holy fuck!* He stepped up to it and gently stroked its amazing fender. *If these were the cars they left at home, what were they driving?* He circled the car once before locating the door to the house. He knocked gently.

"Come in," he heard Mandy call from beyond the door. He could discern the excitement in her voice and felt the rush of testosterone he'd become accustomed to with even the sound of her voice. He opened the door to a mudroom and heard her call, "In here." He stepped smoothly over a discarded pile of shoes and into the kitchen. Mandy was leaning against the kitchen cabinet, her head tilted so that her hair swept down and onto the counter. Ryan did not know what shocked him more, the awesome room he'd just walked into, or the incredibly outrageous red hair that adorned Mandy's pretty face.

He could not speak at first, but when he did, he croaked, "Wig?" He wasn't sure what he wanted the answer to be as he took a step closer. Mandy shook her head *no.* "Sister?" he managed to get out.

"Not home," she said as the very tip of her tongue slid across her lips.

Christ! What was this spit of a girl doing to him? He took a few quick steps toward the kitchen counter. He grasped the red strands, twisting the softness around his fingers, and pulled her face to his. The tang of her toothpaste, mixed with the sweet pleasure of her lip-gloss, played on his tongue. He felt the awesome pressure of her thigh as she brought it slowly up the inside of his left leg, leaving it gently pressed into his crotch; her other leg somehow magically wrapped around his right calf. As he moved from her lips to the soft, smooth curve of her neck, his hand gently cupping her left breast, she breathed into his ear—a small, almost animal, whimper of desire. He could not muster the strength to take her to the leather couch that was only a few yards away—much less carry her to the beautiful bed he imagined her luscious body lying on each night—but was forced to have her right there, against the counter that her mother must have chopped vegetables on.

~

Christy put her head back and laughed.

"No! It's true!" Katy insisted as she handed Christy the joint. Christy took a drag as Katy repeated, "Really, it's true!"

But Christy could not recall what was true and didn't really care, but laughed again and admired the red strands of her hair that fell across her face. They were sitting cross-legged on Katy's big canopy bed. The smoke from the joint was captured in the pink canopy and formed a little cloud above their heads. Between them sat a bag of chips, chocolate chip cookies, a melting half gallon of marble fudge ice cream, and two spoons. Christy's cell phone beeped and she searched around in the folds of the unmade bed before locating it beneath the cookie bag.

She let out a little squeal as she read the text. "Zack and Brandon want to hang out," she told Katy, excited and frightened at the same time.

"Cool," said Katy. Her parents had gone to the game; they had the house to themselves until at least eleven. "Tell them to come over." Brandon and Katy had been going out for three days now, although she'd liked him for a long time. Christy was excited for her, but wasn't sure how she felt about Zack, or any other boy for that matter.

As soon as she hit the SEND button in response, the doorbell rang. The two girls' eyes grew wide. "Oh m'god!" Katy screamed. They'd not even had a chance to fuss with their hair or whore-up their makeup. They flew off the bed and into the bathroom. With eyebrow pencils and lip gloss drawn, they attacked their faces, ignoring the repeat of the doorbell. Within moments the deed was done, and they went down the stairs, laughing and grasping each other in excitement.

The two young men leaned against the railing of the stoop as if they were waiting for paint to dry. When the door opened they did not move a muscle other than the subtle dip of their chins in salutation. "Hey," one of them finally said, and came forward and gave Katy a little peck on the lips. Christy's eyes grew wide, but she recovered quickly and tried to match the *whatever* attitude of the group.

Both boys were tall and lanky—one could easily be mistaken for the other—with legs too long and feet too big—Great Dane puppies on a mission. Their hair was cut close to their scalps, and there was an uneven attempt at a beard on their mildly blemished faces. They ambled into the house, glancing about the formal living room to their left with disinterest, and peering hopefully up the staircase to their right. Brandon came close to Katy and touched her hair with the tips of his fingers. Zack smiled hopefully at Christy. She flushed with excited tension.

"Let's go downstairs," suggested Katy. She escorted the group through the kitchen and down the basement stairs, flipping on lights as she went. The basement was large and totally remodeled into several rooms. In the first room they came to was a ping pong table, which the boys seemed mildly interested in. The second room was lined with inviting plush couches, which elicited much more interest than ping pong. Only when fully into the room were the couches' true significance realized, for they all faced the most amazing 102-inch plasma TV in the history of flat panel TVs. Zack whistled aloud. Brandon covered his mouth to hide the braces that lined his erupting smile. As if that wasn't enough, in the corner, next to the TV, gleamed a brand new Xbox 360!

~

Carol buried her head in Jerry's chest as Jerry groaned aloud. Tom cussed under his breath, while Sarah stared, mouth agape, at the field.

Bob Radcliff stood up and yelled at the top of his lungs, "What the hell is wrong with you fu—" But he never got the last word out as his wife jabbed him sharply in the ribs and he was forced to sit down and rub his side in irritation. *Interception! Unbelievable!* Albany had been running the ball steadily down field, picking up sixty yards, when some idiot made the decision to throw on first down from the thirty-yard line. The pass was slow and wobbly and fell gently into the large and inept hands of New Hampshire's right-defensive tackle. He looked almost stricken by his good fortune before he set his mind to running and lumbered back up the field, knocking Danes down like gnats before tripping over his own feet at their twenty-yard line. Two quick plays and the score was tied at twenty. The extra point was good and New Hampshire took the lead. The Danes could do nothing with the ball after that, and New Hampshire scored yet again. They went into halftime—twenty-eight to twenty.

"I'm going to get some coffee," Carol said to Jerry. "You want anything?" Jerry shook his head glumly. As she and Sarah made their way down the stands, Tom slid closer to Jerry and reviewed the plays of the first half. No one was paying much attention to the marching band or even the scantily dressed cheerleaders that bounced around on the field. When they'd fully reviewed all that was necessary, Tom's talk turned to fitness.

"I think we should take up jogging," he announced. "If Lenny can propel his fat ass down the jogging path, then certainly we can."

Jerry moaned, as if racquetball wasn't bad enough.

"Look," Tom persisted, "the weather's still decent. We should be outside, not stuck in some stinking concrete court trying to lose an eye!"

Jerry saw the logic in that, but was still not thrilled. Certainly there must be an easier way. He was about to suggest liposuction when Tom declared, "Tomorrow! Eight sharp!" Jerry sighed, but did not argue.

Carol stood in the long line for coffee. It had turned much cooler, and coffee and hot chocolate were quickly becoming more popular than cold beer. Sarah had gone to the bathroom. When Carol finally received the two cups of steaming coffee, Sarah had yet to return, so she made her way to the condiment bar to wait. As she was adding just a little sugar to her cup, she looked up and could swear she saw Fran Brown, Katy's mother, come out of the bathroom. She hesitated, then decided to abandon the coffee. She pushed her way through the crowd and caught up to the woman. Yes, it was definitely Fran. "Hey, Fran," she said as she gently tapped her arm. "I didn't know you were coming to the game."

"Oh, hi, Carol. Yes, we try to get to at least one game a season." She smiled, not a care in the world.

Carol struggled briefly, trying to phrase her next question so as to not seem accusatory or let on that her own daughter had lied to her. "Christy is always so excited about going to your house," she said, figuring that if Fran seemed confused she could always turn the words into a more general statement— *Oh, I wasn't referring to anything specific like today!*

To Carol's relief, Fran nodded her head and said, "Yes, Katy was excited too. They always have such a good time together. In fact, I just talked to Katy and they're watching TV and doing each other's makeup."

"So they're behaving themselves? Not burning down your house or having a party or something?"

Fran laughed. "Oh, I'm sure they're making a mess, but I'll have them clean up before I bring Christy home tomorrow."

"Oh no! I'll come get her," insisted Carol.

When Carol returned to the condiment table, she was glad to see the coffees were unmolested. She considered calling or texting Christy, but then Sarah returned and she decided that nothing would be gained by communicating at this time with her youngest. Since she had no intention of leaving the game to physically check up on the girls, she let it go, and they went up the stands to rejoin their husbands.

~

It wasn't just the red hair that made all eyes turn their way as they walked into the club. It was more the way Mandy carried herself—the tilt of her head, the set of her shoulders, some enticing force or power she emanated. He'd been victim of it the very first time she'd entered his orbit, back when her hair was a chocolate mane. He'd been sitting at the party, enjoying the music and the beer, when he felt the air shift and there she was. His world had altered—and was still off keel. He felt sorry for those who longed for what he had, and he felt proud as he took her arm.

They worked their way to the bar. He ordered a beer and a rum and coke. Even though her wristband indicated she was under twenty-one, the bartender did not give him a hard time and took his money without question.

The music was loud and it beat within Amanda's chest. She'd been to this particular club many times, but this was the first time she'd been here with Ryan, and her body sizzled with anticipation. The chance to show him off, the chance for him to see her dance—she knew she was the best dancer in the club, probably the best in Albany, perhaps the world—but the music was so loud and it beat within her chest so hard that she thought that she might scream. She drank her rum and coke greedily, knowing it would help to calm the beating. She dragged Ryan to the dance floor before she flew away, knowing that everyone was watching her—that everyone wanted her and wanted to be her—and she danced to the beating as no one had done before. Soon there was another rum and coke, and Ryan was laughing and she was laughing, and there in the corner of the room was Jason Radcliff, a boy from her class. He was so messed up that he was actually puking in the corner, and they laughed at that. And then there was some bitch in her face—some old girlfriend of Ryan's saying nasty, bitchy things about her *beautiful* red hair—and Amanda was on her, knocking her to the floor, ripping at that bitch's blonde hair. Ryan was trying to pull her away, but he could not remove her from her prey; he could not overcome her superhuman strength. It took two or three people to drag her away, people she would kill if only she could break away — she would kill everyone in the place and burn it to the ground!

Back outside, in the cool, quiet night air, Ryan's strong arms held her from the back, pinning her arms to her sides. She felt safe. Her superhuman powers drained. Her body went limp, and Ryan guided her to the car.

~

Nothing in Zack and Brandon's sixteen years could have prepared them for the pure pleasure they were feeling now — nothing on TV, the Internet, or print came close to the real thing. They'd heard other boys talk about it, but this was something that must be experienced directly; no words could ever do it justice. This was reality at its finest; the sensation was awe-inspiring.

Zack moaned aloud with satisfaction. "Awesome," agreed Brandon. Niko Bellic had just neatly blown the head off of some punk, his head flying back and then bursting over the screen. How many people had they killed so far? And they hadn't even attempted driving yet — Zack didn't care what it took, he was definitely getting *Grand Theft Auto IV*, even if he had to steal it!

Katy did not stifle the yawn that burst from her mouth before she said, "You guys really have to leave now. It's nearly eleven. My parents will be home soon." This was the third time she'd said it and she was beginning to get annoyed. This had been the lamest night ever, watching two stupid boys murdering people for hours! She looked at Christy in desperation. Christy shook her head in disgust before getting up and planting herself in front of the obnoxiously large screen.

"Move!" both boys yelled.

Christy met their yell and added a little volume, "You have to leave *now*!" And with that she unplugged the Xbox. The boys sat open-mouthed and deflated, game controls dangling from their limp and tired hands.

~

As they made their way back to the car, Jerry and Tom, arms

around each other's shoulders, sang, *"Purple and gold, our flags are waving high...."* Carol and Sarah walked a few feet behind, and although they did not join in the singing, they were smiling and happy. The coach must have ripped the boys a new one during halftime because they came out on fire and dominated the remainder of the game. The final score was forty-eight to twenty-eight.

They all piled into Carol's old Volvo wagon, Jerry in the driver's seat. He never subjected his good cars to the football parking nightmare. They drove home in pleasant silence, all tired and content. As Jerry dropped them off at the front of their home, Tom turned to Jerry and pointed his finger at him, "Eight sharp! Be here at eight and ready to work off all that crap we ate." Jerry waved his hands in surrender and headed home.

~

Ryan sat at the foot of his mattress and watched Mandy stare at the ceiling. He'd brought her here, to his apartment, because he couldn't leave her the way she was—he certainly couldn't take her home at this point. It was after eleven. Her parents were most likely home by now. Her face was blotchy, her eyes were red and swollen from crying; there was the distinctive scratch across her cheek from her battle with his ex. At least she was quiet now, almost catatonic. He was beginning to feel less freaked out. Certainly his ex was out of line, but Mandy's reaction had totally freaked him out. She really hadn't had that much to drink, didn't appear drunk. He didn't even think she'd finished her second drink. They'd smoked a little weed in the car on the way to the club—maybe it was the combination of the two? She was, after all, so young. (He forgot that sometimes.)

He rubbed his hand into his face. What was he doing with this girl? This *high school* girl? And what was he going to do with her *now*? He got up and paced around the small room. He just needed to buy some time, get her in better shape before her parents called the police or something. There were others at the club who knew her. It wouldn't be long before they'd find out what happened if they started asking. He spotted Mandy's purse and pulled out her cell phone. "Mandy," he said. "Who's your best friend?"

When she didn't answer he asked her again. The only response he could get out of her was, "You." He flipped through her phone log and noted more CALLS TO and CALLS FROM — Kelly more than anyone else.

~

Carol was brushing her teeth when she thought she heard her cell phone beep. Jerry was still downstairs, so she rinsed out her mouth and went to retrieve it from the bedside table. As she read the text, she frowned — Amanda will be sleeping at Kelly's tonight. Amanda had added a little graphic at the end of the text with a smiley face whose eyes popped out as little hearts. *Odd. Well, whatever.* Carol would take what she could get. She texted back, K and added with some difficulty, LOVE YOU. U 2 came back and Carol smiled as she put down the phone.

~

Katy picked up the ice cream container off her bed, carried it dripping into the bathroom, and tossed it into the tub. She and Christy shoved the soiled bedding out of their way and snuggled under a clean blanket from the linen closet. They spent the next four hours in adolescent prattle until falling asleep in a tangled mess of hair and smeared eyeliner — Brandon and Zack slept in their own beds, dreaming of fiery car wrecks and blown-apart heads.

~

And what of Lenny Couch? He was alone in his rented bed, in the little one bedroom apartment he was subleasing; and because he never did get his medical question answered, he lay there awake, worrying about his ass.

4

Seven-thirty a.m. seemed unreasonably early for a Sunday morning, and as Jerry dragged himself out of bed and quietly searched for suitable running attire, he cursed his brother. Why had he, once again, allowed Tom to talk him into foolishness? Jerry would have happily—and realistically—surrendered to his aging body had it not been for his brother. But he pulled on his old sweats without waking Carol and padded into the kitchen for coffee and cereal. Deep down he knew that a little struggle would do him good.

Jerry pulled up to Tom's at seven-fifty-nine with satisfaction. Jerry felt even more pleased when Tom, who was already stretching in the front lawn, looked up from his leg-pull in surprise, and checked his watch and was even more surprised. Jerry had just ruined a perfectly good opportunity to annoy his brother. He got out of his car and joined Tom, smiling smugly as he said, "You look surprised to see me. You did say eight, didn't you?" Tom's obsession with punctuality had long been a source of contention, and Jerry felt a little victorious.

"I guess after all these years, I've finally got you trained," retorted Tom dryly.

Jerry narrowed his eyes at his brother. *Damn!* He'd have to give that point to Tom. It was too early to spar with a pro, so Jerry did not respond. He joined Tom on the lawn and stretched his stiff, old body.

The local park, with a well-maintained jogging path, was a few blocks from Tom's house, so they began to make their way toward the path at a slow, easy jog. By the time they reached the entrance of the park, they were already puffing, and Tom was feeling an uncomfortable tightness in his chest and an ache in his right knee.

"You okay?" Jerry asked him.

They stopped at the entrance of the jogging path. "Why? Do I look like I might be having a heart attack?" Tom made his voice sound light and mocking, but he was eager for an answer.

"No ... just out of shape."

"Come on, then," said Tom in irritation, and they began down the path. They ran in silent personal misery. When they finished jogging two miles, they slowed to a walk, and Tom puffed, "I think that's pretty good for our first time out."

He was limping noticeably now. Jerry looked at his knee. It was red and swollen. "You better put some ice on that," Jerry told him.

"I don't believe that fat little fuck ran ten miles," said Tom. Jerry looked at him in confusion. "Lenny Couch!"

"Oh! *That* fat little fuck," Jerry laughed. "Why do you let him get to you?"

"I don't know! But it makes me dislike him all the more."

And, as always, the way Tom said these simple words made Jerry laugh. Nobody, not even Carol, could make him laugh like Tom could.

As they limped home, Jerry realized that a week had not gone by without him and Tom seeing each other other than Jerry's first year at UAlbany. It seemed a little weird, and yet ... why weird? When they were growing up it was just the two of them. The only stable thing in their young lives was each other. Wasn't it natural to want to hang on to that? They'd lived together through college and most of Jerry's med school years. Jerry had even lived with Sarah and Tom their first few years of marriage, helping with the babies and the rent. He wondered if he'd still be with them if Sarah had not introduced him to Carol—now that would be weird, bordering on pathological! He felt a sudden rush of sentimentality and gratitude toward his brother. He looked at him, about to say something mushy, but then saw how badly Tom limped—the grey hair that mingled with his natural light-brown, the small lines creasing his face—and Jerry felt something else: fear. And all that he could manage to get out was, "You better put some ice on that."

"Yeah, I heard you the first time," said Tom.

Jerry felt mildly rebuffed and the sentimental moment passed.

Once back at Tom's, they went into the kitchen. Tom sat at the table and moaned as he put his leg up on a chair and stared at his knee in irritation. Jerry got him a bag of ice and set two glasses of water on the table. He dug around in a cabinet and fished out a bottle of Advil. He shook out two for himself and put the rest of the bottle next to Tom's glass of water. He sat down across from Tom.

"This sucks, Jerry. It really does!" Tom rubbed his forehead with his hand. "It was that stupid curb we went over—right at the beginning."

"You can take three, four if it's really bad, but you should eat something." Jerry grabbed a banana from the bowl on the table and placed it next to the glass and the Advil. Tom just gave him a dirty look.

"Middle age sucks," said Tom.

Jerry smiled at him. "You're way past middle age."

"No, I'm not!"

"Tom, you're an accountant. Do the math. Do you really think you will live to one hundred and four?"

Tom waved his hand at Jerry in irritated dismissal. "Whatever! You suck!"

Jerry just laughed.

They both looked up at the sound of someone's approach. It was David. He wore nothing but a pair of sweatpants, his hair messed from sleep. He was a young version of Tom—tall and well-built, rugged in his handsomeness. He went right for the coffee, and only after he sipped his life-giving liquid did he take in the scene: both men at the table, sweaty and beat, the Advil, the ice pack on his father's knee. A smile crept across David's face, and he stretched his arms above his head and pulled his chest out, feeling his twenty-one-year-old muscles ripple, and did a slow turn. He knew he looked awesome. David ducked quickly as the banana flew across the room. He laughed heartily.

"Get some clothes on, dammit," said his father.

David laughed again and flexed his muscles as he picked up the banana. "Thanks for the banana, old man," he chuckled as he walked back down the hall, coffee in one hand, banana in the other.

Jerry smiled and shook his head. Tom glared at the departing back and was tempted to throw another piece of fruit at his son, something of more significance, a cantaloupe perhaps—if he could lift the damn thing! "I need to get that kid out of my house," he told Jerry. Then as if replacing one nemesis for another, Alby came hobbling into the room and sat down right in front of Tom, pinning her green feline eyes on him. "Jesus," moaned Tom. Jerry laughed. Alby switched her tail, and ever so slowly raised what was left of her right leg and pointed it at Tom.

"That is so bizarre," observed Jerry as he watched the cat. "And she only does that to you?"

Tom rubbed his head again. "Yes," he groaned. Tom had an unfortunate history with Sarah's cats. The first, many years ago, was Albert. Tom, accidentally on purpose, ran him over in the driveway, something that Sarah had yet to forgive him for. Alberta (shortened to Alby) was Tom's replacement-apology kitty. She'd had all four legs when he'd picked her out of the litter ten years ago, but then there was the ill-fated incident with Tom and the lawnmower—something that neither Sarah nor Alby had forgiven him for.

Tom picked up his good leg with the intention of giving the cat a little kick, when Sarah walked into the room. "Tom!" she yelled, and gave him an exasperated look.

"Oops." He put his leg down quickly. "Just stretching." He gave her a boyish grin. She shook her head at him. "Don't be mean to me!"

Where Are the Cocoa Puffs?

he begged. "Can't you see I'm injured," pointing to his knee. Sarah looked at his knee without sympathy.

"He has had a bad morning," offered Jerry.

"You two really ought to take this fitness thing a little slower," she said as she poured herself some coffee. "You know, you're not young anymore. Coffee?" she offered. Both men shook their heads. Tom reached for a new banana, popped four Advil in his mouth, and followed it up with a water and banana chaser. Sarah glanced again at her husband's knee before heading to her office. "I guess David will have to mow the grass today."

Tom turned to Jerry after she'd left. "And that's as much sympathy as I'm going to get. Thirty years ago she would have helped me to bed, brought me the newspaper, handed me the TV clicker, provided me with ice packs, food, sympathy sex—now all I get is a reprieve from mowing the lawn."

"She offered you coffee."

"It's not the same as sympathy sex," he mused.

"Well, I need to get going," said Jerry as he stood up from the table with a groan. "Is there anything, other than sex, that I can do for you before I leave?"

Tom shook his head with exaggerated sorrowfulness. "No, I'll manage somehow."

~

Jerry pulled into the garage and, before he stepped into the mudroom, remembered the Sunday paper. He went back to the front of the garage and stepped through the door that led to the front of the house. He noticed the old Jetta and the girl with the bright red hair kissing the driver of the car parked a house away. It was inconsistent with the neighborhood, so he glanced up again as he bent to get the paper. The girl, who by now had stepped out of the car, stood stockstill by the open door and stared at him—a deer caught in headlights. Even as recognition registered, comprehension did not, but some instinct made him move quickly to the road and in front of the car to block any possible escape. He looked at Amanda, still wide-eyed and stunned, and saw the scratch across her cheek. He stepped up to the driver's side of the car and indicated to the young man behind the wheel that he wanted the window opened.

Shit, shit, shit, was all that went through Ryan's mind as he slowly rolled down the window. This thought immediately changed to, *I'm so fucked. I am so fucking fucked.*

Once the window was down, Jerry extended his right hand and said with a smile that neither matched his eyes nor tone of voice, "Jerry Benson. And you are?"

Ryan reached for Jerry's hand awkwardly through the window, and as he felt the firm grasp of the other man's hand, he said, "Ryan Downing. It's nice to meet you, Dr. Benson." If Jerry was impressed by the use of his formal title, he did not let on, but nodded his head slowly in contemplation, finally releasing his grip on Ryan's hand. Jerry looked away from the young man, and met Amanda's gaze. Her face was now set in stubborn defiance. He smiled at her slightly, then returned his attention to this *Ryan Downing* fellow. "Why don't you come in, meet the rest of the family?" He watched with pleasure as Ryan's face shifted, almost imperceptibly, from discomfort to panic.

"Thank you, sir. Normally I would, but I have some things I have to do this afternoon."

"Sure, sure, I understand." He smiled his most welcoming smile. "Tonight then. Come for dinner. I insist. We'd love to have Ryan for dinner, wouldn't we, honey?" he said as he looked back at his daughter.

Amanda immediately grabbed at the chance to win back her place with Ryan, a chance to at least see him again, to prove to him that she wasn't crazy. Although he wasn't unkind, he'd barely said a word to her all morning. Neither one of them had brought up the events of last night. It's not like she hadn't had the right to act the way she did. That fucking bitch should never have gotten in her face—but still...maybe she'd overreacted...a little. She nodded at her father, then leaned down through the car door, her hair sweeping forward and said, "Come?" her bottom lip slipping between her teeth.

Ryan looked at her, saw the need in her chocolate eyes, and felt the rush of emotion she elicited like no one had ever been able to do before and nodded *yes.*

"Great," said Jerry. "Six then." He stepped away from the car and joined Amanda on the other side. "Nice hair," he said, as he shut the door to the passenger side of the car. He put his arm around his daughter, ignoring her tensing muscles. As he turned her toward the house, he thought of the immortal words of Sun-Tzu: *Keep your friends close and your enemies closer.*

~

Carol sat on the plush leather couch and sipped her coffee as she enjoyed the view of autumn that spread out before her, a painting too amazing to be real. She sighed, taking in the pure pleasure of solitude—no kids; no husband. Do people who live alone embrace their peaceful existence? Would she, if alone in life, be too crippled by loneliness to realize the splendor of solitude?

She'd never planned to marry—certainly never to have children. If she'd learned anything from her parents' miserable marriage, it was that marriage could be darn right miserable. And if you were brave enough to get married, then it was best not to bring children into the whole sordid affair. Her early experience with men certainly had done nothing to alter what she'd learned. She'd decided, sometime in her turbulent teenage years, that marriage was for braver or, depending on how you looked at it, stupider souls. But then she'd met Sarah at an education conference, and Sarah had all but literally dragged her home to meet her brother-in-law.

Carol had been almost twenty-nine, wild and free—fighting for women's rights, equal opportunities, equal pay, and struggling to finish her PhD. A man had been the last thing on her agenda, yet she'd allowed herself to be dragged to this woman's home—a need for a mild diversion perhaps? She'd walked into Tom and Sarah's large old house they rented, already angry with this man with whom she was forced to meet—wasn't he, just by being male, worthy of her anger? Looking forward to proving her superiority, she'd walked in with a small 2x4 on her shoulder. Jerry, unaware that she was even coming, looked up from his desk in the corner of the room, psychiatry books spread out before him, with mild interest. In the end, abnormal psychology had won, and he pushed up his glasses and returned to his studies.

She'd been slightly put out, her anger with no place to go, but she'd followed Sarah out to the patio where Tom was grilling steaks—which she would not eat—and fussed over the babies as if she'd liked them. After Tom had good-naturedly called Jerry an *anti-social faggot*, Jerry closed his books and sheepishly joined the group. Somewhere, half-way through dinner, Carol had known that abnormal psychology was no longer on Jerry's mind. Wasn't that some sort of victory?

Jerry proved to be like no man she'd ever met. There was no hidden agenda or game playing; he felt no need or desire to be better than her. He was certainly not willing to defend the male sex or dispute any conviction she might hold dear. He wanted her—without question—but if she did not want him back ... well, he was okay with that too. And if she'd gone after him out of pure obduracy, it didn't matter for long because she'd become hopelessly caught in her own trap. And here she was, twenty-two years later, in her beautiful home, with her cup of coffee at just the right temperature, loving her husband and her girls, knowing that any life she might have envisioned for herself held no relevance.

The first thing that went through Carol's mind as she looked up to the sound of the door opening was, *what has Jerry brought home from the park?* But that, of course, was just a fleeting thought. "What did you do to your hair?!" Carol said, with disbelief. As Jerry led Amanda closer and set her down on the couch across from Carol, the question changed to, "My God! What happened to your face?!"

"Yes," said Jerry, as he joined his wife on the couch. "The hair is painfully obvious, but please, tell us about your face."

Amanda considered her options, and finally blurted out, "Some bitch was in my face."

Jerry and Carol looked at each other in confusion. "We don't understand," said Carol.

"At the club!" she said with nasty exasperation. "She fucking attacked me!"

Carol was about to chastise the language, but Jerry touched her arm lightly and said with disbelief, "You were in a fight with this girl?"

"You are so stupid! Of course, I fought her!"

Carol, who had never had a physical confrontation in her life, sat in stunned silence. Jerry, a victim of his father's drunken cuffs across the face when he was very young, felt as sad and helpless as the child he once was.

"Can I go now?"

And because neither one of them wanted to look at this stranger their daughter had become, they waved her away, and were relieved when the room was free of her.

~

Ryan took a long time trying to decide what to wear. He was glad that the weather was cool and that long sleeves were appropriate—no tattoos would be scrutinized. He finally settled on simple jeans and the light blue shirt his mother had sent him last Christmas that still sported the tags. He threw the tags vaguely toward the trash can and ran his fingers through his straight dark hair. Would a little mousse make it less punkish? He fluffed it up a bit and out of his eyes. It fell back, straight and uneven, across his forehead. Well, whatever, the *doctor* had already seen his hair. He could still bag the whole thing. Why did he care what this man thought of him, anyway? Was it a need to prove himself worthy? He *was* screwing the guy's eighteen-year-old daughter after all. Show his respect for Mandy? Masochism? *This is the most likely explanation*, he thought, as he pulled on his soft leather coat and searched for his car keys. Maybe the good doc could help him figure it out.

~

Jerry set the table in the formal dining room. If they were going to do this thing, they were going to do it fully. Carol had chosen the fine china and crystal water goblets, usually reserved for holidays, which may have been a bit too much—but, what the hell. Although really not a snob, he properly placed the various silver spoons and forks on the table, thinking this young man would be clueless about how to use them. This man—surely the reason for his daughter's metamorphosis—needed to understand the way things were.

Carol was taking the roast out of the oven when Amanda came into the kitchen. She felt the tension in the air before turning her eyes to her daughter. Amanda had showered, and her hair, though just as red, had bounced back to its natural curls, somehow softening the shock. Carol wondered how long it would take before the surprise she felt each time she looked at Amanda would fade. Amanda's eyes were big and glassy with excitement—her nervous, jumpy energy, practically tangible.

"Can I help?"

Carol looked at her, even more surprised. "Sure! You can finish the salad," she said, pointing to the tomatoes that needed to be cut and the nearby cucumber. As Amanda began to chop with such enthusiasm that Carol worried for her fingers, Carol asked casually, "So how did you and Ryan meet? It is *Ryan*, right?"

Amanda nodded her head as she jabbed at the tomato as if to kill it. "At a party."

"When?"

"A few weeks ago."

Carol nodded her head and thought about this piece of information. After a long moment, she asked, "What's he do?"

Amanda shrugged her shoulders. "Don't know."

"Is he in school?" Amanda shrugged. *Did she ever talk to this boy… this man? If not talking, what then?* Carol thought.

"I guess he works somewhere. Maybe takes classes at Albany, sometimes?" Amanda finally offered, distracted by the death of the tomato.

"How old is he?" Carol ventured, knowing she was asking just one question too many.

Amanda chopped hard at the cucumber, slicing it meanly in half. "I don't *know!*"

Carol jumped involuntarily. Amanda swung her way, the knifepoint suspended between them momentarily before she let it drop loudly to the counter.

"I can't do this! I hate cucumbers!"

"Okay...okay," said Carol, trying to make her voice calm. "Why don't you take that vase of flowers and put it on the dining room table."

I can do that. I can do that, thought Amanda as she picked up the vase and carried it carefully to the dining room, breathing deeply, wishing she'd smoked just a little more weed. She just could not seem to slow her mind down or the jumpiness of her body. It wasn't like she wanted to scream at her mother. She really didn't hate cucumbers at all. And her mother, really, she didn't hate her.

She stepped into the dining room. Her father was just putting the water goblets above and to the right of the plates as she walked in. The table looked lovely—made lovelier by the flowers she gently placed in the center. Jerry looked up at her and smiled; Amanda felt her eyes fill with tears.

It hadn't been all that long since they'd celebrated her eighteenth birthday in this very room, used these very same plates. She'd wanted a fancy dinner party with all her best friends donned in their best summer attire—*no jeans allowed* was specifically printed on the invitations. She'd worn her pretty sleeveless green dress, her hair pulled and twisted into a fancy updo, her mother's pearls around her neck. Her mother had made all the food, served them courses as if they were in a fancy restaurant. She'd invited eleven people since twelve fit perfectly at the table when it had all the leafs in place. It had been so difficult to decide which eleven people to invite (five girls and six boys), but in the end she felt she'd chosen wisely.

All the girls had looked beautiful in their slinky summer dresses. And she really wasn't all that bothered by the boys, all of them respecting the *no jeans* request by wearing nasty cut-offs, gym shorts, or sweats. Kenny Frank was the only boy to wear a tie, but he'd failed to wear a shirt—which was okay, because the bright floral print looked good against his buff, muscular chest.

Her best friend, Ally, had sat to her left in a beautiful slinky yellow dress. Jonathan was to her right, wearing one of those stupid tee shirts with a tux painted on it, and tugging at her hair, messing up her 'do and laughing. Everyone was laughing, sticking their pinky fingers out as they drank the sparkling cider from her mother's crystal goblets and saying, "To the birthday princess!" (It was pretty obvious that most everyone had smoked a little something or drank something a little stronger than sparkling cider before ringing the doorbell.)

Amanda had felt like a princess, sitting at the head of the table, smiling as her friends toasted her, pushing Jonathan's hand playfully from her 'do, proud of the wonderful food her mother had prepared.

"I just can't wait for the birthday spanking!" exclaimed Jonathan. Everyone had laughed, even her mother, as she slipped out of the room, carrying away the dirty dinner plates.

Jonathan's hand was on the back of her head; Amanda felt a strand of hair fall free of its constraints. Again, she removed the hand. "Do I get to pick who spanks me?" asked Amanda, making the laughter increase and eliciting hopeful looks from some of the boys.

"Oh! Oh! Me! Pick Me!" cried Alex Simmons from across the table, shooting his hand up and jumping up from his chair.

Chad Finch was suddenly up and grabbing Alex in a good-natured headlock, smashing Alex's dark moussed-up spikes back into his head, as he exclaimed, "Sit down, motherfucker. She doesn't want your hands anywhere near her ass!" sparking a brief, but rowdy wrestling match, which shook the table, spilling goblets, teetering the candles, and causing general pandemonium. Kenny Frank jumped up like a bull with two baby carrots he'd stolen from the relish tray stuffed up his nose and snorted them out and onto the table, which made Jennifer Wiley laugh so hard that she'd fallen off her chair. But Amanda—she hadn't laughed at all.

She'd stood up, more hair falling from her 'do, and screamed hysterically above the chaos, "Stop it! Stop it! You're breaking my mother's things! You're spoiling everything!" She'd looked at the stunned faces of her friends and burst into tears. She'd ran from the room, and it was Ally who'd followed her, fixed her hair, cleaned up her makeup . . . .

They'd managed to finish dinner, cut the cake, even have ice cream, but something had been lost that day, and it was yet to be found. It was no wonder none of them called her anymore, even Ally barely spoke to her at school and avoided her as if she were contagious.

"Amanda?" her father asked.

She looked up from the table, waved away his concern, and said softly, "It looks like Christmas." And then she was thinking of her childhood and the pure, uncomplicated joy of being a child, the love her parents had always shown her. Her father, taking this as some sort of apology, walked over to her. He put his arm around her, agreeing about the table; she fought hard not to cringe and shove him away.

~

Ryan chose the front door this time. He'd thought about bringing a bottle of wine, but quickly discarded that foolish idea and instead came empty-handed, deciding flowers were too *gay* and he was hard-pressed to come up with anything else. He stood there a moment, the large wooden door a solid barrier before him. He adjusted his coat and felt his hair, making sure it wasn't doing something really strange, before tapping the bell gently with his right hand. He tensed to the movement behind the door and adjusted his face in pleasant salutation. Mercifully, Mandy opened the door. The red hair, still astounding, was now in cascading curls and he could not help but lean forward and kiss her lightly, his hand in her hair, hoping that her father wasn't frowning from beyond the door. "Hey, babe," he whispered.

"Hey." She let him into the house—which was even more impressive through the front door. Two large white urns sprouting leafy green ferns adorned the formal entranceway. Off to the right, a dark mahogany spiral staircase led gracefully to the upstairs. To the left, an archway to the formal dining room. He could just make out that the table was set, and waiting for him. Straight ahead, a larger-arched entrance showed a different, but no less spectacular, view of the massive living room and the windows beyond. The view of the valley, the focus the house had been created around, was impossible to overlook even as it was dwarfed by the archway. The kitchen, off to the left of the living room, was not visible from where they stood.

"They're in the kitchen," she said. He kissed her again, this time harder, but not so hard as to be forced to hide or wait out an unwelcome hard-on. He moved away from her and pulled at the imaginary noose around his neck, his tongue lolling out with his imaginary death. Mandy laughed merrily, and they headed for the kitchen.

Carol was pulling out the rolls from the oven as Amanda and Ryan walked into the room. She turned around, her face flushed from the heat of the oven, which helped hide any other flush that might have erupted on her face from the pure sexuality of this young man—definitely man, not boy—who walked beside her daughter. Dark hair, dark soulful eyes, beautiful, but not-too-beautiful cheek bones—he looked like a young Johnny Depp...Jim Morrison perhaps?

Christy felt it too and her fifteen-year-old body did not quite know what to do with itself. Much to her horror, she giggled and had to turn her face in shame.

Jerry made the introductions, seemingly oblivious of the static in the air.

Carol, who normally would have offered her guest a drink (nonalcoholic in this case) and chit-chatted before dinner, felt the need to sit down. She rushed to get the food on the table, handing various bowls and platters to her family to take to the dining room. Once seated, Carol smiled at Ryan, feeling safer with the hard, firm wood of the large table to lean on and half her body hidden from view. "I'm so glad you could join us for Sunday dinner," she said, as if they ate like this every Sunday. Ryan smiled a slightly-crooked-and-damned-if-it-wasn't-sexy smile her way, and thanked her for allowing him to be there. His teeth were the sort of perfect that only braces could endow. His shirt was of a fine linen cloth, Italian most likely. His hair, a curious black, flopped forward in uneven points, slipping down his forehead and threatening his eyes. Shorter in the back, random tuffs of hair stood erect and disorganized. Carol had the distinct—and incredibly inappropriate—urge to run her fingers through that hair.

Ryan picked up his linen napkin and placed it across his lap, and said, "Wow! This looks great." He appreciated the goblets, the softly lit candles, and the delicate china, knowing full well it was for him—not in the way a guest would hope to be honored, but as an intimidation; a challenge. He was up for it. Hadn't just walking in the door been the biggest obstacle?

There was little talk other than culinary chatter as they began to pass the food around. Once the plates were full, Ryan waited until Jerry picked up his fork, not sure if there was to be some sort of blessing before reaching for his own. Amanda sat to his left and sizzled with excitement. He turned her way, his soft eyes shining with admiration, and squeezed her thigh surreptitiously under the table.

Christy sat across from them, her mouth slightly agape. She seemed to suddenly realize this and forced it shut. She reached for the butter and gave her full concentration to buttering her bread.

Jerry missed the thigh squeeze, but had noted the napkin, now neatly on Ryan's lap. He was further disappointed when Ryan reached for the salad fork without hesitation. He began to eat the leafy greens and set the fork carefully on the salad plate as he took a drink of water. Jerry sighed a bit. Then there was Carol's behavior, acting as if she'd never seen a man before—which did nothing to improve Jerry's disposition. He sighed again softly and narrowed his eyes at Ryan, waiting for just the right moment before he said, "So tell us about yourself."

Jerry watched with satisfaction as Ryan, who had just put an unwieldy piece of lettuce in his mouth, looked momentarily perplexed on how to tackle such a broad-based, almost hostile question—and damn if Carol didn't come to his rescue and pleasantly say, "Are you working? Going to school?"

Ryan swallowed with relief and smiled at Carol as he said, "Well, both really. I work at UPS. A package handler." He looked apologetic as he continued, "I took this semester off from Albany. I had to save some money, you know, to get through—"

"And what are you studying? Your major?" Jerry interrupted, with his subtle assault.

Ryan turned to him and met his eye as he said, "Architecture, sir. I have one semester left."

Amanda looked at him in surprise. She hadn't known that. She hadn't even known where he worked. Of course, she'd never asked. Had she even cared?

The room was duly impressed, and Jerry paused with a soft sigh to consider his next move.

"Where are you from?" asked Carol. "Did you grow up around here?"

Ryan gently dabbed at his mouth then placed the napkin back on his lap. "No ma'am. Atlanta."

Well, thought Jerry, that would explain the natural use of sir and ma'am, but he was hard-pressed to pick up an accent. "Is that where your parents are now? Atlanta?" he tested.

Ryan shook his head. There was a hint of sadness in his movement. "No, sir. My father's dead a long time now. My mom's remarried, living in Charlotte."

Jerry felt himself running out of steam. He knew all about the dead parent thing. He was finding it difficult to find fault, so was forced to change tactics. "How old are you?" he asked bluntly.

There was a downbeat of silence, Ryan's eyes meeting Jerry's, and then flickering away. "Twenty-one," Ryan lied in such an obvious way that Christy laughed out loud. Ryan flushed and smiled sheepishly, adding quickly, "Three years ago."

"Excuse me?" asked Jerry, a twinkle in his eye.

Ryan's grin was boyish with embarrassment as he said, "Three years ago I was twenty-one, sir." They all laughed then, even Jerry, and something in the way Ryan said it reminded him of his brother, Tom, and he softened, just a bit, to this new friend of his daughter's.

Ryan felt the air shift and knew that he had survived the initial inquisition, albeit shoddily. The focus moved slightly away from him, and he was able gather his own information about this family, this life that Mandy was part of, and these people who loved her. He covertly studied Dr. Benson as he looked down to cut his meat. He was a decent enough looking man for his age. Not the least bit intimidating, although he'd tried hard to be. Still in good shape, a pleasant, calming face. Ryan imagined he was quite good at his job.

It was obvious that Carol had never quite had Mandy's incredible looks, but Mandy's hair, her eyes, her hot little body, came from her mother. Carol was striking, in a sexy older woman sort of way. He had not missed, nor did he ever, the effect he had on most women, including Carol. It had been part of his daily life since he was fourteen, and although he never lost appreciation for it and used it to his advantage, he certainly did not dwell on it.

Christy was cute, would probably be pretty in a couple years. She was a perfect combination in body and face of her mother and father. It amused him that she couldn't even look him in the eye. Each time he looked her way, her blue eyes were on him, but then shifted away and down, getting lost in the blush of her face. The contrast in the personalities of the sisters was remarkable. Amanda, the nucleus in a crowd, even in this tiny family—and isn't that what took his breath away? Even now he could feel it, the excitement in her voice as she talked—she was doing all the talking—her joy of being alive, as if feeling life more intensely than most.

Mandy grew more animated, chattering excitedly about her plans to study biomedical engineering. After she got her PhD, she was sure she would develop an artificial eye that could actually see, transmitting the images directly to the brain, similar to an electronic pathway, but better than the optic nerve. Once that was done, the next thing she would tackle was the auditory system. A cure for deafness; something much better than cochlear implants. Her parents watched her with amazement, a slight knit to Jerry's brow. Christy was bored and feeling less self-conscious—now that she'd realized that he was only human and not some god Amanda had acquired. She wanted to talk about herself but could not get a word in edgewise. Ryan sat back, a pleasant smile on his face, and thought about the last time he'd seen Mandy naked.

~

It was ten-thirty. Ryan had left about an hour ago. Amanda had wanted to go with him, but they had refused her request. She had, thankfully, not had a fit in front of Ryan. Jerry sat in the living room watching her now. He'd been watching her all evening, ever since the biomedical engineering thing. Carol had already gone up to bed. Amanda was now in the middle of the living room, and she was bouncing—literally bouncing—with energy. "Amanda," he said quietly. "You need to calm down."

"Aren't you." Bounce…her red hair on the wing. "Glad." Bounce… "To see me *happy?!*" The words burst from her mouth, edging on hysteria.

With that, he put his head in his hands and felt the sort of grief that numbs the mind, but takes deep pleasure in residing in your very gut, a swift kick, an expanding pain, the capture of your very soul. The tiny thought that had crept into his head hours ago could no longer be denied. As it grew, it took form and finally was so obvious that he felt foolish for having denied it so long. And now that it was a concrete thing, he knew that he must act. He must get up and act. But he was numb and drained, so he stood up with difficulty. "Stay," he gently told her, and made his way up the stairs and into his bedroom.

"I need to go into my office," he told his wife.

"What? You're not on call." Carol looked up from the book she was reading in bed, her glasses perched on her nose.

He did not want to tell her. He did not want to say the words aloud, as if the words would make it more real, more tangible. If he could only keep it to himself, hide it, treat it, and make it go away. "I have to get some meds for Amanda," he managed to get out, without bursting into tears.

Carol looked at him, a mixture of dread and confusion. "I don't understand."

He really just couldn't get into all of this. Now that things were set in motion, it became imperative that the movement continue. Yet he had to tell her something.

"You know my mother; she was not a well woman." Carol's confusion deepened. She had never known his mother. She'd died years ago from a deliberate overdose of her medication. "Mentally, she was ill." Carol nodded her head. Of course, it went without saying. "And then there's your Uncle Joe...."

There was this sort of fear that invaded Carol's face, and he knew that she understood what he was attempting to say, so he closed his eyes to ward off tears and said, "And that's why I have to go."

"But she was in such a great mood tonight. I can't remember the last time she's been so happy and animated," Carol argued.

He opened his eyes to her, and simply said, "I have to go. You need to watch her."

When he got to his office, he went immediately to the cabinet where he kept the endless supplies of samples that drug reps were always bringing him. He shuffled through the boxes, taking samples of Depakote. He skipped over the antidepressants and briefly considered the antipsychotics, choosing Seroquel over Risperdal. He threw in some Xanax and Klonopin for good measure before leaving quickly with his sack of major pharmaceuticals tucked under his arm. He was grateful, as he made his way back through the tunnel that led to the parking garage, that he didn't run into anyone from the hospital that he knew.

When he returned, it was midnight. The house was quiet, the smell of dinner and candle wax still in the air. The living room was deserted; the lights were off. There was the faint glow from the front of the house. Carol must have left the light on at the top of the stairs, a beacon he went toward in the gloom of the house. All the bedroom doors were shut, and it appeared like any other night when he'd been forced out of bed and called into the hospital, sneaking back in a way that did not wake his family. But this was not like any other night, and he considered which door to go to first in the search for his daughter.

He found Carol in bed, unable to sleep, the gentle light from the bedside lamp illuminating half her face. She looked at him with tired and worried eyes. "I thought you were going to watch her," he said with mild reproof.

"She said she wanted to sleep and insisted I leave." She said this simply, without apology. He could not help the look of exasperation that flicked across his face. She saw it, and her lips tightened with her own disapproval.

Jerry walked down the hall with trepidation. He reached the door, afraid of what he might find—her gone or even dead. He should have taken her with him and admitted her where he knew she would be safe. Fear was living in his gut, but when he opened the door she was there, alive, and was even smiling a bit. "You're not sleeping," he noted, his voice professionally calm. Her eyes were wild and glassy as if she might never sleep again, but her face was tranquil. The glow of her laptop was all that lit the room. He could detect the sweet smell of pot and he understood her need, but he had brought her something better—if only he could convince her of this.

"No! I'm not tired!" He stepped into the room and sat on the edge of the bed. "I was thinking," she said excitedly, "that as soon as I'm done with school that I'd get a job on a cruise ship as a dancer or a singer or both: a singing dancer, singing with dance. I might work in the kitchen, too, making little tarts. I like chocolate, but I could do fruit too."

"Amanda."

"… it would be fun to work in the casino with my tarts and I could dance, up on the bar—do you think they give tips to dancers on a cruise ship? If the boat's rocking does the music beat faster? I think my feet could keep that beat. I'm sure they pay you well, even without tips …."

"Amanda," he said her name louder and touched her arm gently. She pulled away rudely at the touch and looked at him with irritation. "What?!"

He heard Carol at the doorway but did not look her way. "When is the last time you slept?"

"What?"

"Did you sleep last night?" he asked slowly, saying each word calmly and distinctly. Carol came in and sat down next to him.

"I don't need to sleep anymore; I don't have time. I need to practice my dancing," and looked as if she might jump out of bed to dance.

"You need to sleep, just a little, so that you'll dance better."

"But don't you see? I can't! You just have no idea! You have no idea what goes on in my head!" and her face twisted in agony and she began to weep.

He closed his eyes to the pain of her words because he did have an idea of what went on in her head, but only an idea. "I know ... I know." He wanted to reach for her and rock her in his arms, but he could feel her brittleness and did not touch her. He felt Carol lean on him in despair, and he told Amanda he could help her, and went to his arsenal of drugs, picking one from each of the three classes he'd brought. He gave her water and handed her pills and watched as she took them without resistance. He glanced at Carol, and was not sure if her look portrayed bewilderment, condemnation, or a little of both.

"What's wrong with me?" The words were small and frail, laced with fear. And he told her, as he'd told hundreds of patients, what he believed, what he knew, what he did not know, but he kept it short and simple, only telling her what he thought she could handle in her fragile state.

Carol heard the words *brain disease, bipolar, manic depressive illness*, and clutched them as a gift, a pardon, a reprieve from guilt. But then, knowing what she knew from her husband's profession and the sort of people he dealt with, she was seized by another kind of guilt — a guilt of being pleased about being blameless; of wishing a lifelong illness on her child rather than owning up to the fact that she had somehow been a terrible mother. And then another layer of guilt — she was relieved that it was Jerry who more closely carried the rotten genes that they had unwittingly passed on to their child, and blamed him for the sperm he'd placed in Carol when all they'd wanted was a dream.

Amanda heard her father's words and also felt relief. At least she wasn't crazy. She heard him say there was something wrong with her, but then again, he was telling her that she *was* crazy—really *crazy*. Then her father's words got jumbled up and she ceased to listen, and was overcome by the need to tell him of all the books she planned to write.

He listened to her endless blather and watched with satisfaction as she slowed and calmed. Finally, before two hours passed, she shut her eyes and fell into a blissful sleep. He had insisted Carol get some sleep, as his body, rudely transformed during his residency, was used to this sort of thing. It had been decided, before she went to sleep, that Carol would stay home with Amanda. Jerry looked at his daughter for a while before deeming it safe to join his wife and try to get a little rest before starting his day with other people's tragedies.

~

Amanda was having the most amazing dream, a Wizard-of-Oz burst of color, a rich, full saga, heavy with detail—love, hate, and intrigue. It went on the entire night and into the morning light, continuing until she was apparently awake and looking about her room in drowsy, splendid rapture. She closed her eyes again and gave in to the dream, only slightly aware that her mother had again come into the room and then left like a timid, little mouse.

It was some hours later—the urge to use the bathroom forcing her out of bed and the gradual realization that she was late for school—that she had a math test, and that Ryan had promised to meet her after school before he went to work. (This got her mind spinning and her energy pumping.) When she finally located her mother in her office downstairs, she was anxious and desperate to get to school. Her mother seemed resistant to the idea as it was already after eleven-forty and most of the school day was over. Panic was too small of a word to describe the sensation that invaded Amanda's body. But *finally* her mother became reasonable and agreed to drive her in—so that Amanda would not burst—and she relaxed in the knowledge that she would be there when Ryan came.

5

Now that she had been discovered—given the words and the diagnosis—it gave her license to behave in whatever manner she wished. She was crazy and it was a relief to let the power out, to not have to keep it locked inside. With this release, she was able to just hang on and go to school on Monday, stay sane with Ryan—stay just above the bedlam of her mind.

She took the pills her father gave her each night because sleeping was good and the dreams were great, but when she complained about her morning fog and the Seroquel was decreased, she raced about in her mind at night until she crashed into misery. He told her to take it early in the evening, but then she was tired and forced to sleep before all that she needed to think about had been thought. He kept upping the other drug until she felt like all she was doing was taking drugs—pills upon pills choking the very life out of her.

And she hated them for it, especially her mother, tiptoeing around her with those red-rimmed eyes, as if she would shatter—which of course made Amanda shatter—and it wasn't her fault; it was her mother's! (The puffiness under her eyes caused Amanda to scream and break things.) How dare they treat her like she was crazy! All they needed to do was leave her the *FUCK ALONE!*

~

"She's getting worse, not better," Carol complained to Jerry. She had survived—just barely—three days of hell with her daughter, the only reprieve being the few hours she could go to work while Amanda was at school. But now they were safe in their room. It was Wednesday night and Amanda was out with Ryan for a couple hours, giving the house a welcome calm. "Maybe she needs to try a different medication."

Jerry shook his head. How many times must they have this discussion? "It takes time. She's not even up to a therapeutic dose of Depakote yet."

"It's making her worse," Carol persisted, as if she knew what she was talking about, as if she were the psychiatrist with over twenty years of experience. This was one of the many things he found frustrating about treating mental illness: the families' impatience, their constant distrust, made all the worse because they were correct not to trust; he did not really know what he was doing. He could not know if the medication would work. He could not know if the diagnosis was even correct. What the diagnosis even meant. There was no exact science, no lab test or x-ray. He relied on his gut and experience and he was using this, this *not really knowing what he was doing*, to try to save his daughter's life.

"You don't know what it's like! How badly she treats me when you're not here!"

She said it with accusation and antagonism. They had decided that it was easier for Carol to do half-days, to take time from work to babysit their eighteen-year-old daughter, but he knew she resented the implication that her profession was less important than his.

You don't know what it's like. How many times had he heard these exact words from his patients' family members over the last twenty years? And he had always assured them that he did, because didn't all these years dealing with these difficult patients give him perhaps even a better understanding, a more solid medical understanding? And then there was, of course, his mother, her first break when he was very small, certainly giving him the empathy he needed. He had truly believed this. But now, knowing that he'd not understood at all, not understood *at all* what the families were going through, how it felt to lose a family member—his mother, never having quite been his—to lose your child, and yet not lose her, because there she was, in your face, hating you. Not just hating you, but *loathing* you. And there you are, grieving as if she were dead—even *wishing* she were dead so you could get on with it. But she was there, in your face, loathing you.

Maybe if he had spoken these thoughts to Carol—thoughts that shouldn't be said aloud, thoughts that should have not even been thought—things might have gone differently. Instead, what came out of his mouth when he responded to Carol's mistrust and distress and resentment was something else, some manifestation of his own frustration. "Damn it, Carol! It's not the medication that's making her worse," and he said it harsher than he needed to. "You need to give it time. It's not like the brain has a switch that can be turned on by a few days of medication, and suddenly decide, 'Oh! Now I'm going to be normal!'" he continued with mean sarcasm. "You've got to trust me, damn it!" It felt good to say what he always wanted to say but could not to his patients and their families, but the look that Carol gave him, after he spit his frustration at her, made him feel more alone than he had ever felt before.

Carol felt it too, the loneliness, the isolation. The only one she could talk to, now an enemy. She hadn't told a soul what she was going through. Not her mother, nor her brother, not Sarah, and certainly no one at work. And why? If Amanda had just been diagnosed with a brain tumor or cancer, something more tangible, she would have told them, gotten their support, not been ashamed or embarrassed. She knew that Jerry had yet to tell his brother, hadn't even seen Tom—the injured knee a reprieve from Tom's sudden obsession with his body. They'd planned to have dinner tonight, the four of them, but they'd begged off—Jerry, lying to Tom, claiming Carol had a headache, or some such thing. They were too raw for socializing.

It had only been three days since Ryan had come to dinner, and in that time Carol had been called a *fucking bitch* by her daughter so many times that it barely fazed her anymore; it was equivalent to *I hate you* or the slam of a door, a parental hardship that comes with the territory. What bothered her more was the loss of the ability to simply walk across the room; she felt like an intruder in her own home. The tension and hatred seeping from Amanda's pores, flowing through the house, was alien and evil and yet so real that it made the hairs on Carol's arms quiver to attention. And then there was Amanda's sudden raw agony, beating Amanda down, ripping at Carol's heart and tearing at her soul. She was afraid to ask Amanda the simplest of questions, always preparing for the *fuck you*, sometimes getting an almost pleasant answer. Then there were the times Carol innocently made some little statement or joke and was hit with hysteria and verbal violence, an occasional object thrown her way. She never knew what, if anything, was going to come at her next.

~

Christy heard the song of her parents' harsh words but could not comprehend them. She didn't need to; she knew they were talking—no, arguing—about Amanda. Everything was about Amanda, even worse than it had been before, as it always had been. Christy was always in the background, the good child. And now her parents were freaking out, over what? It wasn't as if anything was any different; in fact, if anything, Amanda was nicer to her. She hardly ever made fun of her anymore, didn't put her down. Amanda had even gone into her room the other night, hung out for a while to talk nonstop about Ryan—which was sort of annoying, but it was nice to be her sister's confidant; nice that Amanda felt she could tell her absolutely everything about the guy. This sudden idea of her father's that Amanda was sick (he must be obsessed with his work) didn't make sense to her. All Amanda needed to do was lay off the weed a bit—and all the other drugs that fucked up her mind.

~

"How do you know it's not the drugs?"

Carol was still at it, desperate for some sort of resolution, never willing to go to sleep angry or unsettled. Carol had brought Amanda into his office on Monday for a diagnostic workup, and he'd done the obligatory blood tests and urinalysis; he had sent her across the street for an MRI, an EKG, and he'd considered, but then scrapped, a lumbar puncture, for Amanda was on the edge of hysteria. As he anticipated, all the tests were normal other than the tox screen—the levels of cannabis not surprising; no other street drugs found.

He was tired now. He wanted to go to sleep. "Marijuana isn't causing the manic state she's in. If anything, it calms her down; she's self-medicating." He'd told her all this before. They'd been through all this before and he was so tired that all he wanted to do was sleep, but his wife was like a terrier, with unlimited access to her daughter's doctor.

"Maybe she should be in the hospital," Carol said.

Jerry sighed heavily. "I told you before; I don't think it's warranted. She's not suicidal. She's not a danger to anyone. You don't know how bad things can be at the hospital." Then he told her something he'd told his patients and their families many times over the years, but he said it coldly, without compassion. "You are, of course, entitled to a second opinion." And with that, he rolled his back to her, a period on the end of the discussion. He added an exclamation point as he flicked off his light.

Before his mind drifted off to restless sleep, he wondered again about the inanity of what he was doing—treating his own daughter.

Carol lay on her back in the dark, staring at the ceiling she could not see, and enjoyed the sensation of the tears that rolled slowly down the sides of her cheeks, knowing that she'd been wronged, that he was being a jerk, and that she'd lie there all night and cry just to spite him. Tomorrow, when she was crippled by lack of sleep, he would see what he had cost her. And then she'd find her daughter another doctor—one who wasn't a jerk; one who actually knew what he or she was doing. That would show him for thinking he's God's gift to mental illness.

~

Carol slammed the phone down in frustration. This was the fifth recording she'd reached. Did no one actually answer the phone anymore? It was Thursday morning. She'd spent the first hour of it searching the Internet for local doctors and places she could call that might be able to give her names of a good psychiatrist in the area. She'd picked up the phone, so hopeful and determined. Her frustration was almost immediate. The woman at the local National Alliance on Mental Illness was so nice, as was the gentleman who answered the phone at the National Depressive and Manic-Depressive Association, but both of them said, without hesitation, that Dr. Jerry Benson, if you could get him, was the man to see. The American Psychiatric Association, NYS Office of Mental Health, and the National Institute of Mental Health also had Jerry listed as a first choice.

But she'd managed to compile a list of suitable alternatives, which she was calling one by one, between all her professional duties. (She was, after all, getting paid to work.) Each phone call added more stress. Almost every call was answered by a machine that announced somewhere in the message that they were not accepting new patients. The few human beings she actually talked to were no better than the machines. One woman was quite rude, and another grilled her with questions as if she were conducting a job interview, saying she'd talk to the doctor and get back to her if she decided to accept Amanda as a patient. By ten-thirty, Carol was so distraught that she did something she'd never done before. She called the high school, got Sarah out of the Calculus class she was teaching, and told her everything with blubbering incoherence. Then she blew her nose, washed her face, and went to her eleven o'clock meeting.

~

"Jesus, Jerry! Were you just not going to tell me?" He was hurt and had every right to be. Jerry knew the unspoken vow of secrecy between Carol and him had been broken. Spurred by their battle, she'd sought solace elsewhere—she had, at least, told Sarah. Jerry had just returned from morning rounds, and before he even had a chance to consider whether or not he felt like eating lunch, his brother was in his office, unannounced, looking hurt and a bit frantic with concern, causing Jerry to feel even more like shit than he already did. "Why didn't you tell me?" Tom sat down in the leather chair which faced Jerry's desk.

Why, indeed. Was it a lifetime of protecting his little brother, the unwillingness to turn the roles around, the fear of Tom's easy sarcasm, or just simply the raw fragileness he felt—things too fresh, too painful to reveal? Jerry shook his head, "I'm sorry, Tom—" But he couldn't go on.

"Jesus, Jerry! Sarah says Carol is a mess. And you? How are you? You don't look so good."

Jerry waved away his concern because, really, he didn't matter; he would be fine. Jerry waited for Tom to ask about Amanda. Tom was rubbing his hand across his face, and it suddenly occurred to Jerry that Tom didn't like Amanda; he never had. Before Jerry could truly digest this epiphany, Tom looked up, tears letting go of his lashes and streaming down his face, and said, "I just can't believe our girl is sick." And with that, Jerry let all his sorrow that had been building for days, that he'd been keeping at bay for Carol's sake—trying to be strong and certain of a good outcome—come pouring out.

~

Amanda was having a bad day at school. All the kids were being shitheads. They were all so stupid and fake, and her teachers all hated her, especially Mrs. Williams. She was a total fucking bitch, and if she didn't leave Amanda alone, stop badgering her just because she was a little late then, well it wouldn't be Amanda's fault if she was forced to rip off her face. She couldn't quite understand how everyone had changed so quickly. There was a time, not that long ago, when they all knew and understood how special and powerful she was. They had given her and shown her the respect she deserved, loved her for her quick mind, her fast wit … but now, they all seemed clueless and irritating. Maybe they didn't like her anymore. It just didn't make any sense, and it hurt. A lot. Ryan had texted her, claiming he had to work early and wouldn't be able to see her today. All that she had left in the world was him, and now she'd lost that, and she'd received a *D* on a math test. She had never received a *D*! All she wanted to do was go home, smoke some weed, and take a Seroquel—or two or three—and dream, dream, dream.

Amanda saw Christy walking down the hall. As they got close, Christy waved at her and said, "What's up?"

It felt good to give her sister a little shove, and even better to hiss in her face, "Get away from me!"

"Hey! What's your fucking problem?" retorted Christy.

The kids nearby stopped, and Amanda could feel their eyes upon her, but she ignored their rudeness. She concentrated all her energies, through the amazing powers of her eyes, into vaporizing Christy.

"Whatever!" Christy said and walked away.

~

Sarah saw the exchange between her nieces. She was standing outside her classroom greeting students as they shuffled into her class. The halls were packed with teenagers, but Amanda, with that awful hair, was hard to miss; she had been looking out for her, thinking about all that Carol had told her. She was so angry with Amanda. The girl had always been difficult and now was breaking her mother's poor heart. What she really needed was a good kick in the butt. Both Jerry and Carol had indulged her as a child, let her get away with things her boys never had, and now they were paying the price.

She just wasn't sure she bought into this mental illness thing; Amanda looked perfectly sane to Sarah. It's not like she was going around mumbling to herself, and nowadays it seemed like every other kid in her classes had been labeled with something or other. It was in vogue to be ADHD or ADD/ADHA or ADHD-PI or AARP or whatever! It was ridiculous. If it wasn't a learning deficiency, then it was an eating or mood or coping issue. Wasn't it possible that we were too quick to label, too quick to pass the buck, so to speak, in order to not own up to the fact that we were maybe, just maybe, not doing our children any favors by giving them everything they wanted, letting them go off and do anything they felt like doing without any consequences?

Sarah sighed as she watched Amanda strut down the hall. She saw the black tips of her too long hair swing out with her movement and disappear into Mr. Stuart's classroom, just as the bell rang.

~

When Jerry got home that night, he came right into Carol's study. She looked up from the paperwork that she'd been trying to catch up on and prepared for the question *how's Amanda?* instead of *how are you?* and the obligatory—now, almost painful—peck on the lips. Instead, what came was his hands gently reaching for hers and a gentle pulling as he brought her to her feet. He put his arms around her and his breath in her hair. The gasp of sorrow that escaped from her lips was matched by his own, and when their shared grief was lessened and words were possible, the apology she so longed for was accepted and reciprocated.

"Bill McIntyre is going to see her tomorrow," Jerry told her as they sat side by side on the small sofa in her office. "At four." Carol nodded her head. He'd been on her list, but was not accepting new patients.

"Of course, that will mean getting to camp even later, but—" He shrugged. Neither of them was looking forward to their annual trip to the camp in the Adirondack Mountains they'd bought years ago with Tom and Sarah. For twenty years now, the families had spent Columbus Day weekend together in the mountains, catching the last bit of fall colors and preparing the place for winter. A little mental illness could not impede the slow and steady movement of family dynamics. "I'll come home and get her," Jerry continued.

"No." Carol appreciated what he was doing, but they both knew it would be much easier for her to bring Amanda to Albany. She was only planning to go into work long enough to teach her morning class and spend the rest of the day getting packed for the weekend. "I'll do it, but I'm just worried she won't go." Jerry nodded his head slowly. It wasn't as if she was three and you could just pick her up, kicking and screaming, buckle her into her car seat and that was that. "We could drug her up." Carol said with a sardonic smile. "Tranquilizer dart from twenty feet away. Then Christy and I could drag her to the car."

Carol pictured the groggy bear of her childhood. Marlin Perkins standing in the background while Jim Fowler did all the work, dragging the bear—perhaps to a cage where they could relocate it to somewhere safe. Jim pulling and sweating, Marlin maybe offering a little shove on the rump. Perkins' voice-over: "And unlike the bear, there may not always be someone to remove us from danger, which is why it's good to know Mutual of Omaha is there." Break to commercial....

"If we have to force her," Jerry was saying, "she won't be in any reasonable state for him to evaluate her, especially if she is comatose from a dart gun."

Carol, in spite of herself, laughed. "True. That's very true."

"I'll talk to her," he offered. "Bill will come here if he needs to, but let's see if we can get her there."

Before they could discuss the best way to approach their volatile daughter, Carol's cell phone rang. "It's Amanda," Carol said in confusion. She was here, in the house. She was sure of it, or thought she was. Carol flipped open the phone. "Hello?" Carol looked at Jerry as she listened to their daughter's voice and knew that he could hear that Amanda was crying and desperate. "Where are you?" She could see the dread in Jerry's eyes, and her own fear was causing another ruckus in her gut. She closed her eyes in relief and annoyance.

"Okay, okay. We'll be right there. Okay, okay. I'm going to hang up now." Her eyes opened to Jerry's and she tried to tell him, with a look, that it was okay. "We'll be right there. Okay, honey. I'm hanging up." Carol flipped the phone shut.

"Where is she?" his voice on the edge of panic.

Carol rolled her eyes in her typical exasperated mother fashion, but her voice was tight with emotion. "In her bedroom."

Jerry considered, as they made it up the stairs, that it could simply be the definition of a lazy teenager, calling on the cell rather than expending the energy necessary to come out of one's room, but Jerry was worried that it was more than this. And this was confirmed when they entered her room. He could see immediately that she had crashed into depression, crashed further and deeper than in the past few days. Her sadness was a fleeting thing that landed briefly and flitted away toward agitated mania. But now her eyes were half-closed with the edema of tears. Her mouth twisted into a frown, so consumed by misery that it was impossible to imagine it could ever be elevated to anything re-sembling a smile again. Her misery, like her hatred, a palpable thing.

"Mom," she appealed to Carol. Carol felt a flood of relief. Finally, her daughter's voice held only need. There was none of the horrid hatred and overpowering anger. Finally, her daughter loved her again, needed and wanted her help. A skinned knee and broken heart—the things mothers are best at mothering. "I'm not doing so well," Amanda managed, her voice slurring with the effort of speech.

"Oh, honey," said Carol, reaching her bedside, hugging her, clos-ing her eyes to the warmth and comfort of closeness to her daugh-ter, which she had missed and longed for. She sighed in gratitude as Amanda's arm came up and returned the embrace, knowing that nothing was ever as bad as it appeared. How many times had she endured heartache growing up? Sadness, an easy thing to understand, could be fixed with time and ice cream, perhaps. She released her daughter. "Did you have a fight with Ryan?"

Amanda looked at her, momentarily confused, before shaking her head *no, no, no.*

"Tell us what's going on," said Jerry as he sat at the foot of the bed.

"I'm so scared," she ventured.

"Scared of what?" he asked her softly.

"Half of me, you know, doesn't want to go, doesn't want to leave...." She stopped and it appeared to be all she had to say.

Carol gently rubbed her arm. "You don't need to go anywhere if you don't feel like it. You can stay home from school tomorrow if we—"

"And the other half of you?" Jerry interrupted. When she didn't answer, he added, "Amanda, what does the other half want you to do?" She jumped slightly from his voice, and then seemed to focus on the question.

"The other half says that it is a mistake." She was looking down and twisting a strand of her hair tighter and tighter until it twisted all the way to her scalp, like one might twist a weed to free it from the earth. "I shouldn't be here." Carol reached out and gently freed the strand of hair, only to have Amanda take up a new one. "I should never have been here. It's wrong for everyone, but—"

They waited, the only sound being the almost audible screaming of her thick strands of hair as they rubbed against each other. "But, you don't want to die," he said, and Carol sucked in her breath with shock. Amanda looked at him. She nodded her head, and fresh tears poured from her eyes. "Well, you need to listen to the half that tells you that you don't want to die, that you want to be here, because the other half is sick and playing a terrible joke on you."

"But if the other half is so sick, then I shouldn't be here."

"Why? Why do you think that?"

"Because if I'm here, and all the other sick people are here, then the sickness will continue, get worse and worse, and more people will get sick, defying the natural selection of things, you know? Before you know it, everyone will be sick."

"And you think that if you kill yourself you can somehow stop that?" he asked. Amanda nodded.

"But don't you see that you are alive and you have a responsibility to that life. I know it's hard to see it right now, but you will get better." He said it with conviction. The sound of his voice saying this gave him the strength and hope he hadn't felt in the last few days while thinking of his mother and most of his patients (he only saw the most dire cases). He hadn't been thinking of the thousands of people who lived quite successfully with this disease, forgetting that, when they were doing well, these people lived better than the average Joe, and that they had some insight and appreciation for beauty and maintained a creative zest that only a little madness could elicit.

"I get better and the disease continues," Amanda said, holding on to her theory.

"You don't need to die to stop that."

Carol could feel her heart beating in her chest; she could feel her tears slowly rolling down her cheeks, and she wanted to scream in agony, to grab her daughter, to clutch her to her chest, to keep her safe, to keep her alive. She couldn't believe that Jerry could talk about—no, examine—the advantages and disadvantages of suicide as if he were leaning against a podium in a ninth grade debate club.

"Just simply don't have children," he countered.

Amanda grasped onto that. "That's true. I don't have to have children."

"And if the medication works, and you get better, why not have children?" he continued. "They, most likely, will not get sick. But if they get sick, then there's medication." Amanda was crying a bit harder now, but he continued. "And, who knows, one day there will be a cure. And even if there's never a cure, the disease—the good side of manic depressive illness—has been the source of innumerable additions of beauty to this world, including you. You're a beautiful addition to this world." He, of course, was crying too.

~

Jerry went in for his first two patients on Friday, but then he had his receptionist, Betty, cancel out the rest of his schedule. He was home in plenty of time for Carol to make her eleven a.m. lecture. Amanda was still sleeping. Carol had already called the school and made arrangements for Christy to pick up any school work for Amanda. Jerry warned Carol that it might not be possible for Amanda to return to school right now. Carol was beyond distraught, as if school were more important than the health of their child, but he knew it was a barometer for her—if she can't go to school, then what *can* she do?

In reality, it would be more unusual for Amanda to be able to go to school. Almost all of his young outpatients were homebound and homeschooled by parents, or tutored for at least a small amount of time, until the medication took hold; until they slipped into fragile recovery. In any case, he'd let Bill and Amanda make that decision. He'd give up control to Amanda's new doctor and play the role of an involved parent, knowing he was doing the ethical, if not more difficult thing.

He checked on Amanda at ten, ten thirty-seven, and again at eleven twenty-one. He paced about the house in-between, making a few phone calls, attempting paperwork, packing the car for their trip, going back up the stairs, peering at her sleeping face, watching her chest move with each breath (yes, she was still alive), and tiptoeing back down the stairs to fritter away a few more minutes before checking on her again.

At eleven forty-five, he heard her voice as he made his way, yet again, up the stairs. She looked up at him, her cell to her ear, and he could tell immediately that she was better, was already cycling out of depression and heading toward—who knows what. "Okay. I'll see you then," she said sleepily. She closed her phone and announced flatly, "Ryan's on his way over."

There was nothing about the way she said it that resembled a question; he didn't tell her that it was fine, but only nodded his head in recognition of her statement. What difference did it make whether he was here? She was alive, wasn't she? No suicide attempt. They'd survived the night without a trip to the hospital.

"You want some waffles? I'll be glad to pop one in the toaster," he added, lest she think he was going to make some from scratch, which he knew was one of her favorite breakfasts. On Sunday mornings—the only time he ever cooked anymore—he made homemade waffles with real maple syrup and eggs on the side with fresh fruit. There was really no reason he couldn't make some now, but before he had the chance to edit his offer, she shook her head *no*; she wasn't hungry. "How are you feeling?" A shrug of her shoulders; a sigh from his lips, which he tried to hide with a yawn. "Coffee? I think I'll have another cup." Another shake of her head. Well, thank goodness Ryan was on his way!

Jerry intercepted Ryan in the front yard. "I need to talk to you." He led Ryan through the kitchen and down into the basement. If Ryan thought he was going to be given a tongue lashing or have a shotgun put to his head, he didn't let on. He followed Jerry good-naturedly, ready for anything—but not ready, as it turned out, for what Jerry had to tell him.

Jerry sat Ryan down in one of the old couches they'd thrown down there years ago. He sat across from him on a small wooden chair that he pulled close, closer than Ryan would have liked. Ryan also didn't like the way Jerry rubbed his chin, trying to decide how to begin, or the tired, worried look in his eyes. By the time he finally spoke, Ryan was longing for a shotgun, and holding his breath for what was to come.

"Amanda's sick," Jerry said, and before the thought of cancer and chemo—her losing her beautiful hair—could take hold of Ryan's mind, Jerry continued. "Have you ever heard of manic depressive illness? You may know it as bipolar disorder."

"Sure, I guess so." Wasn't that something that crazy people had?

Other than Bill McIntyre, who didn't really know Amanda, Jerry realized that Ryan was the first one he'd told directly. Ryan, most likely, hadn't a clue what he was talking about, so he switched into his doctor mode. Ryan nodded dumbly, as if he understood. He was told that it was a brain disease, that there was no cure, but could, in all likelihood, be controlled with meds. Jerry told him that Amanda was in a mixed state—she wasn't necessarily excessively happy or sad, but restless and irritable, volatile and quick to tears.

"Surely, you must have seen some of these behaviors?" It was more of a question than a statement, so Jerry waited for an answer.

"I guess so." Of course he had, but wasn't that just Mandy? Wasn't that the thing that made her so much of a rush—the unpredictability, boundless energy, and boundless sexuality? Even the violence and flood of tears—wasn't that just a part of her personality? What was this man trying to say? That she was a disease and not this girl who he was crazy about—maybe not *crazy*, but—

"Are you saying that Mandy...isn't Mandy?"

Jerry had forgotten that he called her Mandy. The irony suddenly hit him, that Ryan would call her by another name, having met her, most likely, in her manic state. Jerry raised his hands in a gesture of uncertainty. How could he begin to answer that? "I think it's fair to say that," and he made a small movement of acceptance of the name, "Mandy is Mandy, but the extreme swings and excessive aggression or excitability, intense restlessness—these sorts of things will soften with treatment."

"Well, that would be good!" They both laughed in concurrence, and again Jerry found himself liking this young man—at least enough to be upfront with him.

"There is also the possibility that she won't get better. She could get worse, regardless of treatment; no matter what the final outcome, the getting there won't be a pleasant trip. Right now, she's very fragile and vulnerable, and if you are going to stick around, then you *must* stick around until she's at least more stable. If you can't do that— and let me tell you, if I were you, I'd run like hell—then you need to end it now." He said this bluntly and meant it, but mingled with the knowledge that he wouldn't wish a relationship with an unstable manic depressive on his worst enemy was the uncertainty of what was best for Amanda. Could she handle Ryan breaking up with her now?

"I don't want to stop seeing her."

"You understand what I'm saying?" Jerry said.

"Yes, sir."

"Twenty-five percent of manic depressive patients attempt suicide. Ten percent succeed." If he said this to shock Ryan into the seriousness of what he was talking about, it worked. Ryan sucked in a breath, and for a moment Jerry thought he might cry. Jerry had to look away from this young man's face for fear that he, himself, would cry, and two men crying together in an old, dirty basement was really just too much.

"What can I do? You know...to help?" Ryan asked.

Jerry was relieved to be asked something reasonable, forcing his emotions back in line. "Just what you're doing now; be there for her."

"How about if she flips out?" He was remembering the scene at the club. "What do I do then?"

"The worst thing you can do is react to her rage or violence with rage or violence. Just make sure she's safe, but get out of her way. The rage comes on fast but burns out quickly. Don't take it personally. It's not really about you or something you did." He made sure he had Ryan's full attention when he added, "Alcohol and street drugs like marijuana may seem to help, but really they make it worse. You should discourage these things."

Ryan looked at him a bit hopelessly, "She's, you know, a—" and whatever Ryan was going to say was interrupted by a sudden tune. "It's Mandy," he said. "It's her ring."

Jerry recognized the song immediately. *"You are like a hurricane..."* Ryan's cell phone sang.

"Neil Young fan?" he asked with a smile. *"... there's calm in your eyes..."*

Ryan shrugged. *"... and I'm getting blown away..."* "Seemed appropriate," Ryan said as he fished through his pocket for his phone. *"... to somewhere safer where the feeling—"*

"Hey," Ryan said into the phone as he stood up and brought it to his ear. "No, I'm here. Yeah. Here in your house." Ryan stood still for a moment. "Well, in the basement, actually, with your dad."

He cut a look at Jerry and Jerry shook his head ever so slightly. *Can this kid just not lie?* Ryan seemed to regroup. "Yeah." Jerry watched him as he paced gently. "You know how guys are with plumbing and that sort of thing." Jerry rubbed his forehead with incredulous amusement. Ryan shot a collaborative grin at Jerry. "Yeah, you're right. He's a little weird." Another pause, the slow pacing again, before saying, "Yeah... No, I'm coming up now... Okay... Sure." He popped the phone back in his pocket and turned back to Jerry. "She wants me to come up. To her room." He looked at Jerry for guidance, for permission.

Jerry nodded his head with consent. "Do you know where it is?" he asked, and if he were testing, it was subtle and lacked conviction.

"No, sir," which was the truth.

"This is a lot to take in," Jerry said as they made their way upstairs. "If you have any problems with her, questions, you let me know."

Ryan made his way up the beautiful staircase that led to the bedrooms. When he hit the landing he had to turn left and walk across the open hallway, banister railing to his left. The first bedroom, straight ahead, was the master bedroom. The door was open and the windows were facing the valley. The large bed was neatly made. It was a lovely room, the sort of room he'd imagined. The master bedroom stretched across the expanse of the house, including, he assumed, large closets, master bathroom, probably a Jacuzzi or some such thing. The hallway made another left turn, so that the entire thing was U-shaped, and it was along this final bend that the girls' bedrooms could be found. The first door was slightly ajar; he could see just enough to note the chaos—Christy's room. The second door was a shared bath. The third door—Mandy's door (right where Dr. Benson said it would be)—was closed. He knocked lightly.

"Ryan?" He opened the door and stepped into the gloom. It was good-sized, only slightly smaller than his apartment. The curtains were drawn on the two windows, and it took him just a moment to locate Mandy. She sat near the head of the delicately curved white iron bed. The bedding was in disarray about her; her face was puffy and drained. He stepped across the large butterfly-shaped rug that adorned the light hardwood floor, and in a few steps he made his way to her, noting, to his surprise, that the room was relatively neat.

"How you feeling?" he said as he kissed her lightly.

"Okay. Better."

Ryan ran his fingers through her hair and glanced at the small pile of empty medication sample packets on her bedside table and the glass of water. He took in the wads of tissues strewn about the bed before returning to her tired face.

"So what's going on? What's up with you?" She shrugged. He waited. "What's with all the pharmies?" he said, indicating the bedside table. Her eyes grew big, frightened. She did not answer. He picked up the packets—Xanax, Seroquel, Depakote. "You have some pretty good stuff here ..." he said as he shifted the packaging lightly between his fingers. "I don't know about this Depakote stuff, but the others—"

He knew all about pharmies, the most popular source of entertainment these days with a lot of young people, personally something he was never really into. He looked back at her and gently pointed the packaging toward her. "What's up?" he asked again, this time with a little more insistence.

Amanda stared at Ryan's face, used her powers to penetrate the depth of his eyes, looked into his very soul, and all she could see was concern. "My father thinks I'm fucking crazy!" The words burst from her mouth before she could give them much consideration, but after she spoke, she felt a fear as cold as ice slice right through her.

He dropped the packets back onto the nightstand and leaned toward her, gently grasping the sides of her sweet face between his hands. He took in her brown eyes, large and shiny with moisture, and whispered, "And you? Do you think you're fucking crazy?"

"Maybe," she whispered back and began to cry.

It was less than an hour later when Jerry looked up from his spot on the couch to see Amanda and Ryan coming down the stairs. She had showered and even managed a little makeup. "You should eat something," he told her. "Why don't you two make yourselves a sandwich? There's turkey in the fridge."

"We're going out," she said.

He glanced at the clock. It was one-forty. "Amanda, you've got a doctor's appointment at four."

"What?!"

"Remember?" he said calmly. "We talked about it last night?"

"You never told me about any fucking doctor's appointment!"

Jerry sighed and Ryan shifted uncomfortably on his feet. "You need to go to this appointment. You agreed to go last night. It would not be fair to Dr. McIntyre to cancel last minute."

"I need to get the FUCK OUT OF HERE!"

Ryan turned to her, brushing her arm and bending his head to talk softly in her ear, "Hey, babe. Don't talk to your dad like that."

Jerry waited for the burst of violence and the verbal outburst. He could see Amanda struggle and then, to his relief, deflate to pacification.

"How about I take you to the doctor?" Ryan suggested. Then he looked at Jerry. "I could take her."

Jerry narrowed his eyes in consideration, pretty sure he could trust Ryan to get her there, but not sure how he felt about passing the buck, so to speak. How involved was he willing to let Ryan become? She'd only known him a few weeks. Taking her to the psychiatrist seemed a bit much. But after the week they'd been through—well, he'd be willing to sell her to Ryan, for a reasonable price. "Will you go if Ryan takes you?"

Amanda shrugged. "Sure she will," said Ryan. "Just tell us where to go."

Just then they heard the door from the garage open, and Carol stepped in, flipping through the mail as she walked into the kitchen. She looked up to see the small gathering—her husband on the couch and, standing near him, Amanda and Ryan. She wondered if they knew what a striking couple they made.

"Hi, Ryan," she said with a smile as she threw the mail on the counter and stepped into the living room to kiss her husband hello. "How are you feeling, honey?" she asked Amanda, who answered with a shrug. Carol looked at Jerry and raised her eyebrows in question.

"Ryan's going to take Amanda to her appointment," Jerry told her with feigned enthusiasm.

She turned to Ryan. "Is that so?"

Ryan nodded. "We'll go grab a bite to eat somewhere, hang for a while. There's plenty of time to make it by four," Ryan offered.

"Well, you'll need to bring her right home after the appointment so we can get on the road," said Carol.

"What are you talking about?" Amanda's tone was dangerous.

"We're going to camp!" Carol said with exasperation, and then jumped at the sound of Amanda's scream of protest.

"I'm not fucking going!"

Jerry put his head in his hands. Even Ryan closed his eyes in despair.

"Of course you're going!" Carol said, her own voice dangerous now.

"Ryan took the weekend off to hang out with me!" retorted Amanda. The two women stared at each other with volatile stubbornness.

Jerry was desperately trying to figure out how he could get across to Carol that what was important now was to get Amanda to this doctor's appointment; the rest could be sorted out later. He didn't want to make matters worse. But before he could come up with the proper wording, Carol said, "Well, I guess Ryan will just have to come with us then!"

Jerry and Ryan looked at Carol in surprise. Even Amanda was taken aback. "Only David's going. There's plenty of room," Carol said as if the matter were closed. She looked at Jerry and he smiled. It was a brilliant idea. They'd been dreading the long weekend, anticipating the stress of keeping Amanda's explosive moods in check. This was a brilliant idea indeed.

6

After much discussion and debate, it was finally decided that the young people would drive the old Volvo with David at the wheel, and Jerry and Carol would drive with Tom and Sarah in their car. Group dynamics, such as they are, always create delays. By the time Ryan and Amanda returned from the city and the final packing was done—the last-minute bathroom runs, the *oh-wait-I-forgot-my-iPod* trips back into the house—it was six-forty before everyone piled into their designated cars and the engines turned. It was pre-arranged to stop at Roxie's Diner for dinner in Warrensburg, about half way to the camp. David took off first (as if this were a race) and was gone out of view before Sarah could get her seatbelt on. "Damn kid," muttered Tom. He was feeling a bit hot and grumpy. What he really needed was a cold beer.

Sarah sat in the front seat with Alby sitting comfortably on her lap. Tom glanced over and watched as Sarah gently rubbed the cat's head. Alby had her eyes closed in pleasure. Both of her legs, her good one and her bad one, stretched out over the console, almost reaching Tom's thigh with her longer leg. He could see her claws kneading the air in delight, and he swore if she stuck those little needles in his leg he would—well, he didn't know what he would do, but it wouldn't be pretty. Tom had long ago given up trying to talk Sarah into leaving the cat at home when they went to the camp. (Couldn't cats live like a week or two on their own?) She claimed that camp was Alby's favorite place to be, as if the cat could talk or something.

Jerry sat, a bit uncomfortably, in the back seat. There wasn't quite enough leg room in Tom's new Prius—a car he was so proud of, with all of its conceivable gadgetry, like driving around in a spaceship. Despite all of its technology, it was a car too small for Jerry. He was generally ignoring the conversation around him (Sarah and Carol talking—Tom silent in his grumpy-after-work mood) and he was, of course, musing about Amanda.

He hadn't had much of a chance to talk to her about her appointment with Bill. She'd ignored his questions and handed him a couple of prescriptions with an appointment card for next week and disappeared to pack her things for the weekend. He'd given Ryan a questioning look, but it was clear he either wasn't talking, or knew no more than he did. Jerry noted with satisfaction that Bill had not altered the medications, other than increasing the Depakote. He wanted to call Bill, but there hadn't been time and he felt the frustration that normal family members must feel, not having a clue what was happening behind those closed doors. But he was consoled; he knew he had the privilege of access to Amanda's doctor. Whether Amanda signed the privacy waiver or not, Bill would talk to him. He'd just have to wait until Tuesday.

Jerry let go of his musings when Carol slid closer across the seat, placing her hand on his thigh. She leaned in and kissed his neck. He put his arm around her as she whispered, "We can make-out, just like in high school."

He lifted her face to his, kissed her lips, and whispered, "I didn't know you in high school." She just smiled, no doubt remembering other times in other cars with other people, and kissed him again.

"Hey! Cut it out back there!" Tom's eyes were in the rearview mirror. "What do you think you're in high school or something?" Sarah turned her face to the back seat and smiled. Carol and Jerry just laughed, and kissed each other harder. "Hey! Really! This is a new car. No slobber."

"What do you think they are, Tom? Dogs or something?" asked Sarah.

Alby, disturbed by Tom's chiding, stood up and carefully made her way to the back seat. "Hey!" said Tom. "Don't let her just walk around! She's going to poke my leather."

"Oh for God's sake, Tom! Would you just shut up!" said Sarah. Alby made her way between Jerry and Carol, jumping lightly onto the back trunk cover.

Carol leaned in close to Jerry again and said, loud enough for all to hear, "Blowjob, Dr. Benson?" Tom knocked his head once and then twice against the steering wheel while everyone else laughed.

~

David's eyes flicked to the rearview mirror again. They were still going at it. Couldn't they just keep their hands off each other for another couple hours? He turned to the backseat. "Hey! Do I have to get you two a fucking room or something?"

Ryan looked up from Mandy's lips and smiled at David. "Okay. Sure. That'd be great."

"Fuck you, Downing," said David with a smile, and turned back toward the road. He'd seen Ryan around at clubs, parties, and such. He didn't know him all that well, but hadn't heard anything negative about him either. The real losers—the druggies, the pushers, the players—you heard about them.

"You're just jealous," he heard Ryan say, his voice just audible over the music. "You've got two gorgeous women in this car and both of them are totally unavailable to you."

"Actually, there's no law in New York State that says you can't marry your first cousin," David said. He reached over and squeezed Christy's leg.

"Oh! Yuck!" squealed Christy as she turned bright red.

"Oh! My! God!" Amanda screamed with laughter. "You totally looked that up!"

David laughed heartily. (He had looked it up, the day Amanda turned seventeen.)

Amanda disentangled herself from Ryan and dug around in her purse. She pulled out a cute little pipe with a tiny green lizard on it. Ryan watched as she carefully placed a small wad of the green-black sticky leaves she removed from a small plastic bag into the pipe. He thought about what Dr. Benson had told him about street drugs, but *really*, what was he going to do—especially when it was one of his friends that secured it for her.

She lit the pipe with a gentle suck from her lips and handed it to him. He took it, mingling with her fingers longer than was necessary, and took his own tiny hit. David's hand reached back from the seat and Ryan handed it forward. After David was done, he offered it to Christy.

The music vibrated in the car as the sun disappeared behind a distant mountain. The car zipped down the road as a light cool breeze blew in the open windows, blowing through their hair. The pretty little pipe made its brief visits to everyone, glowing in the setting sun. Amanda closed her eyes, her head sinking into Ryan's lap. She stretched her legs to rest her feet on the car window, watching the silhouettes of the trees as they whipped by. Ryan's fingers got lost in her hair as he wished she would turn her face toward his crotch so he could lean back and close his eyes to some *real* pleasure. Christy leaned her own pretty head against the back of the seat, glancing at David, admiring his strong jaw and handsome profile, wondering what it would be like to kiss him—to kiss anyone. David continued to watch the road as he set down the pipe, tapping his fingers against the steering wheel to the bass that pounded through the car; wondering, as always, when the next opportunity for sex might come up.

~

"Fifty-six!" announced Tom with joy. Jerry had to admit he was impressed, but Tom's little game he was playing with the gas mileage was no doubt slowing down the trip. On every hill—and there were a lot of them considering they were in the foothills of the Adirondack

Mountains—Tom would watch in horror as the consumption graph on the screen dropped from around 75 mph to below 20 mph as the car made its way up the hill. He would then ease off the accelerator, causing the car to drop to a crawl as it tried to make it up the hill with four adults—one of them being the idiot behind the wheel.

"Tom, I'll pay for the gas. I'd like to get there before midnight," said Jerry as he leaned forward.

"You're missing the whole point," insisted Tom. "It's not the money; it's the challenge!" But Tom was busy doing the math in his head—what he paid for the car minus what he would have paid for a similar non-hybrid car plus the price of gas minus what he was saving plus how many years it would take before it actually made him money....

"Can't you do something with him?" Jerry appealed to Sarah.

"Unlikely," said Sarah.

Alby settled comfortably by the back window. She stretched across the trunk cover, lightly pawing the back of Carol's head. Carol reached her hand back over her head to tickle Alby's chin. She could hear the cat's elated purring. They were about an hour into the trip and Carol was getting hungry. They should have been there by now. Carol's other hand moved to her stomach and lingered there. She suddenly leaned forward and said, "You know, Tom. At the rate we're going, I'll have starved to death before we get to Warrensburg."

"Well, that will save him some money, too," said Sarah.

"I told you! It's not the money! And who said I was paying for dinner?"

~

"Do we have any food in this car?" asked David. "I'm starving!"

"It's all in the back and up top in the car carrier," said Ryan, who'd helped pack the car.

David sighed. "Well, we're almost to Warrensburg anyways."

Christy moaned. "We're not going to Rotten Roxie's are we?"

"Duh," answered Amanda. "We go there every fucking year!"

"God. I hate that place!"

"What's with all those stupid bear pictures anyway?" asked David. Christy and Amanda laughed. "Yeah!" yelled Amanda over the music, but louder than she needed to. "Who the fuck wants to eat at a place where they have pictures of bears eating out of garbage cans?"

"Especially when the bears are eating rejected Rotten Roxie's rations!" added David. They all howled with laughter, even Ryan, who hadn't much of a clue what they were talking about.

"If the place is so bad, why do you go there?" asked Ryan.

"Our parents think we love the place," answered Christy.

"Yeah, one of us, probably Casey like when he was three or something, said it was his favorite place in the world and they've been dragging us there ever since," said David. "That's probably why Casey begged off this year: to avoid Roxie's." He said this a bit wistfully. (Matt hadn't come for Columbus Day weekend for two years now.) He was missing his brothers already and wondering if he would bother coming next year. He reached in his pocket and threw Christy his cell phone. "Text my Mom and tell her we're going to Subway, will ya doll?"

"They're going to be pissed," warned Christy as she sent the text.

Amanda bounced up and down gently in the back seat. She loved Subway.

~

Sarah read the text and slightly frowned. She looked at Tom and he turned his eyes from the road and met her look. "What did he say?"

"They're going to Subway."

"I told you that if we gave them a car, we'd never see them again," said Tom.

"They don't want to go to Roxie's?" asked Carol.

"They've got all our crap! They better show up at camp," Tom continued.

"But, they love Roxie's," Carol said, and stopped as she felt her fragile emotions surge.

"That place sucks!" said Tom. Sarah and Jerry laughed in agreement, no doubt picturing the nasty, sticky plastic table cloths, the dusty, cheap silk flowers; those awful bear photos everywhere, not to mention the greasy food. Carol, however, felt her tears roll down her cheeks and was grateful for the darkness of the car. She was remembering the five happy kids tumbling out of the cars, rough-housing in the parking lot; Tom yelling at them, entering the restaurant and being hit with the smell of pancakes and grease; Casey running to the nearest bear photo and staring with wonder; Amanda pulling on her hand and asking, "Can I have pancakes for dinner? Can I?" her face flushed with excitement, looking down at Amanda's eager face with a rush of love, "Of course you can, honey."

"Why don't we go into Lake George for dinner?" suggested Jerry.

"There's that really cute pub," offered Sarah. They all thought of the dark, rich atmosphere, cool Irish ale, a nice hearty sandwich or steak. And even Carol had to admit that maybe, just maybe, leaving Roxie's behind would be a good thing.

~

David pulled down the lane to their camp at eight-fifty (great time considering the beer run and the stop at Subway). It was a cloudy night so he left the car running with the lights on until locating the hidden keys, remembering the last great party he'd had up here. He hoped the camp wouldn't still smell of vomit and beer. Amanda, Ryan, and Christy were already out of the car. Amanda was walking around in the dark with Ryan in tow, saying, "Look! Look! You can see the lake!" Of course you couldn't see the lake, considering the darkness and the heavy leaf cover clinging to the trees.

The camp—as if the word *camp* could describe the massive A-frame—was situated on the northern end of the east side of Indian Lake. Jerry and Tom had chosen this particular place for its remoteness and price (much more reasonable than Lake George at the time) and although the lake itself was tiny compared to Lake George, the fourteen-mile-long lake was the quintessential Adirondack paradise—still free of crowds, surrounded by gentle rolling mountains; the occasional bear lumbering across the yard (they'd even seen a moose once, early in the morning). They'd owned it for twenty years now, scraped all the money they had together to buy the place—barely able to make the payments those first few years. Now, if they were to sell it, it would be the best investment they'd ever made.

David located the keys under the big rock by the side deck, unlocked the door, and flicked on the lights, illuminating the main room of the camp. It was a large single structure—A-framed wooden ceiling, wooden rafters, big stone fireplace in the middle of the room, large glass windows facing the lake, open kitchen to the right, and pegged wall to the left for coats and shoes and such. The smell of wood, mildew, and a hint of beer vomit hit him, so he opened the windows to the kitchen and the sliding glass doors leading to the front deck before he headed back outside to shut off the car and grab his beer.

When he reentered the camp, Christy was peering out of the front windows, trying to see the lake below. Amanda was still showing Ryan around the place. "This is my parents' room," she said as she opened the door off the living room to the right. Jerry and Tom had added to the original structure—two wings on either side consisting of nice-sized matching bedroom suites, complete with baths and private decks. They disappeared into the bedroom for a few minutes before reappearing slightly flushed.

"Hey, David," she called as he twisted open the top of one of the beers. He offered one to Ryan, who shook his head *no.* "Where'd you say my mom and dad are now?" He put the rest of the twelve pack in the fridge.

"I don't know. They stopped at that restaurant … probably a good hour away."

Amanda took Ryan's hand and pulled him toward the stairs, which led to the loft and the bedrooms above the kitchen area. "I'm going to show Ryan the upstairs," she said with a grin. David closed his eyes for a moment with a tiny sigh and then looked at Ryan, who gave him an apologetic but-you-know-how-it-is smile. Christy turned from the window and looked at David.

He reopened the fridge and grabbed another beer. "Hey, Christy, let's you and me go check out the lake."

The night was warm for early October; their light coats were all they needed. They made their way to the front of the house, David careful of his two beers. By the time they reached the stairs that led down to the dock, their eyes had adjusted to the dark and the going was easier. They might have turned on the outside lights, but that would have ruined the ambiance of the night. They could hear the gentle slap of the waves against the shore and the rustle of the leaves swaying in the light wind. A few desperate crickets chirped—the only memento of summer. Somewhere close there was a call of a bird, an owl maybe, and Christy jumped at the sound.

"It's just a stupid bird," said David.

"I know," laughed Christy. "But it *is* a little spooky out here."

As if he were being putout, he said, "*I'll* protect you." And then they both laughed. They reached the shoreline and walked across the ramp of the dock, going to the very end and sitting. Their feet dangled just above the water. David put the beers between them. They didn't say anything for a moment, both gazing out at the dark waters. He picked up the open beer, took a gentle swig, and placed it between his legs.

"So tell me about Amanda," he said, finally breaking the silence. "Is she really sick or what?"

Christy sighed; she would rather not talk about Amanda. She shrugged. "My dad thinks she is." She dipped her feet toward the water, barely reaching it with the soles of her sneakers. She kicked a bit and sent a small wave out to sea. "I don't know; she's always been *emo*." She fiddled with the zipper of her jacket. "But Mom and Dad were up half the night last night…." She dropped the zipper and turned toward David. "She wanted to kill herself or something."

"Oh man." David rubbed his chin with concern and took another long drink from his beer. "You know Grandma Benson was nuts." Neither one of them had ever known their grandmother. "She *offed* herself."

Christy nodded in the dark. "Our dads are okay."

"Yeah, but what a wild way to grow up." They didn't say anything for awhile, staring out into the blackness. David finished his beer and set it behind him. The clouds broke apart and moonlight snaked across the water.

"Grandpa Benson was a drunk," Christy offered.

David laughed a bit at the absurdity. "Yeah, he basically offed himself too." They both laughed. Christy hit the water again with her sneaker, this time harder.

"Do you worry… you know… about yourself?" asked Christy.

"Naah." And as if to emphasize the point, he opened his second beer. He turned to her in the dark. "Do you?"

She met his gaze. She could just make out his face in the moonlight. "I worry about a lot of things," she whispered, and began to cry.

~

Ryan gently rested his forehead on Mandy's and then shifted, just enough to see her eyes, and was lost—her pupils were big and endless. He kissed her lips and pulled away to look at her again. She smiled and teased his hair between her fingers. They were on the bottom of one of the two bunk beds in the girls' room. They were still interlocked when he tried to gently pull away. She clamped her legs around him, pinning him to her. "Don't leave me," she breathed into his ear. He smiled and relaxed against her.

"I won't," he whispered back. He felt a need to tell her how he felt—to tell her the three words that were in his head—but they seemed too large for him to put in the right order on his tongue. He had never put them together for anyone as a man; he'd only put them together as a little boy for his mother. He dropped his head against her neck and heard her whisper "I love you" in his ear; and he turned his face toward hers and his words slipped out like silk. "I love you too."

~

The first thing Tom noticed as he walked into the camp was the unpleasant smell of stale beer and vomit. He looked back at Sarah, who was coming in behind him with Alby in her arms, and said, "Did you know he's been up here?"

She smelled it too and knew exactly what he meant. "No."

"Damn kid." He placed the luggage on the floor and looked about the room. "Where are they?"

Jerry came in and set a cooler on the kitchen counter. "It smells like Maggie's in here." Carol stepped in and wrinkled up her nose.

"Yeah. No kidding," said Tom, with disgust. Maggie's was an old bar they used to frequent when they were students at Albany. It was a freshman bar, which meant lots of drinking, lots of cute drunk girls, and lots of vomit. Beer was sold literally in buckets, which came in handy for the puking that came hours later.

But before they could discuss the alleged party that had occurred on their property, they heard the sound of feet on the stairs; and anybody who had ever had sex (and they all had) could tell, as the two young people hit the main floor, that, if nothing else, at least sex had occurred.

"Hi," Amanda said sweetly.

Tom smiled a bit. Jerry glared at Ryan, but the boy wouldn't meet his eye. Sarah, who had not gotten much of a look at Ryan earlier, was struck and then weakened by the raw sex that exuded from him. Carol looked at Amanda's glowing, happy face—yes, it was happy; happier than she'd seen it for months—and could not feel anything but gratitude toward Ryan. It wasn't as if the fact that they were having sex was a shock. She'd known Amanda was sexually active for at least a year now, had even brought her to the doctor's and made sure she had birth control. She could sense the shock and disapproval of Sarah, however, and she felt she must say something, but *thank you, Ryan*, would probably be inappropriate. Then there was the very real fear that anything negative she might say would cause Amanda's happiness to burst like angry daggers throughout the room, so in the end she simply said, "Hi. How was your ride up?"

"Good."

"I don't suppose it occurred to you two while you were do-ing…whatever you two were doing…to unpack the car?" Tom said, pausing to enjoy Ryan's discomfort, then adding, "And where, please tell me, are Christy and my son?"

"They're down by the water," said Amanda.

"Sorry, sir," said Ryan, his head bowed in apology. "We'll go right now and unpack the car." He glanced at Jerry, who was still glowering at him, and Ryan frowned again in apology as they stepped by the intimidating group and headed for the car.

"Oh man!" said Ryan as they hit the night air. "That was fucking awful!" Amanda laughed in delight.

Tom went to the deck and peered down toward the water. He could just make out the two figures silhouetted in the moonlight at the end of the dock. They were close to one another. The figures seemed to merge into one, and he sighed heavily and yelled, "Hey! You two come on up here!" He waited on the deck and watched as they got up. They were lost in the trees until he could hear their approach. When they got close, the first thing he noticed was the two beers that David was carrying. The light from the camp, hitting their faces, showed that Christy had been crying.

"Hey, Dad," David said. "You made it."

"That's right." Tom's voice was tight, and David narrowed his eyes and set his mouth at his father. "Why don't you go help unpack the cars, Christy? I need to talk to David," Tom said without taking his eyes off of his son.

Christy looked at her uncle and then back at David. "Umm ... okay, sure."

When she left, Tom looked at the beers in David's hand and then back at his son. By the look on his face, David knew that he was asking about more than just the beers, and it pissed him off. He was tired —fucking tired—of his father always assuming the worst of him. So he took a step closer to his old man, still not breaking his gaze, and said, "Can you just, *for once in your life*, give me a little credit! She's fifteen *and* my cousin!"

Tom, still not ready to back down, said, "Why was she crying?"

"Do you think maybe, just maybe, she might be a little upset about her sister?" he retorted. Tom was rebuked and looked away.

"I'm sorry, David," Tom said, and shook his head.

It took David a second to grasp his victory. His mind flashed to the first and only time his father had ever offered him an apology—the time Tom had accidentally flushed David's pet turtle down the toilet (which really hadn't been his dad's fault; it was David who'd put it in there to swim around).

"Well…okay then," said David. David felt a little weak with his victory. He felt some sort of grownup responsibility as he digested the knowledge that his father could admit that he was wrong; that his father was willing to give him a little credit. And if Tom had had any plans of bringing up the beer smell in the camp, he let it go. Instead, he put his arm around his son's shoulder, and they walked back inside together.

7

Jerry and Carol went to bed as soon as the food was put away and things were somewhat organized. The lack of sleep was taking its toll on both of them; it was a relief to lay their heads on the pillows in a place other than home, to feel a certain kind of peace that comes with getting away and knowing that you're surrounded by a world somehow more real than Niskayuna, NY. Although they were tired, this peacefulness they were feeling shifted into a need that hadn't been felt in quite some time, and they made love—not out of some sort of obligation, but out of desire. Ideally, they might have simply fallen asleep in each other's arms—but that was something for younger bodies and happier souls. Instead, Carol felt the need to talk to her husband.

"Did you notice," she asked as she reached for some tissues, throwing a couple Jerry's way and saving the rest for herself, "that they never asked about Amanda?"

"I noticed." Jerry sighed as he searched around the bed for his underwear. "Well, Tom did ask me, before we got in the car, if things were any better. I told him *no*, but there wasn't an opportunity to say more." He found the underwear mixed up with the sheets at the foot of the bed.

"You know if Amanda had cancer or even the flu, they would

96

ask." Carol, who had not bothered putting her cotton pajamas back on, was beginning to get angry at the injustice. She was mainly feeling disappointed and hurt.

Jerry turned to face her. "You know, there are some excellent family support groups in Albany. I think you should go. There's a twelve-week class for family members. I get a lot of positive feedback from my patients' families."

She sighed. She really didn't want to cry again. "I'd like to be able to talk to my own family. Feel their support."

"I know." He lay down and pulled her to him. "But sometimes it's easier with strangers."

~

Tom and Sarah, who were having their own post-coital conversation, lay side by side in their king-sized bed, watching the shadows of the leaves that danced across the bedroom ceiling. "How many times do you think our boys have had sex up here?" Tom was wondering aloud.

"I don't even want to think about it," was Sarah's response, but then she obviously did, because she added, "All three put together ... probably more than we have."

"Oh man! We should have this place professionally cleaned."

They laughed, and Tom was considering what cleaner might be willing to come out this far.

"Every time I look at Amanda with that awful red hair, I just want to drag her into the bathroom and dye it back. It's as if she wants to look crazy," Sarah said.

"Oh, I don't think it's so bad. Besides, it's only hair. It could be a big ring in her lip or something."

"I suppose. What do you think of Ryan?" she asked.

Tom pulled the covers up to his chest and said, "Seems nice enough. Maybe a little old for Amanda."

Alby jumped up on the bed and mewed *hello*. Tom gave her a look of mild reproach. Sarah wiggled her feet slightly at the cat. She pounced gently and pretended to rake Sarah's foot to threads with her back legs. "Do you think he's too young for me?" she asked with a grin.

Tom turned to her and returned her grin. "So he's the one that got you all hot and bothered tonight?"

Sarah gave him her charming, coy face, and said, "But you are the one who took care of it for me."

He reached over and kissed her lightly. "You are very welcome. I do what I can." He settled himself into the bed. Alby came close and carefully stepped on his stomach. "Is that really necessary?" he asked the cat. Alby responded by making one small rotation before finding a bed on his abdomen. "Jesus!" he said, but did not move to scare her.

"She loves you," Sarah said with a smile.

They were quiet for a few minutes. The only sound was the heavy purring of Alby. Tom was almost asleep when he heard his wife say, "Do you think they're okay? I wanted so much to say something, you know, but Carol looked so shell-shocked and fragile. I didn't want to make her cry, to make it worse."

"Yeah. I don't know. It's a hard thing." She didn't respond right away, and he fell asleep.

~

Ryan watched as Mandy carefully considered which card to put down. She was biting her bottom lip to the point that he could see her skin turn blood-red. To his relief she put down something that he could overtake, thus winning the trick and saving her a couple hearts. It was late. The house was quiet as the night was running into morning. The four of them had taken a little walk, smoked a little weed, and after raiding the fridge, decided to play some cards. They were playing Hearts on the game table in the loft, which overlooked the main living area below. He and David were gently sipping on beers. It would have been a fun and relaxing way to spend the night if Mandy didn't look like she was about to lose it.

Twice now Mandy had been stuck with the queen—once by Christy, who laughed with pleasure, and once by David, who said, "Sorry, kid. It had to be done." The queen had not fallen yet with this hand. Ryan didn't have her, but he was trying hard to claim her for himself, to protect Mandy from getting *the bitch* as David liked to call the queen of spades. He didn't know where she was, but he led the highest club he had, which was a Jack, knowing that clubs had been played twice. It might just be enough to flush out the queen. To his distress, Mandy was forced to take the trick with the queen of clubs, collecting a heart from Christy. This would most likely mean that David held the queen of spades, he reasoned. Mandy took a long time choosing her card, and then finally, to Ryan's dismay, she threw the eight of diamonds. *Didn't she know diamonds had been played three times and had split?* There was nothing he could do but hope that David would be kind.

The scream of agony that burst from Mandy's mouth as David dropped the queen made them all jump, and, to make matters worse, David said, "Fuck, Amanda! It's just a card game." Ryan watched Mandy's eyes flick to David's and her face quickly disintegrated further into misery, and then she was gone. She upset her chair and fled down the stairs and out the back door without a coat or even shoes. Ryan was only moments behind her. David looked at Christy and said, "Jesus!"

Christy looked back at him. She reached for his beer and took a long, slow drink, and then said dryly, "Yeah. Welcome to my world."

~

Ryan could not see her as he hit the outside, but he could hear her as she made her way through the brush behind the house. If only she'd stayed on the driveway and ran toward the road, but no—she was heading into the trees. He took off after the noise, but was quickly confused by the sound of his own movement and had to stop to listen in the dark woods. She was still moving, off to his right now, and he called her name and turned to the right. How was he going to tell Dr. Benson that he'd lost the guy's daughter in the Adirondack Forest? He called again. She didn't answer.

He stopped again and realized he was gaining on her; he had his shoes on, after all. He brushed at the undergrowth, trying to protect his face, feeling the scrape of branches against his arms and face as he made his way toward her. Finally he could see her in the gloom of the night, a movement against the stillness of the forest. He picked up his pace, quickly diminishing the distance between them. He could hear her raspy breathing as she sobbed and tried to run at the same time. "Leave me the fuck alone!" he heard her scream.

"I won't!" This was the second time in the last five hours that he'd said these words.

She slowed to a walk. "Don't come near me!" she warned. She struggled through the undergrowth, feeling the rocks and fallen branches slicing into her bare feet—a sensation she actually enjoyed because it was something real, something tangible. What she really wanted to do was to go back to the card table and take the queen with a "Fuck you, David" and a smile, but now she needed to get away; how could she face anyone ever again? She longed to stop, to drop to the forest floor, to lick at her wounded feet, to allow Ryan to take her—to take all of her until there was nothing left—but then the pleasure of the pain in her feet would stop and what would happen then?

He also slowed to a walk, staying close enough as not to lose her in the darkness. He could see her tripping in her bare feet, staggering, but she didn't stop, and they went on like this for an unreasonable amount of time. He had the sudden fear that they would both be lost in this forest. How many days would it take before they would find their way to the road or for someone to find them?

He took a few quick steps in her direction and was on her before she had a chance to react. But when he wrapped his arms around her, she became an animal trapped in a snare, and it took all his strength to subdue this creature—this thing he loved?—and really, why the fuck was he here? Bleeding, tired, and angry, Ryan wanted to punch her in the head and knock her out, drag her back to her father and say, "Here you go! Good luck!" and walk away. He'd grab his crap (though he hadn't brought that much) and at the first faint light of dawn, he would head down the road and hitchhike back to Albany. Was it only yesterday afternoon that her father had warned, "Run like hell"?

Suddenly she was captured, impeded. She fought while the trees were spinning about her and the cold earth was grasping at her feet. She was mystified by a screaming so loud that she screamed to make it stop, struggling against the cold terror of his embrace, struggling to save some small part of what was left—almost getting away—feeling his arm close to her face and opening her jaws to its flesh. Then the sensation of falling down onto the wet, waiting earth....

He twisted his arm away as she tried to bite him and forced her to the ground. "Damn it, Mandy! Cut it out!" He straddled her, his knees pinning her arms to the ground—the only things still able to move were her legs, which were harmless to him now. He brought his hands to either side of her face, well away from her mouth, and braced himself against the earth, dropping his head toward her chaos, small shushing sounds coming from his throat.

And he waited, catching his breath, resting, holding her down with his weight while her legs thrashed about. Even crazy people had to get tired, didn't they? He felt his heart beating in his chest, heard it—even over her screams—beating in his ears, and he closed his eyes, briefly fantasizing about a straightjacket for her and a warm bed for him.

Amanda felt the weight of his body as she listened to his soothing sounds. She felt the weight of her fear lift as it eased away. She felt safe and angry, hot and cold—her legs still thrashing on their own accord. She wished he'd put his face just a little closer so that she might use her teeth to rip at its sadness. Then, like the coming of a slow train, the thick blanket of fatigue....

It took longer than he would've thought possible, but finally, after a good ten minutes, her legs slowed and her screaming subsided, and he brought one of his hands carefully to her face. "Are you done?" he asked. She was shivering now beneath him, her face passive and vulnerable, and she leaned slightly into the touch of his hand. He risked shifting his legs and pulling her up into his arms. Instead of resisting, she wrapped her freed arms around him and clung like a small child.

"You're freezing," he said, holding her in the dark forest. His knees were wet and cold from the earth—the wetness soaking into his jeans. A fall breeze hit his face, cooling the burn of his scratches, gently blowing his hair into his eyes, rustling the leaves of the surrounding trees—the only sound he could hear on top of the *I love you, I love you, I love you* that she repeated over and over into his ear.

~

There was a small suggestion of dawn when Ryan and Amanda finally stepped up to the back door and went into the camp. She had not stopped talking the entire journey back. And it had been a journey—Ryan felt like a brainless Davy Crockett or a faggy Daniel Boone, close to tears himself at times. He was never a wilderness kind of guy. He grew up in Atlanta, for Christ's sake. Mandy kept insisting that she knew these woods and yammered nonsense while trying to tell him which way to go. Ryan just wanted to tell her to *shut the fuck up!* But finally, by some sort of miracle, he found the road and realized they were closer than he'd thought. There, before them, stood the most beautiful structure he'd ever seen—the Benson Camp.

~

Jerry was lost in a dream. It was a rather pleasant trip into the absurd, involving chipmunks, of all things—a complicated, enchanting tale—so that when the hesitant knock on the bedroom door roused him from his sleep, he could not seem to fathom where he was or what had caused him to wake. By the time he realized he was at camp, there was another soft knock, and he looked toward the window. It wasn't quite dawn. His brother had gone too far. He knew Tom was all hot to start their kayaking early, but this—well, it was beyond rude! Jerry staggered to the door and flung it open, ready to tell Tom off, but was shut down by the very tired and faintly bloodied face of Ryan.

"I'm sorry, Dr. Benson, but I didn't know what else to do." The now familiar, but nevertheless unpleasant, shot of fear went through Jerry, and he stepped from the bedroom and scanned the room with his myopic eyes, locating Amanda, who looked worse than Ryan, but was nonetheless swaying gently in a slow, beautiful dance about the living room.

"Hang on," he told Ryan, and went to retrieve his glasses. Carol stirred, and he told her to go back to sleep. Ryan was near Amanda when he returned, and as he stepped closer, Jerry asked with dread, "What happened?"

Ryan closed his eyes with fatigue. "The queen of spades. That's what happened—*the fucking bitch*."

Jerry had no idea what he was talking about. He watched as Amanda continued her slow ballet. "Did she take her meds last night?"

Ryan shook his head. "Don't know."

Jerry glanced toward the kitchen and saw that the glass of water and pills he'd left on the kitchen counter were untouched. He went to his stash of meds and took out an extra Seroquel and a Xanax. He retrieved the water and the pills from the previous night.

"You can't imagine what it was like, Dr. Benson," Ryan was saying, standing there like he might cry.

Jerry returned from the kitchen and placed a hand on Ryan's shoulder. "Call me Jerry." Ryan nodded with acknowledgement and sunk into the nearest couch.

Jerry approached her slowly. "Amanda, you need to sleep now." He extended the glass toward her, and her hand went out fast and sent the glass—plastic, thank goodness—thudding across the room. He patiently retrieved the glass and refilled it at the kitchen tap. "Okay, Amanda. This is how it's going to be," he said slowly and firmly. "If you don't take these, I will have Ryan help me, and we will drag you to the car. I will tie you up if I need to. I will drive you back to Albany, where Dr. McIntyre will admit you to the psych ward." And although she was as psychotic as he'd ever seen her, he knew that she was hearing him. "There they'll shoot you full off all sorts of drugs, put you in a padded room, or tie you to a bed. And there you'll stay without seeing Ryan or anyone else until you are stable and more reasonable. Is that what you want?"

Ryan put his head in his hands and thought he might be sick.

Amanda stopped her movement, and Jerry extended the glass to her again. She took it, and he handed her one pill after another until they were gone and in her body. He took the glass, and she continued her dance. "I've got this. Get some sleep," he said to Ryan. But he appeared unable to move, so Jerry went to him and gently helped him up by his arm. He put his arm around him and led him toward the stairs. "I'm sorry for the night you've had," Jerry told him. He pushed him up the stairs until his own strength took over. Jerry watched him until he made it to the landing. "Thank you," Jerry called up the stairs. Ryan gave him a *whatever* wave of his hand before disappearing out of view.

As the daylight strengthened, Amanda became more coherent. Jerry listened to her talk about the injustice of David, the flight in the woods, the getting lost, the heroic part she played in getting them home .... Jerry was able to piece the rest together in a more lucid and much more likely scenario. It made him feel sad and guilty knowing that all this was going on while he was sleeping peacefully.

He eventually got Amanda up the stairs and into a bottom bunk without waking Christy, before the rest of the household woke up. As he pulled the covers up to her sleepy face, she said, "You know Dr. What's-His-Name—"

"Dr. McIntyre?"

"That's right. He said I should try to take some Seroquel, you know, in the morning—that it might help?"

"I think that's a good idea." Jerry felt a flood of relief. This was the first time she'd verbally acknowledged her meds in any positive light, thus acknowledging her need; her illness—which was critical to recovery.

"I don't want to be so tired though."

"Try a half of a pill or a third."

"That's right. That's what the doctor dude said."

Jerry nodded his head and smiled. "That doctor dude knows what he's talking about."

She was quiet then and shut her eyes. He was about to get up and leave when she said, her voice very small and sad, "Do you think he'll break up with me?"

Jerry shook his head. "I don't know."

"I won't blame him if he does."

Jerry frowned and thought, "I won't either." But he didn't say it out loud. In a couple of minutes she was asleep, and Jerry slipped away to make some coffee.

8

The morning dawned bright and clear. A few white, puffy clouds hovered near the horizon, and a soft mist caressed the lake as they pulled the kayaks into the water. A great blue heron, startled by the commotion, complained loudly and coarsely before taking off like a small pterodactyl. They watched as it winged its way down the lake and disappeared around a small bend in the shoreline. The water was a mirror; the astounding autumn display of the western shore perfectly reflected in the water so that if it were a photo you'd be hard-pressed to tell which way was up. They eased their bodies into the boats and pulled away, cutting the image of the sky above; their paddles licking quietly at the lake. They turned south, hugging the water's edge.

The original plan had been for all of them to go, but Carol did not feel comfortable leaving Amanda, even though Jerry insisted that he'd given her enough sedatives for her to sleep at least eight hours. But when they checked on her before he left, she was no longer in her bed. They found her in the boys' room, all three occupants fast asleep — Amanda wrapped in Ryan's arms, and David only a few feet away. Carol frowned at her husband, but then shrugged it off with him and tiptoed out of the room.

Sarah begged off once she found out Carol wasn't going. She knew

Tom was on a mission that she did not wish to join. She wasn't thrilled at the prospect of paddling back alone once she had enough. So it was just the two brothers. Tom was determined to paddle the entire shoreline, which was considerable—the lake was fourteen miles long with many tiny inlets. It was generally a seven to eight hour paddle, depending on the conditions and how many of the inlets they explored. They'd done it many times—when they were younger.

Jerry was disinclined to be gone so long, but Carol assured him they'd be fine between Ryan and David (if Amanda became difficult) and Jerry's orders to give her a half of Seroquel with the Depakote when she woke up. But still, Jerry felt ill-at-ease. He popped his cell phone in its waterproof holder—although coverage was spotty at best—and told Carol he'd call even if he needed to knock on someone's camp and borrow a landline. But, as they made their way across the water, the stillness only interrupted by their gentle movement, the morning serenade of birds, and the soft pop of an occasional fish as it kissed the water's surface; the beauty of the place enveloping him, he began to relax and gave himself over to Tom.

They paddled with determination for the first two hours, saying very little and waking up to the day. Their muscles cramped with disuse at first, but then they stretched and opened up to the task. As they hit their rhythm, they skimmed across the water almost effortlessly, watching the amazing shoreline go by and the migratory birds float lazily out of the way, taking off in small groups heading south. A weak autumn sun rose in the sky and Jerry felt a sort of peacefulness he had not known for some time.

They were three-quarters down the east shore when Tom slowed and sat back in his kayak and waited briefly for Jerry to come alongside. "Those two cups of coffee that felt so good a couple hours ago—well they don't feel so good now." Jerry nodded and they made their way close to shore, searching for a place to pull out. After watering the earth, they returned to their boats. They rowed at a slow pace, and Tom began to talk.

"This thing … this thing with Amanda … it's really tough."

Jerry nodded, agreeing to the obvious.

"I wish … you know … there was more I could do."

"This helps," said Jerry as he lifted up his paddle and indicated the outside world with a light swing of the blades.

"Yes, it's nice out here." Tom made a few gentle strokes with his paddle before continuing on. "When you were at college and Mom—" He stopped and looked at Jerry. "You know … died." Tom looked away and down the lake. "I've always wondered if there was something more that I could have done, you know, to stop it."

Jerry took in a breath and was struck by the poignancy of what Tom was saying, but was irritated that the conversation had turned so quickly from his to Tom's issues. After all, the woman had been dead for over thirty-four years. But Jerry assumed that Tom's rumination was mixed up with his concern for Amanda, mixed up with the fear—a fear Jerry shared—that Amanda would, of course, end up like their mother: never really being well and choosing not to go on.

"There was nothing you could have done. She was very sick for a very long time. You were seventeen. Even Aunt Betty could do nothing. Nobody could. There are so many better meds these days," he added, wondering who he was trying to convince. "She might still be alive, or might've died an old woman if they had the same treatments back then."

Tom was quiet for a long moment, his kayak barely progressing forward. "How strong is this inheritance thing, you know, the genetic aspect?" he asked. Jerry felt annoyed again and paddled hard for a few strokes, pulling away from Tom and collecting himself before attempting to answer.

Who specifically was Tom concerned about? Himself? Christy? His own boys, most likely. But why did that bother him? It was a natural concern. Jerry felt the sting of disregard, and his own anger at the injustice. Approximately fifteen percent—depending on what study you believed—was the probability that Tom or he could have developed manic depressive illness. There was maybe a three percent chance that their kids could develop it. Three percent! (Not that these statistics meant anything now.)

Why him? Why Amanda? Why *not* one of Tom's kids? The thought of substituting one of Tom's boys for Amanda slapped him with guilt. If he could, he would in a heartbeat. This thought played across his mind and he indulged the fantasy for a moment, choosing Matt as the victim, before another thought suddenly hit him. This couldn't be real. No! This just *wasn't* happening. Not to him. Not to his child. After all, damn it, it just wasn't fair! It was some sort of stupid mistake that had been made, that *he* had made, and Amanda was actually fine!

"Jerry?" Jerry had stopped paddling and Tom pulled up beside him.

"Yeah—I'm sorry. If you are worried about your boys, you shouldn't be. The odds are way in their favor, especially as they get older." Jerry submerged his right blade deep into the lake and pulled against the water, feeling the kayak leap forward a bit awkwardly, then right itself as he brought the left blade into play. Then he paddled as if he could leave everything behind.

~

David was the first to wake up. He stretched his arms out above his head and glanced toward the other bunk, seeing Ryan's sleeping form, not remembering hearing him come in. He didn't see Amanda until he got out of bed, shaking his head with mild disapproval. Even he wouldn't have the balls to sleep with his girlfriend in her parents' house. (Well, at least if they were home.) He slipped on his jeans and an old sweatshirt, and quietly left the room.

His mother was reading on the couch and he could see his aunt out on the deck, leaning on the railing, her eyes to the lake. "Hey, Mom." She looked up and smiled as he helped himself to the last cup of coffee. He glanced at the clock on the microwave; it was eleven-fifty. "Where's Dad?"

"Kayaking with Jerry."

He nodded his head and sat down on the couch, facing the lake. Sarah was about to ask him what they did last night, but then Carol came in from the deck. She smiled warmly at David. It was no secret that of the three boys, David was her favorite—a feeling that he shared for her. She had always been his go-to adult when his parents were being pains-in-the-ass, which seemed to be the constant state of affairs when he was younger. Lately, they'd been a bit more reasonable.

"So the first to rise from the younger crowd," said Carol.

"Yes, that's me, the early bird," he said as he yawned loudly, not bothering to cover his mouth.

"So what did you four do last night?" asked Sarah. Carol felt a little surge of apprehension. She hadn't told Sarah about last night's events; she wasn't even sure if David knew all that had occurred. And why did it matter? They were all family, weren't they?

"Just hung out...played some cards." And his answer was complete, to Carol's relief.

Sarah nodded slightly and returned to her book. Carol stepped toward the kitchen to get out some things for lunch. Her head was in the refrigerator when Christy made her way downstairs. "Mom!" she heard as she stepped from the fridge, lunchmeat in hand. "Where's Amanda?"

She could hear the concern—maybe subtle panic—in Christy's voice; nonetheless, she hesitated with her answer just long enough for David to call from the couch. "No worries. She's in my room with Ryan."

Sarah's head came up from her book and Carol sighed with an embarrassment that mingled with despair. She wondered if David was clueless or just being mean. Christy looked at David and back at Carol, waiting for some sort of response, some sort of disapproval or verbal reprimand toward Amanda. Carol looked away and said weakly, "She had a very rough night."

Carol looked back at her daughter and saw the disbelief and something else—disgust? "Well," said Christy. "I'll remember that if and when *I* ever get a boyfriend!"

Carol was immediately angry. "That's not fair and you know it!"

"And it's also not fair that Amanda gets to do whatever she wants just because she's crazy or something!"

"That's right!" retorted Carol. "None of this is fair! But the last thing I need is you being a brat!" Christy's face fell from anger as if she'd been slapped. Carol closed her eyes and turned from her daughter and held onto the counter for support. Sarah and David looked at one another and then studied the floor.

"Don't you see," Carol said quietly. "Don't you understand that Amanda—" She had to stop. What she wanted to say was that Amanda might never get better; that she was capable of committing suicide. Whether she and Ryan shared a bed was really not all that important in the grand scheme of things. What was important was that she got better. What she did say—what she was able to say—was, "Don't you see that Amanda needs to get better?" Carol blinked hard trying to hold back her tears.

"Whatever! I'm going for a walk," said Christy, and she headed for the door.

"I'll go with you," said David, jumping up from the couch, bringing his coffee and not looking at his mother or his aunt.

Carol heard the door open and shut, and closed her eyes and waited.

"Kids are tough, aren't they?" was what she heard from Sarah. Carol nodded her head without looking up from her neat little stack of lunch meats—each in its own little plastic bag, one slice of meat laid down upon the next. "We caught both Matt and Casey, you know, with girls in our house." She was at the other side of the counter now, not quite in the kitchen. "But we just laid down the law—put a stop to that whole thing."

Carol turned to her. "So you think that was it? They just stopped having sex?" Her voice was measured, her sarcasm tempered.

Sarah blinked once. "Well, no, but at least they showed us the respect we deserved ... demanded."

Instead, they fumbled in the backs of cars and in public places, risking bodily injury and arrest.

Carol set her mouth and nodded ever so slightly, and turned back to her meat. It wasn't really that she disagreed with Sarah; it was just that, well, sex wasn't the issue.

"You know, Carol, it's okay to just say *no*."

Carol gave the meat a very dirty look. *Just say* no! Carol bit back her anger before saying something like: *Go to Hell, Sarah! To hell with you and your high-school-math-teacher priggishness and your holier-than-thou answer to motherhood!* But as Carol rested her fingertips on the cool, wet plastic of the lunch meat, she realized that her sister-in-law could not understand how it felt to be afraid, mentally and physically, of your own child. She could forgive her for that. Yet how could Sarah totally disregard Amanda's illness? Carol felt herself step away, retreat from their friendship to somewhere safer, and, instead of condemning her to purgatory, she said, "Would you like turkey or ham?"

~

Ryan woke up slowly and felt the warmness of Mandy's body. He sensed the lingering odor of her shampoo and tightened his arms around her before fully waking. As he realized where he was, the horrible memory of the earlier events returned to him. He didn't understand how she came to be in this bed with him, or how he could want to make love to her and also want her gone.

He slowly extracted himself from her. She didn't wake. He picked up his duffle bag off the bedroom floor and quietly headed for the door. He opened it and closed it with care, then made his way to the bathroom, which separated the two upstairs bedrooms. The hot shower, although a bit spastic, felt wonderful, and he lingered longer than he might normally have. When he stepped out of the bathroom, freshly dressed and feeling much better, he carried his duffle bag with him. When he got to the top of the stairs, he did not know what to do with it, so he left it there, at the top of the stairs—for now.

Carol looked up from her sandwich at the sound on the stairs and saw that it was Ryan, his wet hair falling gently into his eyes and his head tilted down in unease. As he got closer, she saw the faint scratches on his face that Jerry had described. She took in the smile that he tried to give her and her heart was full of gratitude and compassion. She appreciated his awkwardness and she wanted only to make amends for her daughter's behavior, to make him feel welcome and comfortable, to even beg him not to leave—not now. She stood up, deserting her sandwich and stepping toward him. Carol ignored Sarah's gaze as she looked up from her own lunch. "What can I get you?" Carol asked. "Coffee?"

"Yes, please. Coffee would be great."

Carol stepped to the pot and rinsed it in the sink before refilling it with fresh water for a new pot. She heard Sarah ask, "How did you sleep?"

"Fine. I slept fine, thank you."

"Those bunks are pretty small," Sarah continued in a not-quite-cordial tone, and Carol turned from the sink. Now Sarah had gone too far, and Carol shot her a look that said, "Shut up!" and she wondered if Sarah would be any less of a bitch if she knew exactly what had occurred last night.

Even Ryan was a little annoyed, and he stared at Sarah a bit longer than was socially acceptable before saying, "Thank you, ma'am. I had plenty of room."

"You heard me say earlier that Amanda had a particularly difficult night last night, didn't you, Sarah? Ryan was up all night with her." She looked at Ryan and smiled weakly. "For that, I am very grateful. Thank you, Ryan."

"No problem," he lied.

"Well, I'm glad you got some sleep," offered Sarah with a smile. "I'm sure Amanda will feel better today," she said with forced brightness. She returned to her lunch, and if she was the least bit ashamed by her behavior, it was not apparent. Carol was considering saying something else as she measured out the grounds and hit the brew button on the coffee machine. Then the camp door opened, and the welcome sound of Christy's melodic laughter filled the room.

"You're unbelievable!" said David, with his own rich laughter. He punched her gently and she laughed with glee. The coffee pot made its familiar gurgle, and David turned his attention from Christy and said, "Coffee! Thank you, Jesus!" making them all laugh, and the mood was immediately lifted. Everyone was hungry, and there was much more to do than stew about Sarah and Amanda. Carol went back to the refrigerator and removed the lunch meat again. She put out the bagels and cream cheese, bread, pickles, mayo, and everything else that was necessary to satiate this group.

~

Amanda woke up alone and struggled to gain a hold on the despair that buried her. She forced her way up, but then anxiety overrode despair and she knew she was on another rollercoaster of a day—which initially had been a hell of a fun ride, but now she just wanted to get off. She just wanted to get off! And where was Ryan? No longer on this trip with her, but gone. Gone! Because he could get off; he could leave the amusement park, her fucked-up life!

The anxiety increased until she could feel a scream that had to be freed. She took her pillow and let the agony explode into the soft white down and she hit herself in the head with her small fists. Dissatisfied, she took her tiny hands, wrapped them in her hair, and pulled until she could feel the satisfying pain and the letting go.

~

Jerry called Carol from his cell phone a little after one. The reception kept skipping in and out as she assured him all was well and that Amanda was still sleeping. He reminded her about Amanda's meds—as if she would forget—and said they should be back in a couple hours. Sarah wanted to go into the village and do a little browsing in all the cute little shops. She insisted that Carol come with her because David would be there for Amanda and Carol needed to get out, which was all true, but still….

Carol made her way up the stairs with Amanda's pills and a glass of water. When she opened the door, Amanda was sitting up in the lower bunk, looking a little ragged but okay. "Hi, honey," Carol said as she crossed the room. "You okay?"

Amanda shrugged. Carol handed her the pills and she took them. Then Amanda said, with agitated hopelessness, "They aren't working."

"Your dad says it takes more time."

"I don't think I have more time."

Carol opened her mouth to speak, to say something soothing and comforting, but she was paralyzed by trepidation and couldn't seem to move her tongue toward a response. She longed for Jerry and his reasonableness, his never-failing calmness.

"Where's Ryan?!" Amanda asked in desperation.

Carol noticed the clumps of hair lying like long, skinny red snakes across the sheets and felt the fear swirl through her. She wanted to reach out, pick up each clump, and hold it in her hands; to somehow push it all back into Amanda's head. Instead, she looked up from the bed and into her daughter's frantic eyes, and was thankful to be able to say, "He's on the dock with David and Christy. We all had lunch." She saw the scratches on her face, and when Amanda looked away, Carol's eyes fell on her feet. She gasped lightly.

Amanda followed her gaze, and said, "Yeah ... they're sorta fucked up." Amanda reached down and poked fretfully at one of the cuts. "What did he say? Does he hate me?"

Carol had a hard time pulling her attention from Amanda's feet. Both feet were red and slightly puffy. There were numerous smaller assaults on her upturned soles and several larger angry cuts. There was a large pocket of blood, bright red against the pink of Amanda's big right toe. The sheets were dotted with blood. "No. Of course he doesn't hate you. We need to soak those cuts and get your feet cleaned up." Amanda's feet quickly shifted away and under the sheets as an exasperated sigh pushed through her lips. Carol forced her eyes away from the blood-stained bedding and met Amanda's frantic eyes. "He hasn't said anything, honey. I'm sure he doesn't hate you."

Anxiety eased from Amanda like honey, slowly and sweetly. She fell into tears and reached for her mother. Carol lost herself in her daughter's arms, feeling Amanda's sadness and hopelessness mix with her own. If only she could speed up time and sail away to somewhere calm, happy, and closer to sanity.

~

"We need to have a fire tonight," Christy said as she picked a flat rock from the beach and tried to skip it across the water as Ryan was doing. Her rock hit the surface, made a weak attempt at rising, but then sank, sank like a stone. "How do you *do* that?" she asked as she watched his rock skip and skip and skip in a dance across the water.

He laughed. "It's all in the wrist. Like this," he said, choosing a couple of flat stones from the beach. "Watch. You see what I'm doing with my wrist?" He did a couple of instructional twists of his wrist and arm, but did not let the rock go. "Here, try it. This is a good one," he said as he handed her one.

She extended her arm, her hand opening for the stone, and his fingers touched her lightly as it passed between them. Instead of looking away, she smiled at him. "Like this?" she asked, mimicking his movement.

"That's right," he smiled. "Now try it again, but this time let it go." The stone hit the surface of the lake and bounced up in a beautiful, horizontal float. It sailed forward and repeated the flight three times before coming to a gentle rest and fluttering to the bottom of the lake.

"Oh my God! I did it!" and she jumped with delight and gave him the brightest smile he'd yet seen on her face.

"I knew you had it in you," he matched her smile.

"Is it too early for a beer?" asked David, who was sitting on the dock. "My coffee's cold."

Ryan looked up at the weak sun, still high in the sky but dipping toward the distant shore. "Too early for me."

"Let's gather some wood for tonight," suggested Christy.

David shrugged in agreement. "I'd rather have a beer, but whatever," he said, getting up and heading toward shore. He looked up at the camp and stopped. Ryan and Christy followed his gaze. It was Amanda. Her hair was wet with flowing curls from a recent shower. Her body was looking awesome in her tight jeans and little sweater. She was gingerly making her way toward them. Christy sighed. She'd been having fun with the guys. David smiled at the beauty of his cousin, and Ryan felt his breath catch in his throat and felt the stirrings of desire, which seemed to supersede anything else he might have been feeling. The sudden thought of what it might be like to never see her again brought a twinge of unbearable sadness, which was quickly overcome by the fact that she was making her way toward him.

Christy and David acknowledged her approach and then headed into the surrounding woods to collect firewood. Ryan held his breath, felt the smooth weight of the stone he was holding, and let it drop to his feet. This was it: the moment he'd considered and worried over since he left her this morning. He had waited all this time for her to wake, to come to him, so he could tell her how it was. He hadn't counted on her sanity. Even from this distance, he could tell that she was not the same girl who tried to bite him in the woods hours earlier. She was the girl he'd told, only yesterday, that he loved. And so he took a few steps toward her.

Carol watched from the deck as Amanda made it to the lake level. She watched as Ryan moved toward Amanda. She held her breath and braced herself. Jerry had told her that he'd drive Ryan home tonight, if he wanted to go, but that would leave Carol here, alone with Amanda. Carol could just as easily drive Ryan back and just stay in Albany. Let Jerry deal with the fallout. She watched as Amanda placed her forehead against Ryan's chest. Ryan hesitated before placing his arms lightly around her. He looked up at the leaves of the surrounding trees, then closed his eyes to the pressure of her head against his chest. He brought her face up gently with the tip of his finger until she was looking at him, and Carol swore she could almost hear him sigh before tilting his head into acceptance and bending down until his lips were on Amanda's. Carol brought her hand to her mouth and closed her eyes in thanks to gods she did not believe in as her daughter wrapped her arms around Ryan. She stepped back and into the house and told Sarah that they could go shopping now.

9

Jerry and Tom made the final turn around a bend in the lake and could see the dock before them. Jerry was relieved because he was tired and his shoulders ached; the blister on his right hand had opened up and was seeping onto his paddle. As they drew nearer, the familiar feeling of unease crept over him, just as it did each night now when he was done with work and pulling into his garage, unsure of what he would walk into. As they drew nearer yet, they could see the impossibly large pile of wood that the kids had collected on the beach. To Jerry's relief, he saw that all four kids were there—not three or two, but four. When they were in speaking range, Tom called out, "Are you planning to burn the whole place down?" Jerry saw them all laugh—four kids, not three or two, but four. His relief was complete.

"Seriously," Tom said as their kayaks slid against the shore. "Take about half that away. You'll burn the whole forest down."

Jerry stepped carefully out of the front of the boat. Before he could lift the bow to drag it out, Ryan was there, pulling the kayak ashore. "Thank you, Ryan," he smiled. He caught the young man's eye with a look that asked many things, but what came out of his mouth was, "How are you? Did you get some sleep?"

Ryan nodded his head slightly as he looked at Jerry through his crazy bangs, and with his slightly self-conscious smile, he said, "Yes, sir. I'm feeling much better. We both are."

Jerry nodded and turned his eyes to Amanda, who was bending down and retrieving a branch that had freed itself from the pile. She picked it up, jumped in the air, and threw it like a basketball player toward the top of the heap.

Ryan stepped over to help Tom with his boat, and Tom thanked him kindly as he shot his son a disgusted look. David was still supervising the construction of the bonfire, oblivious to the idea of helping with the boats and totally unconcerned with the threat of forest fires. Tom sighed, shook his head, and headed up to the camp for a shower before it was time to start dinner.

Carol and Sarah came back from shopping a little after five, pleased that their husbands had actually followed instructions and had dinner well under way. The young people were out messing around in the kayaks, splashing more than paddling, and Carol watched from the deck for a few minutes and smiled. Then she turned on the gas and lit the grill.

They ate on the deck even though the evening was cool. The sky, framed by the trees reaching over the deck, stretched above the mountains of the western side of the lake and was pink-streaked and alive with wispy grey clouds. The citronella candles flickered in the slight breeze and the scent of mossy earth mingled with the candles and barbequed chicken. Small brown bats dipped and fluttered almost silently above their heads—sweet whispers of the night—shooting out over the lake and darting back as if it were a game.

Sarah poured a glass of wine for herself and offered the bottle to Carol, who took it with a smile and filled her glass. David closed his eyes in pleasure from his long-awaited beer, which slipped easily across his tongue and into his throat as he tilted his head back. He smiled and then laughed as Christy's piece of chicken got away from her, skittering along the table, coming to a stop in front of Ryan, who picked it up and put it on his plate. "Thanks," he said.

"If you are throwing away your food," said Tom, who sat to

Christy's right, "can I have your corn?" He reached for it, and Christy squealed and laughed, slapping at her uncle's hand playfully.

"No!" she laughed. "It was an accident!"

"Oh!" said Ryan, who was just taking a bite of the meat and smiled. "Did you want it back?" Christy laughed again with pleasure and Amanda shifted a bit in her chair. Ryan, oblivious to the danger, laughed and offered the slightly gnawed drum stick back Christy's way.

"No! Keep it!" And everyone laughed—everyone but Amanda.

Amanda tilted her head toward Ryan, who sensed her movement and moved toward it. Jerry, his own beer in his hand, looked across the table at his daughters bracketing Ryan and relished the ephemeral calm. He turned toward Carol, who looked back with hopeful, un-troubled eyes, and he smiled. If only it could be so simple—to believe that this was the beginning of the end; that some jarring of neurons had taken place or that the drugs had kicked in; that it had all been a mistake (maybe PMS or an adolescent upheaval of sorts)... if only....
He gave her an encouraging smile nonetheless.

Ryan was enjoying himself. He no longer felt the unease of a stranger, but felt relaxed and welcome. Maybe it was the night and the beauty of the place that brought on the contentment he was feel-ing, or maybe it was the beer that was already three-quarters gone. Maybe it was the warmth of Mandy's thigh as it rested against his own. He looked about the table, at this family, and he marveled at how he had been—what? Thrown? No... forced, really—into these people's lives. Now he found himself unwittingly ensnarled yet thor-oughly enjoying himself.

How long had it been since he felt any real sense of family? He hadn't seen his mother for almost two years. Sure, they talked often, but she had her own life now: her husband and her stepchildren. He had no brothers, no sisters; even cousins were scarce. His extended family was scattered about the country. He remembered the painfully awkward holidays he'd spent with his mother's sister as a boy. His two cousins, Rebecca and Aaron, were older and had a propensity for cruelness. He found his younger stepbrothers equally annoying and his mother's new husband judgmental. It had been a relief to refuse any family gatherings. He'd always been cool with that. He had a lot of friends and had never spent a holiday alone. This whole thing was somehow different with this family. And even though he had want-ed—had been determined—to leave Mandy and this alleged illness behind today, he felt for her and was enjoying himself.

He turned to her and placed his hand on her leg. She leaned ea-gerly into him, closed her eyes, and tried to calm the anger she felt. She fought hard to swallow the urge to scream at Christy and shove her away from her boyfriend. Yes! He was *her* boyfriend! She lifted up her face to him and he smiled. The smile was only for her, and she felt a little of her anxiety fall away.

~

Tom insisted that they decrease the size of the bonfire, so they did a little. David knew, relative to some of the fires he'd had up here, that this was nothing. But his father was here being a pain-in-the-ass (his favorite thing to be). Amanda danced around, squirting lighter fluid onto the base of the pile until the bottle was empty, but she still continued to dance like an Indian woman performing a fire dance. Christy joined her. Ryan and David laughed. Amanda grabbed Ryan. The three of them danced until David lit a match and threw it, and they all had to jump back at the roar of the flames. The trees singed, and Tom, who'd been watching from the deck, said, "Damn kids!"

Tom returned to the living room. "You have the number to the lo-cal fire department handy?" he asked as he sat at the downstairs game table. No one really answered. Sarah smiled over the rim of her wine glass as she sipped. Jerry shuffled the cards, and Carol refilled her glass of wine.

"What are we playing?" asked Jerry, the cards smoothly flipping through his fingers. "Bridge?"

Carol made a face. "Too much thinking." Sarah frowned with disappointment.

"Hearts?" Jerry asked, an ironic smile on his face.

"Funny," said Carol. "No."

"Euchre?" offered Tom. Sarah shook her head. If she couldn't play bridge, she wasn't playing Euchre. "Go Fish?" asked Tom with irritation.

Jerry smiled and passed out one card to each of them face down and quickly followed with a card face up. "Five-card stud. Jacks are wild." He looked at the cards. "Your bet, Sarah." She had a two of hearts showing.

"What are we betting?" she asked.

"How about your shirt?" suggested Tom.

She shook her head at him. "Behave."

"I'll get the chips," said Carol.

~

The fire was relaxing into itself now, with only an occasional snap of irritation. They were sitting back in their lawn chairs watching the flames. The boys sipped on their beers and the girls occasionally reached over and helped themselves to the bottles. Christy was threading a ridiculous number of marshmallows on a stick that was laboring dangerously under the weight. Amanda was packing her little pipe. Ryan leaned close and said softly, "You know, your dad says that this makes things worse for you."

Amanda stopped what she was doing and looked at him blankly for an uncomfortable moment before saying, "Well, he *would* be wrong." She saw Ryan sigh, so she added, "It keeps me from wanting to kill people."

How could he argue with that? He had no choice but to accept that she knew, or would at least learn, what worked and what didn't. He took the pipe from her when she was done, and he was grateful for the sweet burning of the smoke as it hit his throat. He anticipated the way it would make him feel in these beautiful woods, next to this beautiful girl, with this amazing fire crackling before him.

~

Jerry was losing badly. His pile of chips, which had at one point been substantial, was quickly dwindling. Tom sat before his own small pile and frowned at his cards. He looked at his wife suspiciously. She smiled back sweetly, innocently. Jerry and Carol had already folded right before Jerry went to the fridge for another round of beers. He poured some crackers and peanuts into a small bowl. When he returned to the table and passed the beers around—the women had switched to beer as soon as the card game had begun in earnest—Tom still had not made his bet. "Damn you, Sarah! What do you have?"

"Are you calling?" she asked calmly.

"I'm asking! As your husband! What the fuck do you have?" Sarah just laughed. He looked at the chips he had left and the chips in the center. He could make a substantial comeback if he could only win this hand. If he folded he'd still be left with enough chips to continue, but if he called and lost... well, he'd be done. He looked again at his king in the hole, the two kings sternly looking up at him, and the happily smiling jack, which was still wild. She was bluffing! There was no way she held a straight flush. He studied the board: three, four, and seven of clubs... damn if she didn't have a jack too! Goddamn Jerry and his wild cards! He hated wild cards. It took away from the purity of the game. He bit his lip. There was no way! She was bluffing! "Call!" he said, shoving the remainder of his chips to the center of the table.

He stared at his wife and then flipped over his king. "Four of a kind," he said with assurance. Still, he could not read her face, and she dragged it out even longer as she reached for her beer. She took a sip before slowly taking her card from the hole and flicking it gently to the center of the table. The six of clubs came to rest, and Tom buried his head in his hands, while Jerry and Carol laughed. Sarah gathered up her winnings.

"You buying more chips, Tom?" asked Jerry.

"What! Are we playing for real money?"

Jerry shrugged as if to say *why not?* then said, "It's your wife who's winning. Doesn't it all go in the same pot?"

"True," agreed Tom. "Honey, can you spot me a ten?"

Sarah slid him over some chips and said, "Oh! Let me show you what I bought today." She jumped up from the table and had to steady herself a moment—they had been drinking all evening after all—and made her way, wobbling a little, to retrieve the package from her bedroom.

David came in from the deck, greeting everyone with a smile, and went directly to the refrigerator. He collected the remainder of his twelve pack (they'd have to make a beer run tomorrow) and grabbed a bag of chips. He turned to the disapproving face of his father and was forced to stop and slowly let his eyes travel along the trail of empty beer bottles and wine glasses that decorated the game table. "Can anyone here spell *hypocrisy*?" he asked, not knowing if anyone could in their present state, so he just laughed. What a wonderful difference three months could make, the three months since he turned twenty-one.

"No beer for the girls!" was all his father could say.

"Yes. Really, David," Jerry threw in. "No beer for them."

"No worries! There's barely enough for me!" And he left.

Tom looked at Jerry. "And that's supposed to make me feel better?"

Now Carol was feeling a little raw. At first the wine had resided pleasantly, but with the introduction of beer and the lateness of the night, she felt like she'd been put through a grater. It didn't really seem fair that Sarah was winning so convincingly at cards. Carol felt slighted by the card gods; her life held such little pleasure right now. Surely the card gods could have smiled on her; instead they'd smiled on Sarah, the one who had shown a total lack of compassion toward her daughter—which was really a childish way for Carol to feel. Nevertheless, it was exactly how she felt. Sarah came back into the room and proudly placed that thing she'd bought today in the center of the table.

"What the hell is that?" asked Tom.

Carol smiled.

"Isn't it adorable?" asked Sarah.

Jerry narrowed his eyes at the thing. "What is it?" It was some sort of animal, that was not in question, and it was constructed with an assortment of forest debris (pine cones and bark). There was at least one thistle and some brown thing that looked like it might have come out of the back end of a bear. It might have been all right if it were small, but it stood at least ten inches tall — too tall to hide behind a lamp.

"It's a beaver, of course!" And Sarah was hurt by their lack of love for this creature. "It's adorable," she insisted, and looked at Carol for backup — since it is an unwritten law that two women always come together against men for this sort of thing — but Carol was feeling a little raw and drunk, and she truly hated this beaver.

"It's ugly as hell," Carol said, and burst out laughing and was joined by the men.

"You told me you liked it in the store."

"I lied!" she howled and had to bend down and hold her stomach as she laughed.

Now it was Sarah's turn to feel slighted. She picked up her beaver and whispered apologies to it as she carried it to the kitchen counter. When she returned, the three of them were wiping tears from their eyes and trying to get their laughter under control.

Sarah sat back down and fiddled with her chips. "I hate you all," she said, and tried to sound light about it. "You know, Jerry, it's not like you have the best taste."

Carol looked at her. Was she implying something?

Sarah waited a beat or two and added, "Remember that awful lamp he brought home, Tom?"

"No."

"Sure you do! It was bright red with a lava lamp in the middle of it."

"Well … maybe …."

She looked at Carol. "That was way before he brought you home, back when it was just the three of us. Me and my two men," she said wistfully.

It wasn't even true! It was Sarah who had brought her home, not Jerry! Carol was reminded, once again, that she was the fourth one allowed into this tiny group, making her feel somehow less important.

She resented the insinuation that Sarah, in some way, had once had the choice between the two brothers and had chosen Tom, leaving Carol with what—one of Sarah's rejects? Even though Carol would never have been interested in Tom—if she were totally honest with herself, she might have had sex with him *once*—she still felt the sting of insult. All this because she didn't like Sarah's beaver? She found, once again, that she was fighting off tears. After all, she was raw and slightly drunk, so she excused herself to the bathroom.

"What the hell is wrong with you?" Jerry hissed as soon as Carol had left the room. "Why would you say that?"

"What? What did I say?" Sarah looked at Jerry and then at Tom, waiting for him to protect her from his brother's attack. Tom didn't look at her but reached for his beer instead.

"You know how hard things are right now," Jerry continued, and then he stopped for a moment and added, "Or maybe you don't, since you haven't once asked her about Amanda."

"What are you talking about?" Sarah was confused. How did Amanda suddenly get into this?

"You haven't once asked how Amanda's doing!" Jerry's voice was still an angry, quiet hiss, which was somehow worse than if he'd been screaming. "How Carol is doing!"

"You know, I just don't understand this illness thing. Amanda seems fine to me."

"Well, she's not. And if you ask Carol, she'd tell you why she's not, and if you can't understand, ask your husband." Jerry looked from Sarah to Tom, and continued, "He can tell you what it's like to live with someone with manic depressive illness." Tom glanced at his brother and then looked away.

Sarah turned her eyes back to her husband who was now studying the lip of his beer bottle. Suddenly, Sarah wanted to cry. How could Tom just sit there and let Jerry attack her? And it wasn't like she hadn't wanted to ask Carol, it's just that she didn't want to make her more upset. "I just didn't want to make her cry."

"Well, maybe that's exactly what she needs! Someone to cry with.

Other than me." Jerry was done. He sat back, reached for the scattered cards, and began to put them away.

~

The fire was quickly dying with the midnight moon. The day was breaking, but it was still too dark to search for wood. With the dwindling heat of the fire, they were all getting cold and running out of world problems to discuss and solve. David stood up, stretched, and yawned. "My bed is calling me." He looked up at the camp. "I think they've gone to bed," noting the decreased light of the main windows. "We're safe."

The fire hissed in protest as they threw a little lake water its way. They deserted their empties, which clicked gently against each other under their feet as they shifted around the fire, folding up the chairs to ward off the dew. David pulled out his little flashlight, and they made their way up the stairs. Even though her father had insisted she come up and take her meds a couple of hours ago, Amanda wasn't the least bit sleepy. She hadn't been alone with Ryan all day, so when they got to the camp, she announced that she and Ryan were taking a little walk and asked to borrow David's flashlight. "Don't lose my flashlight," he said as he handed it over a tad reluctantly. And they were gone, Amanda dragging Ryan by the hand, and all that David could see was the little light bouncing away in the dark.

"Hey! No! Not back in the woods!" said Ryan as she left the drive and pulled him down a tiny path.

She smiled at him in the dark and laughed, "No, this is good! You'll like this." But he wasn't so sure, so he pulled her back and she resisted. "Really," she said, digging her feet into the dirt and pulling him with all her weight. "Trust me!" When he didn't relent, she stepped toward him and pressed her body into his and said again, "Trust me." He sighed into her hair and let her pull him into the darkness.

All that Ryan could see was the tiny spot of light that bobbed before him as he walked a step behind Mandy. Thank God it was just a short walk into the woods; it didn't give him much of a chance to get too freaked. She stopped and waved the beam of light across a wooden ladder and then up into the trees, faintly illuminating a wooden structure amongst the branches. "My tree house," she whispered. And then he understood.

She lay lightly across his chest, on top of the old mice-infested blankets that someone had left up there (probably David), and ran her finger slowly across his jawline. "I told you you'd like it." He moaned with tired satisfaction, but the faint light of the flashlight was casting eerie shadows of spider webs across the ceiling, and although he tried to concentrate on Mandy, the place was creeping him out.

"We should go back, get some sleep," he suggested.

"No! Let's sleep here."

Ryan imagined the spiders dangling down from the ceiling while he slept and the mice scampering across his chest. "No way! Absolutely not!"

She laughed and pouted, resting her chin on his chest. "Chicken shit," she said.

He ran his fingers through her hair and rested his hand on her head asking, "So, what's it like? What's it like in your head?"

She raised her head to look at him before flopping down next to him and looking at the ceiling. "Busy," she said. "A lot going on."

He studied the ceiling with her a long moment before asking, "And last night? When all that was going on? What were you thinking?"

"Thinking? Nothing. I don't remember."

"You don't remember what happened or you don't remember thinking?"

"I don't know! Both?" She was beginning to stress out. She felt his arm tighten around her and waited for his next question. When it didn't come, she offered quietly, "Confusion. I remember confusion."

And, although he wanted to ask more, he did not dare.

~

No one got out of bed early on Sunday, not even Tom. And no one, with the exception of Ryan and Amanda maybe, was all that eager to see one another. When the inevitable bathroom callings tried to force them to stay out of bed, they took one look at the grey dark day and the rain that came down cold and steady and crawled back to bed. Tom finally made his way to the kitchen at ten-forty and started a pot of coffee. He took a cup to Sarah and returned to find his brother looking a little tattered and red-eyed (as he imagined himself to look) helping himself to the pot.

"What ever possessed us to drink like it was our profession?" asked Tom.

Jerry just shook his head — and even that hurt; he was afraid what speaking might do. He took two Advil and threw the bottle to his brother.

One by one the household woke up. Sarah and Carol were quiet but pleasant to one another. As they straightened up from the previous evening's activities, Carol picked up the beaver and placed it gently on the mantle of the fireplace. Sarah asked how Amanda was and Carol had to tell her that she didn't know. As their hangovers gradually lifted, so did the tension between the two women.

The rain continued, and it was decided to prepare the camp for winter. If the weather didn't clear, they'd leave that night instead of Monday. Amanda woke bursting with energy and was determined to go to the movie theater in Indian Lake for the matinee and then out to dinner with Ryan, Christy, and David, so the four men took in the dock and put away the boats in the early afternoon rain. When the outside chores were done, Ryan and David came up from the lake to change and found Christy and Amanda upstairs, ready and eager to leave. Christy was dressed in jeans and a tight little hoodie. She had spent extra time on her hair and makeup and looked older than her years with her tight, smooth belly peaking out from above her jeans and heels dressing her feet. Amanda wore a tight, low-cut black dress with funky black and white striped leggings and even funkier black leather boots. She had her red hair pushed over to one side, twisted and turned so that the black tips flopped across her forehead. An odd assortment of bracelets dangled from her wrists, which jangled a crazy song as she bounced with excitement.

Both of the boys whistled. Ryan had to step close, take her in, touch her, lay his claim on her; David felt the surge between them and felt his own surge of need and misplaced jealousy. He turned to Christy and said, "Can we just pretend, just for tonight, that you're not my cousin?" David enjoyed the blush that spread across her face and he punched her gently in the arm.

Jerry looked up from the football game they were watching, and when he saw Amanda, he sighed. Where did she think she was going? Better yet, where did she think she was? New York City? South Beach? And Christy looked way too old and available.

"Jesus," muttered Tom. Sarah looked up and pursed her lips and was grateful, once again, that she'd only had sons. Carol, embarrassed and confused by her daughters' appearances, did not know how to respond. "Halloween isn't for at least another two weeks, Amanda," said Tom. Jerry held his breath and let it out in relief when he heard Amanda laugh.

"You're so funny, Uncle Tom!" Amanda put on her little leather jacket with the white fuzzy collar, completing the ensemble. Ryan was wearing his black leather jacket and with his hair looking even more interesting than normal—combed to one side so that one eye was hidden; more hair than normal shooting straight up in the back—the two of them could have been on the cover of People—celebrities you know you should know…. Even David, by association, looked a little scary.

"Poor Indian Lake Village," said Carol, taking Tom's lead. "After one look at the four of you, the place may never be the same! Please don't get arrested!"

"Why would we get arrested?" laughed Christy.

"Do you not remember the village?" asked Carol. "Anything other than polar fleece or plaid is strictly frowned upon and may actually be illegal. And the four of you…" she laughed, "well, just be careful." And the four of them shook their heads and rolled their eyes and laughed at the absurdity of these old people as they walked out the door.

The Wizard of Oz was playing at the theater, and it was necessary to get at least a little high before seeing something like that. Amanda didn't remember the witch being quite so scary, or Dorothy looking quite so old—especially to be wearing such a silly dress—but she fell in love all over again with the Scarecrow. He was really an amazing man (man?). He was there with Dorothy almost from the beginning, stuck with her through the entire ghastly journey (even if he was a helpless haystack against those hideous monkeys).

Amanda insisted in the theater, rather loudly, that Dorothy and Scarecrow were totally doing it. Ryan was finally forced to kiss her repeatedly so she'd shut up. But they were all laughing, singing with the songs and having a wonderful time, even if it was at the expense of the other two people in the theater.

By the time the movie ended, the rain had stopped and a faint sun filtered through the reddish grey clouds of sunset. As they walked down the street, on their way to the tavern where they were going to eat dinner, Christy and Amanda started to have an argument. Christy insisted that Tin Man was much sexier than Scarecrow, which Amanda found ridiculous considering he had no penis.

"How do you know Tin Man has no penis?" cried Christy.

"If the guy forgot the heart, he certainly forgot the penis!" yelled Amanda, laughing and leaning on Ryan, who was also laughing with delight.

"Not necessarily! And who says Scarecrow has a penis?" countered Christy.

"Oh, he has a fucking penis!"

"Well, it's true that you can certainly have a penis without a brain!"

"Hey! Be nice," said David.

"But if he does, it's made of straw!" continued Christy. "And what fun would that be?"

But before the argument made a dangerous turn, they walked into the tavern. The locals took their eyes off their beers and took the four of them in, shifting a bit on their bar stools, feeling the power of

Amanda as she laughed and flipped her purse about in the air.

Amanda could feel the power she had and knew that she com-
manded the room. Any of these deer-shooting, beer-drinking, snow-
mobiling good ol' boys would give anything to be with her. Hell, if it
weren't for Ryan, she might have slept with them all. But he was there
and had a power almost as great as her own; between the two of them
the world was theirs to do whatever the fuck they liked. Nothing,
nothing could stop them. All the things that she was going to do,
now, starting tonight, she would begin — that novel that had been
flying around her brain, well, she needed to get some money to start
that, but once she finished that new dance that everyone loved to see
her dance then everything would fall into place, and things wouldn't
be so confusing once she had the money — wait, what the hell was
that hanging from the wall? Why was someone talking to her and
distracting her from what was critical, which was something anyone
who wasn't dumb as shit could see? Of course she wanted something
to drink! Wasn't that why they were here? Were these people just stupid? What she really needed was a pen or a pencil and napkins, lots
of napkins … anything! Order her anything! That thing staring at her
from the wall was freaking her out; its eyeballs were watching her.
Fuck! Things were flying at her now, those eyeballs sending things
her way; some of this just needed to be put down …. *Finally* someone
was handing her a pen and she began to write, already feeling better,
each word adding power to the previous words — if she could write a
thousand words, then that thing would stop staring at her.

Ryan sipped his beer and watched Mandy write. When she was
done with one napkin she would stuff it in her purse and start on a
new one. The tip of her tongue was slipping between her lips in concentration. When the waitress brought their food, she was irritated by
the disruption, but ate and wrote, and did not enter into the conversation the rest of them were having. When the napkins were gone, Ryan
got her more before she became distressed. What he really wanted to
do was read what she was writing, to try to understand what was going on in her head. When she got up, taking her purse and heading

for the bathroom, David asked, "Is she okay?"

"Yeah, she's cool," was his answer. When she came back from the bathroom, smelling of weed, he could tell that she was already calmer, and he didn't question her desire to switch seats with him. He glanced at the large moose head in front of him and swore the thing was staring at him.

10

They left Monday just as soon as everyone was up, the final preparations for winter were completed, and the cars were packed. The driving arrangements were the same, except that Jerry, thankfully, sat in the front seat this time and was able to stretch out his legs; the women sat quietly in the back. As the miles from home decreased, Carol's anxiety increased. The uncertainty of tomorrow played nastily in her mind. She wanted to spend the trip strategizing with Jerry, but could not bring herself to discuss things in front of Tom and Sarah. Was Amanda going to go to school? Should they try to make her go? Should they stop her if she wanted to go? If she went, would she get anything out of it? Would she cause problems? Be disruptive? If she stayed home, what then? Could Carol leave her and go to work? Was she going to spend the rest of her life caring for her daughter when now was the time she should be letting her take care of herself? Was this the way it was going to be? She had spent all those years raising a child, looking forward to the bittersweet time when she would be rewarded by being left behind as Amanda took off into the world, knowing she'd done a good job, that she'd brought a wonderful, beautiful being into the world. Was all this going to be snatched away by this ... illness?!

Jerry's thoughts were of a more clinical nature, calculating how long Amanda had been on the Depakote now (approximately seven days), what her blood level might be—would seven a.m. be too early to call Bill? Amanda's blood really should be drawn tomorrow. Could Carol bring her in? Would Amanda go on her own? He really hadn't seen much improvement, but he resisted the idea that a different drug should be tried so soon. Then again, depending on her blood level, maybe it should be considered—that, of course, was up to Amanda's doctor, not him.

It was a relief when Tom pulled up to the house. The Volvo was already parked in the drive and, not surprisingly, none of the things in the car had been unpacked. Ryan's Jetta was still parked on the road, so they were all there somewhere. Tom was, of course, irritated—really, you'd think they would have at least removed the things from the car. He went into the house in search of someone to yell at, while Jerry, Carol, and Sarah began to sort through the amazing amount of stuff that was in the two cars. It wasn't long before everything was organized and Tom, Sarah, and David were gone, leaving only Ryan, who was thanking them and attempting to extract himself from this family, but couldn't quite do it. So he hung out awhile, watching TV with Mandy and eating an early dinner with everyone. When he left, he promised Mandy he'd see her after school on Tuesday.

~

Amanda couldn't get out of bed Tuesday morning. Jerry and Carol stood in Amanda's room, looking at the dull, tired eyes of their daughter, her face swollen with fatigue, her voice slurred from the Seroquel and a sleep that would not abate. She told them that all she wanted to do was go back to sleep and be alone, so they left—Carol going off to campus and telling Amanda she'd call her later; Jerry going off to find Bill McIntyre before starting his day at the hospital.

The first thing Carol did when she got to her office was call the school and ask to talk to Amanda's academic counselor. She was impressed with herself as she asked to speak with Mrs. Powers—her voice calm, professional, all-business. (This was not going to be hard after all.) But as soon as Mrs. Powers' pleasant, caring voice came through on the line, Carol felt sorrow push up into her throat, and she had to apologize. "I'm sorry—hang on ...." was all she could say through her tears. Assuring her that it was fine, Mrs. Powers waited patiently for Carol to collect herself. Eventually, Carol got the words out that her daughter was diagnosed with bipolar disorder and that she did not know if or when Amanda would return to school. Thankfully, this woman, this angel of sorts, understood what she was being told, had sadly dealt with this sort of thing many times over the years, and knew what needed to be done. She would contact Amanda's teachers, talk to Amanda, put in for homebound tutoring—if that's what Amanda and her doctor wanted. She assured Carol that the school would do all they could to help. Carol, unable to properly thank her through her tears, felt embarrassingly weak and unforgivably fragile as she hung up the phone. Now everyone would know not only that her daughter was crazy, but that she, the most likely source of the problem, was also a bit of a basket case.

~

Jerry found Bill in his office just a little before eight. Bill was in his early forties and a relatively new addition to Albany Medical. He had moved here from McLean Hospital in Belmont, MA, for family reasons, and he was a welcome and greatly needed addition to the staff. Jerry had asked him to see Amanda because he was the best psychiatrist he knew. Plus, they weren't friends; in fact, he barely knew the man, except by reputation and the occasional times when the care of an inpatient overlapped.

Bill came around his desk and shook Jerry's hand warmly. "Hi, Jerry. Sit, please," he said indicating one of the two chairs facing his desk. Jerry couldn't help noting, as he sat down, that Bill's office was nice, but not as nice as his, and this made him both satisfied and ashamed that such a petty, arrogant thought would even enter his mind at such a time. Bill sat in the other chair and turned it toward Jerry, leaning forward casually, with his arms resting on his knees. He met Jerry's eyes with soft compassion and asked, "How are you doing?"

A reasonable and even kind question, but Jerry felt the biting pain from the reality of an honest answer and could not find his voice.

"I'm sorry," Bill added quickly, with a self-reproachful smile. "Stupid question." Jerry laughed softly and felt his discomfort ease off slightly. Bill reached for Amanda's chart. "Thank you for entrusting the care of your daughter to me. It means a lot, coming from you."

"Thank you," Jerry said, accepting the compliment and then adding, "Thank you for seeing her."

"Any improvement over the weekend?" he asked, flipping through the chart.

"No—but no worse."

Bill nodded his head. "Her Depakote level was only forty on Friday…she's at what? Fifteen hundred milligrams per day now? Let's check the level again today." He looked up from the chart and said, "I think we should try to get the blood levels up, you know, before trying a different med."

"I agree."

Bill nodded his head. "I'll call you when I get the level. I'm seeing her again tomorrow," he said as he reached for his prescription pad and wrote out the Rx for the blood level draw. "We'll go from there." He handed Jerry the script.

Jerry knew they were done, knew there was nothing more to say; both he and Bill had a full day awaiting them. But Jerry didn't want to leave. He wanted to stay and beg this man to tell him that his daughter would be fine. He wanted this good doctor to assure him that she wasn't even sick, that Jerry had been nothing but a paranoid idiot—there was no illness. Jerry stared at the script in his hand, knowing that he really needed to get up and leave.

"Jerry," Bill said softly, "I'm so very sorry. You know I'll do the best I can for Amanda. You call me anytime if there is anything more I can do." Jerry made himself get up and shake Bill's hand. He heard himself thank this man, and he left feeling unsatisfied and somehow cheated.

~

When Carol called at a little after noon to check on Amanda, her cell phone went right to voicemail and she did not, of course, answer the house phone. Was she still sleeping? Was she okay? Carol looked at the clock. She had a student coming at twelve-thirty to see her and a rescheduled meeting at one. If she went home she'd miss both appointments... again. The angry, depressed, worried, frustrated mental state she found herself in should have been something that didn't feel so fretfully foreign at this point, but she physically hurt from all the stress, some evil thing tumbling spastically in her chest. When her cell phone rang she grabbed it and was disappointed that it was Jerry, and then anger won out when he told her that Amanda needed to have her blood drawn today in Albany.

"Well, you know what?" she said into the phone. "I don't really care. Your daughter won't answer her phone! I don't even know where she is! I hate her! You deal with it, damn it!" And she flipped the phone shut.

~

Jerry stared at the phone in his hand. She *did not* just hang up on him! He slapped the phone down on his desk and sighed, rubbing his hand across his face. He looked at the clock. He had fifteen minutes before rounds with the residents, then a departmental meeting, several new admissions he needed to deal with, and a huge stack of charts from the weekend he needed to sign off on; he didn't even know how many inpatients he was seeing today. *Shit!* He picked up his phone again and tried home... no answer. He tried Amanda's cell... no answer. *Shit!*

~

Carol heard the small beep of her cell phone receiving a text just as the young woman who sat before her began to cry. "Dean Benson," the young woman said through her tears, "I just don't know what to do ...." Carol glanced at her phone. She could not quite see the screen from this angle, then the screen turned off. It *had* to be Amanda. Jerry didn't even know how to text. Well at least she's alive. (If it was, in fact, from Amanda.) Could be Christy. "I was just hoping you could, you know … if you could just, maybe talk to Professor Young?"

Carol looked up at the tear-streaked face. "Have you talked to her?" Carol asked.

"Well, no … she hates me."

Carol sighed. "You need to talk to her. It's really not my policy to interfere unless there are irreconcilable issues—and you haven't even tried to talk to her." Carol was trying hard to sound kind, but she knew she was failing. The girl looked at her desperately; it was a look she'd seen in Amanda's eyes. Carol closed her eyes in resignation. "Dr. Young is not as mean as she likes to pretend to be. I'll talk to her. I'll let her know that you are coming to see her." Carol smiled. "I'll tell her to be nice." The girl laughed then with relief and thanked her profusely. "Please let me know if things don't improve," Carol said as the young woman got up to leave and Carol reached for her cell.

The text was from an unknown caller. She hit the READ button. It was from Amanda, letting her know her cell battery was dead and she was at Ryan's. Carol closed her eyes, her relief overtaken by her irritation. How did she get there? Probably took the car without asking. But now she had Ryan's cell number, so she saved it in her phone before calling the number from her office.

He answered on the second ring. "Hello?"

"Is Amanda there?" she asked impatiently.

"I'm sorry. Who is this?"

Carol closed her eyes and took in a calming breath. "I'm sorry," she said. She really needed to get a grip. "It's Amanda's mom, Carol." She heard the silence of hesitation.

"Oh! Sure! Sorry. Here she is."

Carol heard Amanda's unenthusiastic greeting and could not hide her irritation. "How did you get there?!" she demanded.

"Drove."

"You can't take the car without asking!"

"Whatever. Sorry."

Carol wanted to scream, to reach through the phone and strangle her. She should be in school if she was capable of getting up and driving into Albany! Another calming breath. "Okay, we'll talk about this later. But now you have to go over to the hospital to page your dad and have some blood drawn."

"Well ... maybe later ...."

"No! I want you to do this now! Do you understand?"

"I've gotta go."

"Amanda! You need to do this! Let me talk to Ryan." But the connection was broken.

~

Ryan traced his fingers gently along the underside of Mandy's left breast. "You told me your mom knew you were here," he said lightly.

She shrugged and drew him closer. "Make love to me again."

He shook his head at her with a smile. "You are insatiable. What did she want?"

"Who?" she said as she nipped at his ear.

"Ow!" He pulled away. "Your mom."

"Wants me to get a stupid blood test."

He nodded his head. "Today?" His cell phone rang again.

"I'm going to throw that fucking thing out the window!" She grabbed for the phone, but he beat her to it.

"Cut it out, Mandy!" he told her as she tried to grab it from his hand. He let it go to voicemail. "Why do you want to drive them nuts? Just get the fucking test."

She smiled sweetly. "Fuck me and I'll think about it."

~

Carol read the text from Amanda when she returned to her office after her one o'clock meeting. Amanda was asking where she was supposed to go for the blood test. Carol shook her head with impatience as she texted back. She'd already told her to go to the hospital; to page Jerry. Her texting skills were greatly improving—she only cussed a couple of times and then pressed SEND. Amanda—or maybe it was

Ryan—texted back, THANX. Carol called the hospital and left a message for Jerry, letting him know that Amanda would be coming in at some point, and then she shut off her cell phone. She was done, at least for today, with all this crap.

11

Amanda's blood level of Depakote had increased to fifty-five, just barely high enough to have a clinical effect. Jerry knew, of course, that each patient was different, that their bodies metabolized the drug at various rates, and that it took time to find the proper dosage. Bill wanted to give it more time—at least another week. It was an easy thing for him to suggest since he wasn't living in their home and didn't feel the stress of the illness seeping into all of them—Amanda seeming, somehow, the least affected, while the rest of them were at each other's throats, or would have been if they had the energy to fight.

Christy spent as much time away from home as possible: staying late after school, throwing herself into her schoolwork and social life—wishing she'd gone out for the soccer team after all—hanging out in the park with some new friends who were fun and cool and weren't all weirded out by shit like some of her older friends were; they had their own fucked-up lives to worry about (divorced parents, alcoholic moms, abusive fathers, drug-use issues). They didn't seem to know, or at least care, that she had a crazy sister. And it felt so good to be away from home. Her mother was driving her nuts, yelling at *her* instead of at who she was really mad at, as if she were afraid or something. It just wasn't fair! She used to be able to talk to her sister, but now there was no one to talk to except David, who was great and all but was obsessed with Amanda like every other boy who couldn't see that she was just a crazy bitch.

Carol was trying not to take all her frustrations out on Jerry, and especially Christy, but it was incredibly difficult. They'd somehow managed to make it through the week and survived another weekend, but she just didn't know how much more she could take. It was impossible to watch Amanda sitting at home all day, not going to school, spending hours on the computer, doing nothing—as far as Carol could tell. She knew Amanda was getting behind in her school work, so Carol had to push and nag to get at least a little work out of her, risking verbal abuse and knowing she was causing Amanda's fragile state to spin into anxiety, but damn it! She had to graduate; if nothing else, she had to at least get through high school. And then there was the frustration from the school. It was already Thursday, over an entire week of education lost since she first talked to Mrs. Powers, Amanda's academic counselor. Nothing was happening quickly—the letter from the doctor, the approval of the board, the finding and setting up of tutors.... Meanwhile, didn't they realize she was getting further behind?

Amanda had never quite realized how amazingly stupid the people in her family were. She had absolutely no tolerance for their ignorance. There were so many important things she needed to get done, but they kept mixing her up, plastering her with pressure and layers of stupidity. Why wouldn't they just get the fuck out of her face? It was easier just to stay in bed.

Jerry was beginning to have his doubts about the Depakote. It had been over two weeks since she'd begun using it. Maybe Lamictal should be added now, but it took weeks of increasing Lamictal to see improvement. Maybe she needed two mood stabilizers—he had patients who had. He didn't know how much more his family could take. Poor Christy. He had tried to talk to her many times, but she just didn't want to hear it. She wasn't accepting the seriousness of Amanda's illness. She felt hurt and abandoned by Amanda and couldn't separate the illness from who Amanda was. Christy was angry. She was angry with her mother, but most of all, she was angry with him. He was, after all, the one who started this whole thing—it had been he who decided her sister was not just a bitch, but actually sick. When Jerry gently suggested that it might be helpful for her to talk to someone about how she was feeling, well, that hadn't gone over well at all. It had been as if he were accusing her of having a mental issue as well, as if he just went around throwing diagnoses at everyone.

~

Thursday afternoon, Carol came home early from work. Amanda had already sent her several frantic texts and called her once in tears, but when Carol got home, Amanda was angry and extremely unpleasant. Carol felt the wave of despair hit her with Amanda's first verbal insult, and she resisted the urge to turn around and return to her office. Obviously her daughter needed her, if for no other reason than to have someone with whom to vent her anger. Amanda disappeared into her bedroom. Carol called Christy, who should have been home from school by now, only to become more distressed by Christy's failure to answer her phone. She made herself a cup of tea and stared despondently out into the valley. The trees were naked now; a storm over the weekend had stripped them of their beauty. Shadowed by intimidating dark clouds, the trees stood dark, empty, and waiting against the hillside. Carol could relate.

"Mom!" a shout came from upstairs, followed by the noise of objects being thrown about. Carol barely flinched. "What the fuck did you do with my purse?" Carol sighed and took a sip of tea. Damn! It was too hot, burning her mouth. "Why the fuck did you take my purse?" Carol felt her heart rate increase—a little.

Carol stood slowly and looked about the room. She didn't see Amanda's purse. Her school books and papers were on the table, but her purse wasn't with them. There were more thuds from above. Heavy stepping, for sure. A crash of something small and fragile. Carol made her way into the den. A sharp, loud scream of frustration came from above. Carol searched the room as she made her way to the computer.

It wasn't here either. She could hear Amanda leaving her room, slamming the door ….

She sat down on the chair and tried to calm herself with deep breaths, and that's when she smelled it, the strong distinctive odor slapping her senses. She saw it now, behind the monitor, the purse that never left Amanda's side, its strap just peaking out. She picked it up, reached inside, and found a little pipe with the cute little lizard, sticky with use, and a plastic bag filled with the green sticky leaves. The pressure of disappointment and anger pushed on her chest and caught in her throat. How many times had Jerry talked to Amanda about marijuana use interfering with her treatment? She had assured her father that she understood, that she had stopped smoking. Did she not want to get better? Was she ever going to stop screwing up her life at their expense?

She held the little pipe in her hand and turned to the sound of Amanda coming down the stairs. Carol stood up. "Amanda! What the hell is this?" she said accusingly, holding the little pipe toward her daughter. "You told us you had stopped!"

"Give that to me!"

"No!" With a few quick steps she was there, grabbing Carol's hand, trying to get hold of the pipe, but Carol tightened her grip. "I'm not giving this to you!"

"You fucking bitch!" And then they were in the heat of more than just a mental battle, but a physical confrontation, for which Carol was ill-prepared. As she felt the pain of Amanda twisting her hands, while trying to avoid the kicks of Amanda's legs, the thought that this just wasn't happening seemed to predominate in her mind. This did not happen to good people like her, to nice families like theirs. Suddenly, a sense of self-preservation and fear kicked in—she needed to get away, to save herself.

"You're hurting me!" she yelled.

"Just give me my fucking pipe!"

"No!" This battle she would not lose. Better to have broken hands than to hand over this thing that seemed to symbolize the failure or success of recovery. If only she could control this impossible moment, then maybe she could control this impossible illness. Carol jerked her body hard to extract herself just as Amanda let go slightly to reestablish her grip. The little pipe went flying, landing hard and shattering from impact, causing Amanda to detonate with rage. With a scream of angry agony, she hit her mother in the face. When the blood from the blow visually slapped back at Amanda, she momentarily saw what she had done and transferred her rage away from her mother and onto the room, grabbing lamps and knickknacks and sending them on trips through the air, then kicking over furniture and freeing pictures from the walls.

"Stop it! Stop it!" screamed Carol, but she took the opportunity to get to the phone and she lifted the receiver. "I am calling the police! Do you hear me, Amanda?" She had her finger on the nine and had located the number one with her eyes, feeling sure Amanda would gain control. "I'm calling the police if you do not stop!" But Amanda just looked at her. Something in her eyes forced Carol to hit the nine and move her finger to the one. Her daughter was coming at her again, so she hit the one twice and braced herself.

~

Jerry was going over a treatment plan with one of his new residents when he heard the page requesting that he go immediately to the admissions desk. He wasn't truly frightened until he saw the look on Janet's face as she handed him the phone. "It's your wife," she said, and the adrenaline was pulsing through his system, preparing him for action as he put the phone to his ear. He listened to the pain and sorrow of Carol's words as she related the story. She was okay and the police were on their way to the hospital with Amanda. He assured her that things would be fine. He told her he would handle things here, that she should stay at home, for herself and Christy, and that she should try to calm down. He said he would call just as soon as he could, and hung up the phone. He did not collapse into tears as he had wanted; instead, he paged Bill McIntyre and made his way to the ER to await the arrival of his daughter.

He had seen a screaming and biting patient forcibly dragged into the ER many times, but never had they had long, bright red hair with black tips flying angrily about that came to rest at the sight of him. Never had he heard these words bursting from one of these enraged patients' mouths, "That's my dad! Let go of me, you fucking pigs! Daddy, help me! Daddy!" And Bill was there, grabbing his arm and telling him something, but he just wanted to go to her, to help his sick daughter.

"Jerry! I've got this!" he said, not letting go of Jerry's arm, forcing Jerry to turn to him, to look him in the eye and listen to what he was saying. "I've got this!" Jerry, relenting in confusion, stepped back and tried not to hear Amanda's screams of *Daddy, Daddy* over and over again as they took her down the hall to the treatment center. He sank into the closest chair and tried to ignore the sympathetic looks and murmurs coming from the staff and strangers in the waiting room.

~

Christy turned to James, the cute eleventh grader who was nice enough to drive her home. "Thanks for the ride," she smiled, and was again so very grateful that she'd finally gotten rid of those horrible braces. No one had braces in eleventh grade! He returned her smile with teeth that weren't quite as straight as her own, but with an adorable face — those amazing dimples were like double quotation marks setting off the sides of his mouth, and his eyes were the bluest blue she'd ever seen.

"Hey, no problem. I just live, you know, right up the road." He hesitated a moment, leaned a bit toward her. "Hey, you know, we should, um, hang out sometime."

Christy's smile grew wider. "Sure, that would be, um..." She almost said, "awesome," but that was definitely too strong of a word, so she said, "cool," which felt stale and juvenile, causing her distress and the desire to leave the car.

But before she could make her getaway, he touched her arm and said, "Give me your cell number. I'll call you." She gave it to him and watched as he saved it into his phone. She got out of the car, wanting to bound up the walkway with pure joy, but she made herself walk, trying to look cool—no, *awesome*—as she was sure he was watching her.

When she stepped into the garage and headed for the door, her cell beeped. He was texting her already! But when she looked at her phone, she saw it was from Katy and she hit READ as she opened the door to the mudroom. IS IT TRUE BOUT UR SIS? There were so many things that were true about her sister.... WHAT TRUE? Christy texted back. She was in the kitchen now. SHE WAS DRAGGED OFF BY COPS. Christy shook her head in confusion. What the hell was she talking about? Christy looked around the room. "Mom?" she called. She dropped her books on the table and deserted her phone on the kitchen counter. She noticed the cup of tea on the counter and walked through the living room, which was a mess. "Mom?" There were sounds of grief coming from the den. Christy went that way and saw all of the destruction before locating her mother in the middle of the chaos, a broken lamp in her lap, crying like no one should ever see her mother cry, and it was more than she could take in, more than her mind could process, and she was tempted to turn and walk away. Instead, she took a step into the room and heard the word *Mom* leave her mouth. Her mother turned toward the word, and when Christy saw her battered face, *then* it truly became too much to bear. "I'm sorry," Christy said as she took a step back and away from the unbearable grief, and made her way to the safety of her room.

~

Ryan was pulling into the UPS parking lot when he got a text. What did Mandy want now? She'd been texting and calling him all day. He'd wanted to see her, really he had, but he had all this crap to do—trying to get things together so he could sign up for classes, trying to figure out if he could afford a better place, considering sharing a place with some friends.... He parked the car and dug out his cell phone.

It wasn't from Mandy after all, but one of his friends. HEARD YOUR GIRL GOT ARRESTED. Ryan hit the buttons quickly.

WTF? he sent. IT'S ALL I KNOW WHAT I HEARD came back. He answered: F! and tried Mandy's cell—no answer. He didn't know Christy's cell number. WHO TOLD U he sent to his friend. BRIAN. Brian picked up on the third ring. "What the fuck did you hear?" Ryan asked.

"Not heard. Saw," said Brian, who sounded like he was stoned out of his fucking mind.

"Saw what, then?" asked Ryan, with impatience. He glanced at the car clock. He was going to be late. He shut off the car and started walking toward the building.

"I was driving by, you know ... saw the fucking pigs dragging her out of the house."

"Fuck! Are you sure? You sound fucking messed up!"

"Hey! I'm not that fucked up, man!"

"Okay ... thanks, man." And he clicked his phone shut. He stepped into the building, thought about turning around, blowing off work, but what would that do? He was just catching up on his bills; he simply couldn't risk losing this job. And it wasn't like the cops were going to give him Mandy even if he figured out where they'd taken her. He'd try to call her parents ... look up their number. They must have a telephone book somewhere in this fucking place.

~

"Mom, everybody knows," said Christy as she picked up a broken picture frame off the floor, the broken glass tumbling out.

"Be careful," warned her mother. "We just can't worry about what other people think," she said, but this was not how she was feeling. Two police cars had responded to the call, lights flashing, sirens screaming—the most excitement that Niskayuna had seen since Rachel Tegal set her car on fire. The crowd that had gathered was really rather small, but things had a way of getting around. She was sure that *everybody* didn't know, but still ... and what was it that they thought they knew? It was most likely not the fact that her daughter was very ill and had to be forcibly taken to the hospital, but something of a more criminal nature. Which was better: mental illness or crime? The phone rang and she grabbed it. *Please let it be Jerry!* "Hello?"

"How are you doing?" he said. The sound of her husband's voice brought back the unbearable tears and she couldn't speak; he seemed to understand this and just continued in his calm, soothing voice, "Listen, they're going to admit her … at least overnight. Just as soon as she gets settled in, I'll be home." He tried another question, "Christy okay?"

"Yes," Carol managed to get out. She wanted him home. She needed him more than her hateful daughter.

"An hour … okay?"

Carol nodded and hung up the phone. She blew her nose in the already-quite-soggy tissues she was clutching. "I'm going to go take a shower," she told Christy, getting up and heading for the stairs. When the phone rang again, Carol did not turn around to answer, but continued on her upward path. After four rings, it switched over to the machine. Christy looked up from the piece of glass she was carefully dropping into a paper bag and heard the sound of Ryan's voice.

"Um, hi … this is Ryan …." Christy took a step toward the phone. "Is Mandy okay? Could you maybe call me? I'm at work. But call my cell. The number is—"

Christy lifted up the receiver. "Ryan! Oh, God! Everything's so fucked up!"

~

As Jerry drove home, he had the sudden need to talk to his brother. He hit the voice command button and asked the car to call Tom. The car obediently complied. "Jerry," his brother's voice filled the car. "I was just going to call you. We need to go bike shopping this weekend. It's the perfect exercise for our old joints. How's Saturday, before the game? Now's the time to buy. Everything's on sale. So Saturday, okay?" And Jerry felt himself smile, his first real smile for days, which was immediately replaced by the threat of tears.

"Tom," he said. "Amanda's in the hospital."

"What?" There was a momentary pause. "Oh, Jesus, what happened?"

"Manic rage. Attacked Carol. Trashed the house. Police had to bring her in."

"Jesus! Where are you? Hospital?"

"Just left. I'm almost home."

"Okay. I'll be over. Give me fifteen minutes."

"Tom, I haven't even seen Carol yet. I'm not sure what I'm going home to."

"Okay. A half hour then."

Before Jerry could respond, Tom had hung up and the car radio came back on. "Rain Drops Keep Falling on My Head" was playing. *What a ridiculously old and stupid song*, he thought and switched it off. He knew he should call Tom back, insist that he not come over, that Carol would prefer that they be alone tonight, but the truth was he wanted Tom there—he needed him there. He was tired of having to be strong, to be the person in the position of authority; tired of being everything for everyone.

He found Christy eating cereal in front of the kitchen TV. He hugged her as she asked how Amanda was. "She's better. Sleeping by now, I'm sure. Where's your Mom?"

"Upstairs."

He nodded. "I'll be back. Save some cereal for me, will you?" He made his way to the stairway, noting the minor trail of destruction through the living room. He stopped when he got to the den, and sighed. He could tell there had been some effort to order the devastation, but it was something that would take more energy than any of them had. He was hopeful that if they kept working, a little bit at a time, sooner or later some order might be possible, along with some acceptance of what had been lost.

He found Carol in Amanda's room, sweeping up some broken glass off the floor. She looked up at him, momentarily. "Let me just finish this," she mumbled through renewed tears, looking away and back to the glass.

"Leave it," he said softly.

"Someone has to do it!" she sobbed.

"Later." He studied her face and gently touched her swollen lip. Just a small cut. She gasped a sob of self-pity as if she'd been hit all over again. He gathered her in his arms and she cried until his shirt was a soggy mess, until his knees ached from standing. He told her it was going to be okay, even though he didn't necessarily believe it, and when her external sorrow was spent, he whispered, "Come eat some dinner with me."

"I didn't make anything."

"Cocoa Puffs. I'm sure we have some."

She laughed, knowing he knew that it had been her favorite dinner—even when boxed macaroni and cheese seemed too complicated, Cocoa Puffs were a godsend. And that's how Tom found the three of them: sitting around the kitchen bar, eating Cocoa Puffs. He grabbed a bowl and pulled up a stool and helped himself. They ate in relative silence for a few minutes. Tom looked casually about the living room at the debris scattered about and, as he crunched the sweet little balls between his teeth, he said, "You two ought to consider getting a maid or something."

They laughed sadly. "You haven't seen the den yet. We need a small bulldozer," Jerry told him with a pained smile.

"Well, they didn't call me Bulldozer in college for nothing. Let's go clean up the crap," he said, scraping the last few puffs onto his spoon.

"No one called you Bulldozer in college," said Jerry with a smile.

Tom looked up from his bowl, surprised. "Really? Are you sure?"

"Quite sure," laughed Jerry. Even Carol laughed.

"Bulldozer!" Christy giggled.

As they stood up and headed toward the den, Tom still had a look of confused contemplation on his face. "It was Jennifer White!" he said with certainty. "She called me Bulldozer."

"Well, I wouldn't know about that," said Jerry.

"No wait…maybe it was just The Bull…or no…The Stallion…Yes! That was it! The Stallion."

"Oh brother," said Carol. Christy laughed with wicked glee.

They stopped at the entranceway to the den and surveyed the damage. Sharp edges of glass hung from splintered frames of photographs. Paintings littered the floor; one curtain was torn and hanging limply from its rod. Dirt, broken pottery, and mangled leaves of potted plants were scattered across the oriental rug. One of Carol's prized orchids, its yellow showy flowers, had been smashed into the rug. Books were tossed from the bookshelf, entire shelves freed of their contents. Broken knickknacks mingled with the torn pages of books. There were dented lamp shades and broken bases, one already uprighted and sitting sadly on a side table, others still prone and crushed on the floor. A figurine of a girl was broken, her face looking upward from the hardwood floor. Two paper bags with shreds of glass barely visible sat next to a deserted and overwhelmed broom. "Nothing a good frat party couldn't produce," Tom muttered as he reached for one of the paper bags and walked across the rug, picking up the larger pieces of glass. The sound of gentle crashing as he dropped each piece filled the room.

After awhile, Christy left them to go do her homework, and they stopped a moment. "We're making progress," said Tom encouragingly. Carol sat down on the couch in exhaustion and watched the two men. They were almost at the point where a vacuum would be helpful. "So when are they springing her?" Tom asked. It was really the first direct reference to Amanda any of them had broached.

"Tomorrow, most likely," said Jerry as he attempted to reshape a lampshade.

Carol sat up in surprise. "Tomorrow?! No! Jerry, you can't!" She began to cry. "I can't see her! I hate her, Jerry! I hate her!" And she hid her face in her hands.

Jerry looked at her with despair and then rubbed his face with his hands. "She's perfectly calm now; she really doesn't belong there. Where else is she going to go?" he asked quietly.

"To my house," said Tom. "She'll stay with us. Just until this all gets..." he looked about the room, "a little less raw."

They looked at him. "We can't ask you to do that," said Jerry.

"Bullshit." Tom gave Jerry a hard look. "Don't piss me off."

"What about Sarah? How will she feel?" asked Carol.

Tom smiled. "It'll be fine. The daughter she's always wanted."

12

Carol closed the door to her office on Friday morning and sighed with relief. Was it just her imagination or was everyone she saw looking at her funny? Did they all know? What were they saying about her? About Jerry? The old cliché—all psychiatrists' kids are screwed up? The worse case of acne she'd ever seen was Andy Jenson's son—Andy Jenson was a dermatologist. Maybe they were all looking at her face, her slightly swollen lip. Could they sense her raw pain? If not, why not? It was all so consuming. Could they not taste it in the air? They should be in here, asking what she needed, offering help, maybe even offering to bring over a casserole. But no one said a thing! She hated them, hated them all. She felt pathetically alone.

Jerry had left early that morning, wanting to see Amanda before he went to his office. He'd called Carol an hour later and told her that Amanda had a good night and she would stay at the hospital the rest of the day. Later on, he'd take her to Tom and Sarah's. He'd probably stay there for a while and make sure Amanda was settled. He told her not to expect him for dinner; in other words, she would be alone this evening.

Carol struggled through the morning, proud of herself for getting through the hours without tears. By afternoon, her façade was strong and stoic—nothing could break her now. She'd been to hell and back. She was amazing. She could get through anything. She walked confidently to her car at five, smiling at the people she knew. They smiled back. They liked her. She liked them. She had to stop at the store, since they were practically out of just about everything. She decided to go to the Price Chopper off Union Street, rather than her usual store.

The first few aisles were fine, even pleasant. She didn't see anyone she knew, and nice music was playing throughout the store. She was sipping the decaf latte she'd purchased from the coffee shop and was munching on a cranberry scone. She didn't know this store as well as the one closer to her house, but she was finding everything okay. She turned down the cereal aisle and realized they'd eaten all the Cocoa Puffs. She made one quick pass down the row and didn't see it. She backtracked and made a slower, more careful search. Where was it? How could there not be Cocoa Puffs? She looked around. There was no one to help her. She searched the shelves again and felt her façade begin to crumble, to cave in, to collapse … oh, dear God … where are the Cocoa Puffs?!

She managed, somehow, to make it through the checkout and to her car. She sat there a moment, breathing hard and trying to prepare to drive. She caught a glimpse of her reflection in the rearview mirror and was slapped with pathetic self-pity. She wept, hiding her face from people rude enough to stray near her car. And she wept without pause.

~

Ryan tried Mandy's cell again at five as he drove toward her house. It still went right to voicemail. Christy said she was getting out today. He hadn't talked to Mandy. Were there no phones there? Was she not even allowed to make a phone call? Even fucking prison has phones! He'd tried the hospital, but couldn't get anywhere there. He finally got through to the psych ward, but was told, by some bitch, that he needed a patient ID number. She refused to tell him if Mandy was even there. There was no way he was going to be allowed to talk to Mandy without that fucking magic number—as if Mandy were only a number, her name holding no meaning. He'd left a message on Carol's cell—no response. Her dad hadn't called him back when he left a message at his office. Why hadn't Mandy called him? Maybe she was so out of it that he hadn't crossed her mind. Was he not significant enough to stay with her? Was he just a fleeting obsession on the road to insanity? How could she have totally consumed his life? He was beginning to feel like he'd been pushed out of a car, left standing on the side of the road, brushing off dirt, watching the car speed away.

Maybe if he'd seen her, made the effort to go over there, then this all wouldn't have happened. Did they blame him? He pulled up to the curb and stared at the house. It stood solid, a fortress where one could close ranks, withdraw to lick one's wounds, and keep out the outside world. Was he the outside world, forcing his way into a place that he doubted ever wanting to go? He turned off the car and made his way, wondering if this would ever be an easy trip—the short walk into Mandy's world.

Christy answered the door and opened it up to him without hesitation. "She's not here. Not coming home…not to here," she explained as they made their way into the kitchen. "Dad's taking her to Uncle Tom's."

Ryan tried to digest this piece of news. What did that mean for him? Tom Benson…now he was a little scary. "Have you talked to her?" he finally asked.

Christy shook her head. "No one has other than my dad."

"I need to see her," he blurted out, almost pathetically, and he saw Christy's eyes mist over. He was unsure what to say or what to do.

Christy had to look away from Ryan. Why? Why does he love her? Would anyone ever love her that way, love her so much that it didn't even matter if she was fucking crazy?!

~

Where the fuck was her dad?! She needed to get the hell out of this place! She paced back and forth in the patient lounge; she'd been doing it so long that there was a fucking path in the carpet, like the neighbor's dog had made along its fence—she was a dog, a dog mad as hell at being confined. "Amanda." She turned to the sound and it was her father. She sucked in her anger, stopped her movement, and then tears of relief sprang from her eyes. She was going home!

He came to her and indicated a chair. "Sit," he said gently.

Fear pulsated through her. Sit?! Why sit? They needed to move, to get the fuck out of here! An animal! She was not a fucking animal! But he was her master, the master of his domain; it was either sit or stay, so she sat.

"Dr. McIntyre said I could go home. Said I could leave." She tried to say the words calmly, clearly, like she was not a crazy lunatic. Her father sat across from her, pulled his chair closer—he always wanted to get so close! He nodded his head, but there was something bad, something hiding behind his nod.

"Yes. You are leaving here but not going home."

Oh my God! She was going to jail! Her fucking mother was sending her to jail! When she was the one that had been wronged; when she was the one whose property had been violated, broken. Of course she'd gotten mad! She'd had every right to get mad. Her adorable little pipe—gone, dead.

"You're going to be staying at your Uncle Tom's for a while."

What? "What?" she said aloud.

Her father was looking her in the eye. His mouth was moving, words were coming out, and she was trying to hold onto them long enough to process, but couldn't. "Your behavior…" *…click, click, click of heels down the hall…* "… intolerable…" *musical notes getting louder—why was there music, anyway?* "… your mother…" *click, click… cell phone—where was her cell phone?… she needed to get her numbers… call Ryan to come save her…* "…will not be tolerated…" *…screaming from somewhere…* "… under any circumstances…" *…some poor fucker, locked up in here.* "Amanda. Do you understand?"

"What? What? What?!"

~

Sarah snapped the clean sheets into the air and they floated gently down upon the bed. She'd chosen a soft purple set of sheets, the closest she had to something girlish. They'd decided on Matt's old room. It was larger and closer to their own than Casey's. The walls still sported posters of football and soccer players. David Beckham gave her an almost cocky smile, his soccer ball tucked beneath his arm, as she tucked in the sheets. Soccer trophies cluttered the shelves along with books, old concert tickets, a stack of Mad Magazines, an old picture of an old girlfriend, even a soccer ball, flat and deflated. Truly, a boy's room. Was that an old dusty condom wrapper behind the bed? Brother! How had she missed that? It must have fallen from the old bedding. She bent down to pick it up. And now Amanda would be here … for how long?

When Tom had come home last night and told her — well … they had argued, of course. Yes, she'd been a bitch, but he should have asked her first before committing to disrupting her relatively calm life. In the end, she'd relented. She'd known Amanda all her life, seen her when she was only moments old, held her sweet little body against her chest, loved her — yes, she had loved her — still did. And now the poor girl was screwed up — even her own mother temporarily lost to her.

Sarah finished with the bed and placed a small but pretty vase of flowers on the bedside table. She plugged in Amanda's cell phone and laptop that Jerry had brought over in the morning. She removed the few clothes that he'd included in the small suitcase and neatly placed them in one of the dresser drawers. She removed the toiletries, including several prescriptions (one of them birth control pills) before pushing the suitcase under the bed. Next she'd have to clean the bathroom. Unfortunately, Amanda would have to share a bathroom with David, and David was a pig.

~

Alby met them at the kitchen door and meowed a greeting, her tail swishing slightly at the possibility of slipping past these people and venturing outside; but Amanda, who knew the cat was never to be let out, scooped her up and held her like a baby, gently rubbing her tummy. The soft warmth of her fur was soothing against her fingers; it helped to stay the anxiety that was creeping like a monster, growing—The Incredible Hulk of Anxiety taking up residence. This house, as familiar as her own, had a new and foreign undercurrent that was curling around with the anxiety.

Sensing all of this, Jerry regretted just walking in as he always had. Should he ring the bell? "Let me go find Sarah..." he said to Amanda, "find out which room you're sleeping in." As he disappeared from the room, Amanda sat down at the kitchen table, still holding the ever-willing cat in her arms. She tilted her head down so that her hair fell around Alby—a game the cat always loved. Her paw came up scooping a lock of Amanda's hair into her mouth, chomping with feline pleasure.

"Hey, cuz." Amanda's head came up and she managed a smile at David's approach—felt better almost immediately from his presence. He sat down next to her, reached into her lap, and tickled Alby's belly. The cat trapped his hand and bit him like a kiss. "She's always loved you," he said, and Amanda was knocked down by gratitude, knocked down by the fact that something loved her.

Her dad and aunt came into the room. "Hi, honey," said Sarah. "You're going to be in Matt's room. Okay?"

Amanda gently placed Alby on the floor and stood up. "I'm going to put my stuff, you know, in the room." She escaped up the stairs with her little bag of crap from the hospital and into Matt's old room. She found her cell phone immediately and pounced on it like a ravenous cat on a mouse. It seemed to take forever for it to power up. She would force herself to learn these numbers, to write them down, because she was lost without this little metal contraption.

He answered on the first ring. "Mandy! Well it's about fucking time!" his words full of concern, full of love.

Amanda texted David asking him if he would let his mom know that Ryan was on his way over. David informed his mother, who looked over her cup of tea at Jerry, who looked back with a shrug.

"It's your house," he said, tapping the lip of his cup with his spoon to remove the extra liquid before setting it in the saucer.

"She's your daughter."

Jerry sighed. Yes, she was…. "It would be best for Amanda to keep things as normal as possible. Let her do what she wants as long as she's safe and not disruptive. I've made it clear to her, and I will tell her again, that any violent behavior will not be tolerated. I will place her in supervised housing if I need to. Do not put up with any abuse, verbal or otherwise."

Sarah nodded her head and turned to David. "Tell her to invite him for dinner. I've made macaroni and cheese." She looked at Jerry for approval, and he smiled with gratitude.

Ryan checked the number of the house again. Yes, he was in the right place, so he put the car in park and shut off the engine. The house was nice. Not nearly as large as Mandy's, but also not as daunting. It was more like the house he'd grown up in before his father died and he and his mother had been forced to move. He saw Tom pulling into the driveway just as he was exiting his own car. He paused and waited for the man to extract his intimidating frame from the Prius. Tom furrowed his brow at him as he looked over the roof of the Prius, but Ryan was brave for his size—and determined—so he walked confidently up the driveway and extended his hand. "It's good to see you again, sir," he said. Tom had no choice other than to grasp Ryan's hand and feel his bravery and determination in the handshake.

Tom's face softened as he said, "I guess we'll be seeing a good bit of one other, then?"

"Yes, sir."

"Have you seen her?"

"No, sir."

Tom looked toward the house. "I haven't either."

"She sounded good on the phone," offered Ryan as they made their way to the house.

They reached the side door to the kitchen and Tom reached for the doorknob. "Well, the whole thing sucks," said Tom.

"Yes, sir. It sucks." Tom held the door open for Ryan, and he entered the house directly into the kitchen, which was warm and inviting. Good smells were cascading through the air. Jerry looked up from his spot at the kitchen table and smiled at Ryan and the head of his brother that towered behind him.

"I found this scary little punk lurking around in the bushes," said Tom as he entered the kitchen. "It was either call the police or invite him in. I figured there'd been enough police excitement in Niskayuna for the week. So …."

Ryan laughed politely.

"Leave him alone," said Sarah to Tom. "Come in, Ryan. If you haven't already figured it out, my husband's a jerk."

Tom stepped up to her side of the kitchen table and bent down, giving her a peck on the lips. "Love you too, dear," he said.

Ryan looked around the room and shifted on his feet. "She's upstairs in Matt's old room," Jerry said.

"Come on," Tom told him. "I'll take you up; I've got to get out of these nasty accountant's clothes."

Mandy wrapped her arms around Ryan as he entered the room. He closed his eyes and let his body melt into hers, absorbing some of her anger and pain. "You need to get me the fuck out of here," she breathed in his ear.

"Can't. Won't," he whispered back.

She pulled away from him and stared at him in disbelief. He slightly shook his head at her and watched her eyes go dark. "What the fuck?" she said.

He shrugged. "Not tonight. So tell me. Tell me what happened."

She drew him near again, and nuzzled his neck. Her words were seductive as she said, "After we get out of here."

He shook his head again. "Not happening."

She shoved herself away from him, pushing her hands hard against his chest. "Fuck you!" she spat. He set his mouth, and gave her his best fuck-you-back glare. "Get out!" she screamed. He dipped his head in acquiescence and was out the door, heading for the stairs before she took her next breath. But he never hit the first step—she was there, grabbing at his arm and pleading with him not to go. "I'm sorry!" she cried. "Please don't go! Don't leave!"

"I don't need this shit," he told her quietly, but he let himself be dragged back into the bedroom. She was crying now and frantic. When she had him safely back with her, she told him her version of what had happened and anything he wanted to know.

Jerry and Sarah heard Amanda's side of the exchange in the kitchen. They listened and waited as things grew quiet. Tom heard, and saw most of it, and waited in his bedroom until Ryan had disappeared back into Matt's room before he ventured downstairs. David was in the den with his iPod blasting in his ears—he couldn't hear a thing.

A short while later they all sat down to a meal of hamburgers, macaroni and cheese, french fries, and salad. Tom and David did their best to keep the table entertained, but the crowd was tough. Amanda sat quietly, pushing her food around her plate. Ryan and Sarah had little to add to the conversation. Jerry tried to let go of his anxiety by trying to convince himself that, all things considered, this was the best scenario; she would be fine here. He could leave here in a couple hours and go back to his house, his wife, and his other daughter. Amanda would be just fine... she would be just fine.

~

Carol had retreated to her bed. She'd not bothered to eat the dinner she'd brought home. She'd stopped by the movie rental place and picked out a DVD she knew Christy wanted to see. She entertained the fantasy of popcorn and licking the greasy fried chicken off her fingers. She pictured a nice evening, hanging with her daughter in PJs, snuggling under a blanket with the popcorn kernels dropping between them, working their way down and into the cracks of the couch. She saw them laughing at all the funny parts in the movie, and crying at anything sad.

When Carol got home, however, Christy informed her that she was going over to Katy's for dinner and then to a movie, and could she please just spend the night? "But I got a movie," Carol said, and she regretted her pathetic words as soon as they left her mouth. They certainly didn't change Christy's resolve to leave. What fifteen-year-old girl would want to spend Friday night with her weak, pitiable mother?

After Christy was gone, Carol had tried to call her mother—she hadn't even told her mother about Amanda yet. The answering machine picked up. In desperation, she called her brother. They chatted amiably for a few minutes. He was five years older and they'd never been terribly close. She hadn't talked to him in months. Another fantasy played in her mind as she waited for him to ask about her family: the fantasy that he would understand. She imagined him having wise and comforting things to say, and that by the end of their conversation she would feel closer to him than she ever had. This would confirm for her that blood and love were mysteriously mixed in a way that could never be understood or truly separated.

The question finally came and she told him things weren't good. Choosing her words carefully, she said, "Amanda's not doing well." A long, pregnant pause enveloped the conversation as she gathered the strength to say, "She's been diagnosed with bipolar disorder." There—the words were out. She became confused when he said something about living with a bipolar, how he knew all about it. Was he telling her that Maryanne, her sister-in-law, was bipolar? "What do you mean?" she was forced to ask.

"Aren't all women bipolar?" he asked flippantly.

Oh…it was a joke. Ha, ha. And that was the end of that little fantasy.

And so she retreated to her bed, even though it was only seven, to truly wallow in her misery. She longed to talk to someone, anyone who understood. She really needed Jerry, but he was with his original family now. She'd been deserted. Carol imagined him sitting happily around the table eating one of Sarah's sub-par dinners (there was not a doubt in her mind that she was the superior chef). Yes, Sarah had him back now. *And* her daughter. Well…she could have Amanda, but she wanted Jerry back! As soon as she entertained these ludicrous musings, she was assailed by a deeper, sadder longing.

She longed to talk to Amanda, to hear her voice, to hear the words, "I'm sorry, Mom. Let me come home." She felt an overwhelming surge of love for her daughter. Of course her daughter was sorry. How could she not be? And Carol would forgive her, because she loved her; and Amanda was worthy of that love—a beautiful, sweet girl who was just sick right now, who was surely racked with guilt for what she had done. Oh, how she missed her daughter! How could she have refused to let her come home? How could she have professed her utter hatred of her own daughter? What Tom must think of her. And Sarah… Jerry too…. No wonder they were all together and she was alone. It was no wonder that Amanda was so screwed up.

Damn if another fantasy didn't roll through her mind—Amanda walking in the door, her hair a chocolate brown again (she'd dyed it back just to make her mother happy). Her beautiful face slightly frightened and contrite, desperate for her mother's forgiveness. Carol rigid at first (not cold, just not a pushover), but Amanda's remorse so pure that within moments they fall into each other's arms and cry. Yes, they cry. Lots of good cleansing tears.

13

"I'm sorry, Tom. We're not going to the game."

"What are you talking about? Of course you are."

"Really, Tom. Carol and I are just not up to it." It was early Saturday morning. Tom was calling about bike shopping before the game. Jerry heard him sigh heavily into the phone. Jerry was on the kitchen phone, the coffee pot he'd been about to fill with water, still in his hand. Carol was upstairs sleeping, thankfully. He'd made it home before nine, but it had been a long night of talking in circles of misery.

"So you're just going to sit around the house and feel sorry for yourselves?" he said with his standard sarcasm, of course, but it was mixed with the kind of reproach that Jerry just didn't need.

"Yes. Apparently so." Jerry did not hide his irritation — part of which was with himself and those three words that had just betrayed his wife. He put down the coffee pot and sat on the nearest kitchen stool. There was another deep sigh from Tom, and Jerry could picture his face through the phone. He was probably rubbing it with frustration. That was when Jerry realized his own fingers were pressing deeply against his forehead, the loose skin sliding against his skull.

"Well, you can at least shop for a bike," Tom finally said.

It was Jerry's turn to sigh. "Maybe."

"Great! You come get me with the Volvo. We'll never get two bikes in the Prius."

"Tom, I don't know if I'm ready to buy a bike—"

"The shop opens at ten. Get here at nine thirty-five. That should get us there right at ten."

Jerry laughed. "You're a royal pain in the ass!"

"Nine thirty-five," Tom said, and he hung up.

~

Tom waited for him in the front of his house. When Jerry continued to gaze at the house even after Tom had jumped in and buckled his seat belt, Tom turned to him and said, "She had a good night. Still sleeping. Ryan left about eleven-thirty. Everything seemed okay between them."

Jerry nodded his head and sighed as he put the car in gear. He wanted to say something, to talk about Amanda, but really, what was there to say? Tom, sensing this, added, "Ryan asked me, before he left, if he could take Amanda out tonight. It cracked me up that he would ask. I think he's scared shitless of me."

"Good," Jerry laughed. "I think he's a good kid, though. I think he's good for Amanda ... especially now." He turned to Tom. "Don't you think he's a good kid?"

"I think he's a great kid. He seems to be crazy about Amanda ... but I guess I just don't get—" he stopped, realizing that he was straying into dangerous territory.

"Why he puts up with her behavior?" Jerry said, finishing the sentence he imagined had formed in Tom's mind.

"Don't get me wrong! Amanda's beautiful, fun, smart ... if I were a young man and she wasn't, of course, my niece ... but still ...."

"Sex isn't everything?" said Jerry, finishing yet another utterance for Tom.

"Jesus, I should just shut up," said Tom.

Jerry laughed. "Tom, you're not saying anything that I haven't thought over and over. Who knows what keeps people together. And whatever it is that keeps Ryan coming back for more, I think it's a good thing. It's all she's got right now. The only thing that's good. You know, not one of her other friends has called that I know of, or come over … even though she hasn't been in school."

"That's rough."

"Yes, it is."

They pulled in front of the bike shop at ten-o-four. Tom checked his watch and smiled. "Not bad, considering you drive like an old woman."

Jerry rolled his eyes. "You're borderline pathological, you know that," he said as he shut off the car.

A tiny bell jingled as they entered the shop. A slight young man, way in the back of the store, looked up from his paperwork and acknowledged them with a can-I-help-you smile. "We're just going to look around for a couple minutes," called Tom. "It's better if he doesn't know we're eager to buy," he whispered to Jerry. "We'll get a much better deal if he doesn't think we're desperate."

Jerry looked at the seemingly endless rows of bikes, the racks of biking attire—helmets, gloves, clips, water bottles, electronic gadgets. "I don't know that I'm ready to buy, and I'm certainly not desperate." He picked up the price tag on the closest bike and flipped it over. Twenty-five hundred dollars?! He raised his eyebrows at Tom. Tom, who was always anally economical, uncharacteristically waved away Jerry's concern.

"We don't need top-of-the-line," he said, making his way through the rows, flipping over price tags, and pressing on the seats of the bikes as if he knew what he was looking for. Jerry followed along. It was becoming quickly apparent that twenty-five hundred dollars was not top-of-the-line. After a few minutes, Tom turned to Jerry and said, "Do you know what the hell we're looking for?"

"Not a clue."

"How much do we want to spend?"

"Nothing."

Tom shook his head at Jerry with frustration. He made his way to the back of the store. "Okay, I think maybe we need a little help here," he told the young man.

"Absolutely," he said, with laidback biker enthusiasm. He stood up and came around from behind the counter. As he made his way through the plethora of biking paraphernalia and toward the bikes, he asked, "What kind of biking do you do?" When Tom looked at him blankly, he added, "Road, off-road, touring, racing, mountain?"

Tom smiled. "Yes! That's right."

The young man smiled back. "Hybrid, then."

It took about an hour to sort through the options. And once the bikes were finally decided upon, there was the endless biking equipment that, really, if you were going to be the least bit serious, you were forced to own. Nobody biked in cut-offs; you had to wear a helmet, a special kind of shoe, clips, gloves, warming boots, short sleeve shirts, long sleeve shirts, ridiculously expensive jackets (which really looked like any other cool outdoor jacket ... well maybe the back was a *little* longer).

Tom held a biking shirt in front of his chest for Jerry's approval. It was the end of the season, so the selection in his size was limited. This particular one was bright orange with blue, pink, and green swirls. "Do I look like the Hindenburg on acid?" he asked.

"People will absolutely see you coming," said Jerry as he sifted through the shirts.

Tom checked his watch. "Jesus! We have to get going. Are you sure you won't go to the game? Skip the tailgate. Just come for the game."

Jerry looked at his brother and sighed. "She's just not up for it, Tom."

"Come without her," he offered meekly.

Jerry shook his head. "I just can't."

"Yeah ... I know. Sorry." He tucked the shirt under his arm. "I guess I'll get this one ... what the hell."

They stood at the counter watching with slight horror as their bills were tallied. "You know, Tom. Jogging was a hell of a lot cheaper," Jerry mumbled as he handed over his credit card.

"Not in the long run, brother dear," said Tom, who was as excited as a kid at Christmas. "Joint replacement ain't free." But when Tom found out the bikes had to be assembled and would not be ready until next week... well, Jerry thought his brother might just cry.

~

Carol made a magnificent dinner. Christy was out again with her friends so it was just the two of them. She'd purchased some beautiful fillets, kissed them with flame, and dressed them with a delicate horseradish sauce. New red potatoes gently smashed with garlic sat prettily next to the steak, and tiny, tender green beans fresh from the garden finished off the plate. There was salad and a wonderful loaf of bread from the local bakery; and the Pinot Noir was one of Jerry's favorites. The candles that gently lit the room should have cinched the evening, but it was too much, too forced, not unlike their first dinner with Ryan; it was somehow just not as good or real as the food at the game. "This is delicious," he told her, smiling gently and sipping from his wine glass.

She smiled back, "Thank you. I got the meat at that new little gourmet shop on Tulip Street—a real butcher shop, complete with a gruff little Italian guy, bloody apron, scary dark stuff under his fingernails." Carol felt a sliver of pleasure when Jerry laughed, and she tried to think of something else clever and funny to say, wanting, more than anything, to hear him laugh again. Her mind drew a blank and she brushed her fingers through her curls, hoping, at least, that she looked good.

"And these beans... they're from the garden?" he asked.

"Yes...."

"Wow."

She watched him as he chewed and hungered for him to tell her how much he loved her, that she was all he'd ever wanted... would ever want.... She tried to impede the despair that was filling up the room, but it had a force of its own, and she had to bring her hands to her face so that she couldn't see—couldn't let him see—how fully it consumed her.

~

It felt good to lie in Mandy's arm's, her sweet body damp and cooling next to his skin, her hair sweeping across his chest, her fingers curling into his arm. Even his little apartment looked good in the dim light of the candle that lit the room. She seemed better today — calmer, less irritable, but still not the bouncy bundle-of-fun that he had loved and hated at the same time. Then again, maybe she was something better … something that wasn't so fluid … something you could hold onto. He turned to her, her body falling away as he shifted. "I have something for you," he told her, and watched with pleasure as her eyes sparkled with excitement.

"What?!" She sat up with a tiny bounce. "What?"

He got up from the bed and stepped across the room. He opened up one of the drawers in the dresser and removed a small box, to which he had carefully applied a tiny pink ribbon. As he crossed the room back to her, she held her hands out to him with the anticipation of a child. He handed it to her, feeling his own boyish pleasure as he watched her discard the little ribbon with exaggerated flair, open the box, and toss the lid across the bed.

"OH MY GOD!" She looked at him. "Oh my God," she whispered as her eyes returned to the box. She gently removed the small and perfect little pipe. She ran her finger carefully along the spine of the little lizard, resting the tip of her finger on its petite, pretty head. She placed it gently back in the box and stood up from the bed, falling into Ryan's arms. "I love it. I love it." She kissed his neck. "I love *you*."

"And I love *you*."

~

Christy tipped the bottle up and felt the liquid sting her tongue. It ripped at her throat, and though she fought it with all she had, she could not stop the gasp and the other obnoxious sound that exploded from her lips. James laughed. She wiped at the tears that sprang from her eyes. "Fuck you!" she laughed back. She swore she already felt the hot warmth of intoxication from the whiskey, mixing with the high from the weed they'd smoked. It felt good and dangerous — who needed control when the whole world was out of control? She took another swig. This one went down with relative ease, and she handed the bottle to James. She sat back against the tree and wrapped her jacket tighter around her. It was cold in the park, but they did not dare start a fire.

"We could go back to my car," he offered. She smiled at him. Finally. She was finally going to be kissed. She was sure that he liked her—she liked him too. There was a connection—deep and almost spiritual. He got her, understood her; wanted to know everything about her; hung on her every word. That deep pain, the loneliness that consumed her—he felt it as if it were his own; wanted to take it away, to fill it with himself. She could have the love she yearned for, the love she needed to stop the pain.

Oh my God, she was soaring with the pure joy of love! He could take her away. Take her away from her fucked-up family, her bitch of a sister, and fill it all with endless love. He handed the bottle back her way. "So, what do you think?" he asked. "Are you cold? Back to the car?"

She took the bottle from him and brought it to her lips, her eyes never leaving his as she tilted her head back. She wiped at her mouth with the back of her hand when she was done and shook her head slightly. "It's nice out here." So he shifted closer, put his arm around her. He would keep her warm. They studied the night air as they shared the bottle. The bare tree branches swayed above them, creaking a bit in their movement. The sky was clear, a half moon rising, filtering through the trees, causing little splotches of hazy light on the ground. She leaned in toward him.

The alcohol was pulsating through her now; the gentle buzz quickly turning into a sloppy unpleasant wave of dizziness; the tacos they'd picked up at Taco Bell, unhappy now in her stomach. But he set the bottle down and was leaning toward her, gently lifting her face with his soft, warm hand, and she looked at him. His eyes were open. As he came closer, she saw his lips part slightly—his lips, wet and fuzzy as they grew closer—a soft (was it slimy?) tongue peeking out from those wet, wet lips. And then those lips were pressed against hers. That tongue (yes, it was slimy) was pushing into her mouth, and she could actually taste the onions of his taco and the cheap whisky as she felt the upheaval of disgust. She shoved him away just in time but couldn't get quite far enough away before what was left of her dinner exploded from her, making an awful noise, dousing the ground, and oozing into his shoes.

Any notion (and there'd been every intention) of getting her naked disappeared—POOF!—from his mind.

14

Tuesday, Bill McIntyre called Jerry late in the day to let him know that Amanda's Depakote level was up to ninety. Was there any improvement? Maybe. She was definitely coming down. Her manic speech was gone, as was her constant need for movement, but her irritability was considerable—a nervous, mean energy rather than a happy, manic one. How much of the irritability was due to the illness? How much of it was due to her issues with her mother? What about not living at home? Maybe tensions between her and Ryan were the problem. It was anyone's guess.

She and Carol had yet to see each other. Carol unrealistically hoped that Amanda would be lost and needy in her shame, but Amanda was stubborn and defiant, still smarting from her mother's intrusion and the loss of her precious pipe. In Amanda's present state, Jerry was unable to negotiate some sort of peace. So, Amanda would continue to stay with Tom and Sarah.

Carol had finally succeeded in getting the tutors in place. Sarah would tutor Amanda in advanced calculus, bringing the work to Mark Kenny, Amanda's regular math teacher. Another tutor would be coming three times a week to the house to handle her other subjects. Physics, however, was still in question, and Jerry knew Carol was working on that. She didn't need physics — or calculus for that mat-ter — to graduate. Perhaps it would be dropped. He'd seen Amanda after her new tutor had left Monday night. She'd liked him. That was hopeful. She and Sarah planned to do some calculus today. He'd stop by on his way home and see how it'd gone. He knew how hard Carol was working with the school, knew that Amanda's graduation was her obsession, something she felt she had some limited control over. And if she failed the see the bigger picture, did it really matter? Because, really, big or little ... was there even a picture? Mental illness: as unpre-dictable as dropping a spinning top onto uneven asphalt ....

~

Amanda loved her new tutor. What was his name? Well ... it re-ally didn't matter. He was young (younger than Ryan) and cute! And so funny! It seemed like forever since she'd laughed. He'd be seeing her three times a week for all her subjects, except calculus. Working with Aunt Sarah in calculus was okay too, even though Amanda knew more about calculus than her aunt. But that was okay; she didn't mind setting her aunt straight on a few things. It was strange, but it felt good having some work to do, and it wasn't like it was hard. She could do anything after all, especially with everything being so insultingly easy. She had a paper due for economics, so she knocked off five pages on her computer. When her fingers were eager for more, she wrote another six pages for her calculus class, because really, you couldn't say enough about infinite limits; and perhaps she'd get some extra credit. She looked up from her work and found her father in the doorway of her bedroom.

"Hi there," he smiled. "What are you working on?"

"A paper for calculus," she stated flatly, and returned to her screen. What did he want now? At least Aunt Sarah and Uncle Tom left her alone.

"You have a paper to write for calculus?"

"Extra credit, obviously!" Christ! He was dumb as a rock!

Jerry considered whether he should brave another question, but decided against it. "Well, I just wanted to stop by and say hi before

I headed home." He tried to sound upbeat and positive. He thought he'd succeeded in hiding the sting of her cold words, but he saw her face twist over to pain and he knew that he'd failed. Guilt was something she did not need, something that would not help her, so he risked rejection and stepped into the room, hugging her briefly. "I love you, Amanda," he said, and felt her arms hug him, quickly, and stiffly back. "I'll see you tomorrow," he said as he kissed the top of her head and left.

Amanda sighed with relief and frustration after he'd gone. Why did he have to be so annoying? She really didn't want to be mean, but, Christ, it was impossible not to be annoyed when everyone was just so fucking annoying! She finished off the calculus paper and printed them both out. She tried to read her book for English, but it was so boring; the words would just not keep her attention. How could anyone write something so stupid? And who the fuck was this Steinbeck dude anyway? He died like a thousand years ago, or something! What could he have to say that anyone would want to read about now? She threw the book in the general direction of her desk and stood up from her bed and paced about the room as she texted Ryan.

WHATS UP.

WORKING, was his answer back. Well, duh! She tried to call him, but he wouldn't pick up. I'M WORKING BABE, came to her phone in a text. She threw it across the room.

~

Jerry kissed Carol hello at the kitchen sink. She was rinsing off lettuce for the salad. Her wet hand made a damp spot on his chest, but he ignored the cool sensation. Rather than letting her go, he drew her closer, extending the kiss to more than just a kiss. She responded by dropping the lettuce from her other hand into the sink and slipping her hands under his arms, snaking her fingers up his back until they were high on his shoulders where she could get the leverage to pull her body into his. They enjoyed the embrace until it was time to either break away or get serious. Finally, Carol pushed away with a flustered laugh and said, "My goodness, Dr. Benson." He laughed in return and gave her butt a little squeeze. "Later," he promised, before heading up the stairs to change his clothes. And she held on to that promise, because it had been forever. It seemed like a lifetime ago since they had made love (not since camp, and that really did feel like a lifetime ago).

Jerry knocked on Christy's door after he'd changed and then risked the safety of his bare feet as he stepped through the rubble of her room to join her on her bed. He sat at the foot of the bed and she smiled politely from the head of the bed, setting her history text aside. "Yes... may I help you?" (His brother's sarcasm.) He was forced to smile.

"Just checking in." Truth was, he was worried about her. She'd been especially quiet and withdrawn since the weekend. Carol had tried to talk to her and gotten nowhere. "Hanging in?" he asked. "Everything okay?" She shrugged. "Anything you'd like to share?"

"Is this how you talk to your patients? Because if it is... well, you sort of suck." She smiled.

He laughed. "Is there a better way to get you to talk?"

She thought for a moment, then shook her head. "No... probably not." Just then her cell phone beeped and she looked at it. "It's Amanda," she said as she read the text. "She wants me to go to dinner with her. Wants to borrow a car so we can go."

Christy looked at him. Her face was noncommittal. Amanda hadn't said a thing about this when he'd seen her less than a half hour ago. How did he feel about her driving? "Your mom's made dinner," he said. Was Amanda capable of driving responsibly? She'd always been a good driver. It would be good for Christy to see her sister, try to reestablish connections. Good for both of them.

"I haven't seen my sister for days." Christy smiled to herself. Her sister missed her, wanted to see her!

He nodded his head in thought. "I guess if you want to go... as long as you stay in Niskayuna."

Carol wasn't so sure that she agreed with Jerry. Would Christy be okay driving around with Amanda? It wasn't like they hadn't driven off together a hundred times before, but still. And Jerry had already said *yes*. Right now Amanda was walking down to get the car and she also wanted to get some things from her room. She would be here any minute now and Carol would see her, and she would see Carol. Carol felt anxiety flutter around urgently in her chest. She sat at the kitchen counter weakly and waited. Jerry came up behind her and gave her shoulder a little squeeze. She leaned into him slightly. "Should I hide?" she asked.

"Definitely not!" And as he said the words, the door to the garage opened and Amanda stepped in with her shoulders back, head up, and face set. It was not the face of Carol's fantasy, but a *fuck-you-don't-talk-to-me* face. They watched as she marched past the kitchen counter without a glance their way.

"Well, hello there," Jerry said.

Her eyes flicked in their direction. "Hi." She did not break her stride.

Carol swallowed her fear. "How are you, honey?" she asked.

"K." And she was gone, through the kitchen and up the stairs.

Well ... at least they were talking again.

~

"So where are we going to eat?" asked Christy. "Let's go to Applebee's." She loved Applebee's, and she thought it would be an okay place to talk. The music wouldn't be too loud and she really wanted to talk to her sister. She needed to tell someone what had happened with James. Christy had been unable to bring herself to tell Katy, and thank God James hadn't told anyone because if he had ... oh, she would know. She went to school Monday morning fully braced for the first "Hey, it's the Puckering Puker!" or "Watch out here comes Ralph ... no, no it's Chuck!" or worse yet "Hurling Whore!" But nothing. Nobody said a thing. She had to give James some credit there, but still, he didn't go out of his way to talk to her; he was even just shy of ignoring her.

Amanda hadn't bothered to answer her, so she said again, "Let's go to Applebee's." Christy was buckling herself into the Volvo and Amanda was flying down the driveway, snapping the car into drive, turning up the radio, flipping open her cell phone to check for texts, changing the radio station, checking her face in the mirror, running her fingers through her hair, and picking up speed before she bothered to respond.

"I need to buzz down to Albany first."

"What? Dad said we had to stay in Niskayuna."

"Fuck him."

"I'd rather not," said Christy dryly. "Where are we going?"

"UPS. I need to see Ryan."

And then Christy understood. This had nothing to do with her. They would not even have time to go a restaurant; she had to be home by nine. And although she knew it was pointless, she ventured, "But I'm hungry."

"Who the fuck said we weren't going to eat?"

Christy sucked in a breath. She wouldn't cry. No ... she just would not cry.

~

Although they had the house to themselves, Carol did not even consider cashing in on Jerry's earlier promise. No, she was too busy entertaining the tragedy of both her daughters being killed in a traffic accident. It had all the makings of a really bad made-for-TV movie. Of course, she'd blame Jerry; and they'd have to deal with all that—the blame, the guilt ... that could suck up two thirds of the movie. They'd probably end up in divorce, but how would the movie end? Would she end up with some sexy, understanding man? Perhaps a widower she met at a bereavement support group ....

Would all of Niskayuna show up for the funeral (funerals)? Could the funeral home hold all those people? She pictured people pouring out onto the sidewalk and everyone crying. It would be a double funeral, of course. Would they get a burial discount? Two for one?

~

Christy watched Amanda melt into Ryan's arms. Were they going to have sex right there in the parking lot? How long could his break from work be? She was hungry and tired. She just wanted to go home. She sunk down in the seat, almost positive that Ryan didn't even know she was there, and turned up the radio.

~

"You okay, babe?" he asked, pulling away from her embrace. He still wasn't sure how he felt about her being here. But there'd been no stopping her. It seemed like a long way to come for the fifteen minutes he had before he needed to return to his shift.

"Better now."

"It's cold as hell out here," he said. He took her hand and led her toward his car. As he got close, he hit the unlock button from his remote and opened the passenger door for her. He went around to the driver's side and got in. "What's up?" he said, turning to her.

She answered him by running her right hand up his leg and pulling him in for a kiss. He returned the kiss but rejected the possibility of sex in the parking lot. The last thing he needed was to risk one of his coworkers seeing them. The endless ribbing would be bad enough, but there was always the chance his supervisor, who was an ass, wouldn't approve of sex on UPS property. He felt Mandy's hand venture into his crotch. He pulled away from her kiss. "Slow down there, girl," he said with a smile. This made her press him all the harder. He laughed and removed her hand and kissed it. "No … really. My boss. We can't. Talk to me. Tell me what's going on."

"Come on, Ryan," she moaned and tried to kiss him again.

Now he was getting a little mad, and he evaded the kiss. "No, I mean it." He was still keeping his voice light, almost pleasant.

Her eyes flashed to fire. "Who the fuck's going to know?!" Her words were hateful, belittling.

"I'm not fucking you here, Mandy!" his anger apparent now. Why was she here anyway? Just for sex? He'd been at work since four, lifting fucking boxes for four hours straight. He still had hours to go. He truly didn't need this shit.

"What the fuck is wrong with you?!" she yelled.

"What the fuck is wrong with *you*?" he retorted. Of course, he knew what was wrong with her, but he was mad and tired, so he added, "Take a fucking pill or something!"

He might just well have slapped her because she brought her hand up to her face as if she'd been slapped, feeling the sting of his words, feeling for swelling. Ryan hated her; and who could blame him? *Take a fucking pill!* There weren't enough pills in the whole fucking world to help her... there was no help. She felt the pressure climb to her throat — a scream, a sob — she wasn't sure what, but she wasn't going to wait around and find out. She was out the door, slamming it shut, and gone across the parking lot back to the Volvo, which was still running, throwing it into drive before Christy even had a chance to sit up.

Ryan sat stunned and angry in his car. What had he done? But, really, what *had* he done? Nothing! He had done nothing.

"Really, Amanda, you should slow down a little." And to Christy's surprise, she did a little. "You and Ryan have a fight?" she asked carefully. Amanda was crying now, slimy black mascara tears running down her cheeks. Christy noted the tiny nod of her sister's head. "I'm sorry."

"Thanks," Amanda said weakly.

Christy was encouraged. "You guys will make up in no time."

"How the FUCK WOULD YOU KNOW?!"

Christy slid down in the seat. The car was going faster again. She just wanted to go home. She closed her eyes. Really! She just wanted to go home. A few minutes later the car slowed and turned as Amanda pulled into Taco Bell. "What do you want?" Amanda demanded.

Christy opened her eyes. Taco Bell! Christy was never eating at Taco Bell again. "Nothing." Amanda was pulling up to the drive thru. "I don't want anything."

"What the fuck are you talking about? What do YOU *FUCKING* WANT?!" Her voice bounced around in the car.

"Chicken burrito. Get me a chicken burrito," Christy whispered. Her heart was beating so loudly that even over the radio she was sure Amanda could hear it.

Amanda placed the order and managed to pay without causing

the poor kid at the window irreparable trauma. She grabbed her own food out of the bag, placed it on her lap, and then threw the bag with the burrito Christy's way. Amanda ate and drove and passed her hand through her hair, repeatedly checking her cell phone while changing radio stations. She looked at Christy. "Why aren't you eating?" she said calmly.

"I'll eat later."

Amanda sighed. "Sorry! Sorry I yelled."

Christy looked at her. Amanda gave her a weak, sad smile. Wow! Christy didn't think Amanda had ever told her she was sorry about anything — ever! "It's okay," Christy said. They didn't talk the rest of the way home.

~

Christy threw the bag with the burrito in the trash as she walked through the kitchen. Carol looked up from her book with relief. Jerry called from the couch, "Where's Amanda?"

"Gone. Walking."

"I told her I'd drive her back to Tom's," Jerry said, but Christy was already up the stairs. They heard her bedroom door slam shut. He and Carol looked at each other. "Oh boy," said Jerry. He got up. "I'll go talk to her."

"No. Let me."

Carol knocked lightly on Christy's bedroom door and opened it without waiting for an answer. Christy was lying on her bed with her face to the wall, crying. Carol made her way across the room and sat down on the bed, shoving Christy's body over a bit with her hip to make room for herself. She placed her hand on Christy's shoulder and said, "What did she do? What did Amanda do?"

Christy did not answer and Carol was beginning to think that she wasn't going to. But then she heard one of Christy's soft sobs turn into more of a sigh, and she spoke in a barely audible voice, "You know, Mom ... it's not always about Amanda."

Carol was quiet for a moment and then she said, "Then tell me what it *is* about." There was a long pause and Carol waited, shifting in the bed to make herself more comfortable. It was early. She could wait a very long time. The pause turned into more than just a pause and Carol shifted again, pulling her right leg up onto the bed and leaning back until her back rested gently on the foot board. "I can wait a very long time," she finally said. There was another long, exaggerated sigh from Christy. She wasn't crying anymore. A few more moments slipped by and Carol, never very good at waiting, added, "I'll bet you that there's nothing you could say or tell me about that I haven't thought or done myself."

Christy just snorted a *boy-are-you-wrong* laugh.

"Try me," Carol challenged. It had been Carol who watched her father walk out on her when she was nine, only for him to be killed in a car accident two months later (saving her mother the hassle of a divorce). It had been Carol who had grown up angry and defiant, who smoked her first joint at eleven, dropped acid for the first time at fourteen, and lost her virginity shortly thereafter to some guy at a party (she never quite got his name). Carol was the one who had tried just about every drug known to mankind; who used her right to choose at seventeen; who finally decided by eighteen that she was done—yes, *done*—with men (other than the occasional need for sex) and that she was done, very done, with the drug scene. Yes, Carol had every confidence that she could challenge her fifteen-year-old daughter who had grown up in a stable, loving home with both her parents in Niskayuna, NY. "Try me," she repeated.

"Oh yeah?" said Christy, turning slightly toward her mother. "How about puking all over the first boy who ever decided that maybe, just maybe, you weren't totally gross."

Carol, unfazed, shuffled through her files of hazy memories. "How about puking down the back of your friend while he was driving and causing a minor, but nonetheless complicated, car accident?"

Christy managed a little smile. "How about if that puking was during the first and only kiss you're ever going to get?"

"Oh yeah? Well, what if your first kiss was with a big, fat, smelly guy with zits the size of pepperoni slices?" Christy laughed, in spite of herself, and Carol joined her. "Just imagine the image of big, red pulsing pepperoni zits coming at you," Carol added, feeling inspired by the laughter. And it felt good to laugh at the tragedies of youth.

"Why?" Christy laughed. "Why did you kiss him?"

"I have no idea!" Carol laughed. "And that was one of the smarter things I did when I was your age."

"And what about Dad? How about the first time you kissed him?"

Carol smiled at the memory. "Well …."

Jerry heard their laughter and felt excluded. He wanted to join them so that he could laugh as well, but he knew it didn't work that way, and he would not begrudge Carol this moment—this increasingly rare moment of laughter with her daughter. He took solace in the fact that this newest drama with their children was apparently ending well, and that later, after Christy had fallen asleep to dream her adolescent dreams, he and Carol would be alone and untroubled enough to enjoy the pleasure of that relative peace.

~

Amanda lay with her back to the bed and tried Ryan's cell phone again. It went right to voicemail. It was two-thirty a.m., and he should be home by now. He should have been home for quite a while. He should have been home with his own back against his own bed, staring up at the ceiling, his hand behind his head so that you could see the dark soft hair of his underarm. And he should be laughing, his cell phone pressed against his ear with his other hand as he stared at the ceiling—laughing and talking to her before he fell asleep ….

She checked her computer again and saw that he wasn't signed in online either. He had no landline to try to call; there was no way to contact him. Amanda sighed.

He had texted her earlier and said he was sorry for getting mad, and she had of course accepted his apology, but he hadn't called her. (Did he think *she* should have apologized?!) He had apparently turned his cell off and then done what? Gone right to sleep? Maybe he met someone at the gas station on his way home … was with her now, pressing his body into this gas station bitch ….

Amanda jumped up from the bed and paced about the room for a few minutes. She could walk back home with the hope that her father had failed to remove the keys from the Volvo she'd left parked in the driveway. But, fuck! If her father found out—well she'd never use the car again. And once she got to Ryan's, what then? What if he really was with someone? What if he wasn't, but just hated her now? She flopped back down on her bed in misery.

A few minutes later, she heard David come home—the opening and closing of the kitchen door, his footsteps going up the stairs, banging around in the bathroom, and finally, the growing quiet of his bedroom. She should have gone out with him, gotten the hell out of the house, but now that he was twenty-one, he could go places that she couldn't—certain clubs and bars that wouldn't allow eighteen-year-olds.

Amanda felt herself dip—no dive—into depression. That terrible feeling of agitated hopelessness swallowed her whole. She had built up just enough agitation to overcome the weight of despair, just enough energy to give in to it and end it all with some crazy, stupid act. Jumping in front of a train sounded nice—if only there were a train. (Good ol' Anna Karenina…she had it lucky—there were so many trains back then.) Taking too many pills could work—there were plenty waiting for her right there on her dresser. The Grandma Benson Express was ready to leave the station…but she wouldn't let that thought get a hold of her, so she jumped up and paced briefly around her room before heading for the bathroom.

David wasn't quite asleep. He was savoring the tail end of his light buzz from the night at the club. He was enjoying the slight spinning of the room and thinking about some cute girl he'd met—what was her name? Jess. Yes, that was it. They'd danced, drank a bit together. She was a sophomore at Albany. Cute. Just as cute as she could be. She'd given him her number. He might just have to call her ….

He must have been asleep because he didn't hear the door to his room open. He was brought into consciousness by the slight shifting of his bed. "David?"

He sat up to the sound of his name in her voice. "Amanda?" And she was there sitting near him on his bed. He could see her hair framed in the glow of the LED of his computer, printer, and clock radio; he could smell her sweetness, practically tasting it in the air. As his eyes adjusted to the dark, he could just make out her lovely face made all the lovelier by its soft vulnerability and apparent need.

One of her small, soft hands came out and landed—a small moth on his chest and pressed until it was more than a moth, becoming something real and tangible and he had to hold his breath at the sensation. "I can't sleep," the sweet words came fluttering out of her mouth and into his ears. Her tear-streaked face turned up to him and he could see her lips part with just a sliver of a crack, and all he needed to do was bend down, just a very small distance, and his lips could meet hers in the dimness of the room and nobody, not one soul, would ever have to know. And with that kiss, every fantasy that had ever played across his mind would continue to play out, becoming a reality. And it was here, right here, for the taking. He brought his arms up from his sides and drew her in, pressed her pretty face against his chest and held her, bringing one of his hands to her head and feeling the silken pleasure of her curls beneath his fingers.

Amanda put her arms around him and let him take her in. She felt the warmth of his bare chest against her cheek and noted that his frame was larger than Ryan's, wiggling her nose slightly to the tickle of his chest hairs and sighing into the comfort, because she knew that she was safe, that he would protect her from herself and that she would survive this moment. She sighed again as he placed his hand on her head, lingered a moment and then patted her in comfort as you might a small child.

"You know," she heard him say somewhere near her left ear. "I can't sleep either. How about we go out for an early breakfast? Denny's okay?"

~

David ordered a Lumberjack Slam breakfast and Amanda ordered Moons Over My Hammy, not because she liked ham or even eggs especially, but because she wanted the chance to say it out loud to the waitress. "I want Moons Over My Hammy!" and she laughed with glee. The waitress, already pissed with her lot in life—having to work the third shift at Denny's to feed herself and her small child—was not entertained or the least bit inspired by the clever menu, but wonderful David joined Amanda's laughter. They spent the next fifteen minutes trying to come up with something better or at least as good, but they were hard-pressed at three-forty in the morning after a night of mild drinking on David's part and a night of rollercoaster manic rides on Amanda's, so the best they could come up with was Jumpin' Flap Jacks and Love, Love Me Stew—which were both admittedly pretty lame.

The ham and eggs thing really wasn't half bad and the coffee was hot and kept coming and really ... did it really matter if she ever slept again? But eventually the food was gone and Amanda's stomach was churning from way too much coffee. She looked over at David's red-rimmed eyes and knew that he was beyond tired, knew he did not possess her superhuman strengths, so she dug through her purse and threw a twenty on the table. "I'll buy," he offered, but she shook her head, stood up, and reached for his hand.

As they walked to the car, she put her arm around his waist and leaned her head into his arm. "Thank you, David," she said.

"Anytime, cuz ... anytime."

He started the car and drove through the quiet streets of Niskayuna. As he turned onto Moe Road he picked up speed. He reached over to the console and flipped the radio on. "Wading in the Velvet Sea" was playing, so he turned it up. (He had always been a big Phish fan.) "Take me to Ryan's," he heard her say over the music. He looked her way and turned the music back down.

"What?"

"Take me to Ryan's. Pleeeease."

He laughed as his eyes went back to the road. "No, thank you."

"No, really. Take me to Ryan's. He'll drive me home later."

He flicked his eyes her way. "You're a piece of work, you know that!"

"Damn it, David! Turn the car around!"

David slowed the car down a bit as he negotiated a curve and prepared for the possibility that the light ahead just might turn red. He did not look her way as he said, "I am not fucking driving you to Ryan's!"

He was confused by the sudden rush of noise, the sudden influx of cold air, and he automatically pressed the brakes further, not quite slamming them into the floor of the car, looking over to the noise and seeing Amanda fly out of the car, only her feet visible now as his foot went down against the breaks as hard as it could go.

At first, the sensation was awesome—the rush of sound, flying through the cold morning air, looking forward to hitting the earth. But the impact was not the awesome impact that she'd imagined. There was the second assault on the earth and the images of gravel-sky-grass-sky-grass-sky before finally coming to a halt somewhere between the grass and the sky. And then there was the attempt to suck in air, but not being able to!

David banged the car into park and was out the door and running toward her before her body came to a rest. When he reached her, her eyes were not quite looking at him but were opened in breathless panic. "Amanda!"

She felt just like the fish, the beautiful fish that Casey had caught all those years ago and had held up so proudly for David to see—Matt yelling from the deck, "Awesome trout!" Her seven-year-old eyes had watched as they marveled over it, watched as Casey just dropped it onto the grass, her standing over it and watching its poor mouth gasp in the unfriendly air. She watched the panic in its eyes—yes, even fish with no discernable facial features can have panic in their eyes.

The boys returned to the dock and took up their poles while Amanda reached down to gently pick up the lovely creature. She stepped into the lake and lowered her hands. "Hey! What are you doing with my fish?!" She gently released her grasp on it as the sound of their poles hit the dock. Their feet ran along the wooden planks, but her eyes never left that lovely fish.

Casey had yelled, "Hey! David, grab that net!" as the fish lay on its side, momentarily suspended in time, opening its mouth to the sudden pleasure of oxygen, righting itself. The boys got to the shore as the fish floated in front of her legs, inches beneath the surface. "Come on, baby," she urged. There was the sudden splash behind her as they entered the water, net in hand, startling this creature; and Amanda watched with pleasure as it darted into the depth of the lake, back to its life. She didn't even care when they dragged her out of the water, threw her onto the grass as if she were the fish, and used their fists to show her their displeasure — no ... it didn't even matter at all.

This is exactly how she felt now: like that fish; all she really wanted to do was to be able to take a breath of fresh, clean air and then dart back into life.

15

Carol picked up the marker and considered for a moment, the tip of the pen poised over the name tag. Finally, she brought the pen down and wrote in large sweeping letters: **CAROL**. Nothing else. As she stood up and pressed the sticky tag to her chest, a pleasant woman, perhaps in her late fifties, extended her hand to her. "Welcome..." she said as her eyes flicked to the name tag and then back to Carol's face. "...Carol. I'm Margaret. I talked to your husband on the phone?"

Carol took her hand. "Yes... hello," Carol returned the smile as best as she could.

"Daughter, right? Diagnosis bipolar. Husband's Dr. Benson?"

"Yes." Jerry had just told her about this class yesterday, had just found out that it was starting. He'd made a call and made sure they'd make room for her. If she didn't come now it would be another six months until the next class. She really would have preferred to wait, but Jerry had been adamant that she should do this now.

Margaret cocked her head at her ever so slightly. "He didn't come?"

"Well... you know...."

"Yes, of course. He knows all this. But, you know, he might gain some insight, a different perspective, perhaps?" Her head cocked a little more, dropping her silvery brown hair forward, before adding,

"And he's dealing with all this, just like any other family member." Her head came up. "But, it doesn't matter." She waved her hand in dismissal. "Welcome! Pick up the handouts." She pointed to a table. "And there's coffee, tea, some cookies." And she was gone and off to the next person.

Carol stirred her decaf and flipped through the large pile of handouts she'd picked up, and watched as others came in—welcomed by Margaret—and picked up their own paper pile to join her around the tables that were loosely forming a circle in a room that wasn't quite large enough. She smiled a bit nervously and made eye contact with each new arrival, marveling that these were just normal people—people you might see walking in the park, the grocery store, or at the office. Ordinary people…like her.

At seven sharp, Margaret joined the group. "Okay, well, we're going to get started. There may be a few late-comers, but we have a lot to cover and we only have twelve weeks. Welcome to Family-to-Family Education Program, sponsored by NAMI Albany. I'm Margaret LoBello. I've been teaching this class along with Vicky Thompson," and she indicated the woman to her right, "for twelve years now. The first thing we're going to do is go around the room and introduce ourselves and talk briefly about our family member. I will start." She sat back, bringing her hands up to her chin and made eye contact around the room. "My son is thirty-three. He first became ill and was diagnosed with schizophrenia at nineteen, during his second year at RIT. This diagnosis was eventually changed to bipolar disorder. He has spent most of the last fourteen years in and out of various mental hospitals. His longest hospitalization was two years. He's attempted suicide four times—that we know of—and is currently living in a group home north of Albany. And at this moment, he is well." She said all this without the slightest hint of apology, embarrassment, or shame. She picked up her cell phone and checked it briefly, smiling slightly at the room before adding, "But, of course, I haven't talked to him today." And everybody in the room relaxed into their laughter.

There were twenty or so people, some of them couples, and they all made their way around the room, telling their stories of their children or siblings; there were a couple of people whose spouses were ill. Their tales were longer than Margaret's and emotionally sloppy, some awkwardly stoic, some left unfinished due to uncontrollable tears, some laced with deep anger—all of them sad; all of them unfair.

When they got to Carol, who was used to public speaking, she felt sure that she was ready, but it started badly. She cleared her throat nervously and said, "Hi, I'm Carol Benson," and was immediately flustered. She hadn't meant to use her last name. Some of these people might know her and make the connection with Jerry. Their family members could very well be Jerry's patients—but that was silly. It wasn't as if her last name was Rumpelstiltskin or something. And really, what difference did it make if they knew?

"My daughter, Amanda. She's nineteen … no," a slight laugh, "eighteen. She's, well … she's been diagnosed with manic depressive illness, bipolar, whatever."

Cripe! She sounded like an idiot. Why did they have to change the name anyway? Especially to a name that a lot of professionals, including Jerry, did not like (he much preferred the more descriptive term, *manic depressive illness*). Bipolar disorder, manic depressive illness—pick a name, damn it!

Carol apologetically glanced around at the faces in the room before continuing. "She was diagnosed … let's see …." Oh my God! Had it only been a little over three weeks? She sighed heavily. "I guess just about three weeks ago." There was a tiny collective gasp from the room—yes, this was new; yes, she was raw—she hadn't even figured out what to call the damn disease yet. "Anyways, it was just so sudden, you know?" And everybody nodded. "Well, Amanda was always stubborn—harder than our younger daughter—but I was totally unprepared … I just never knew … never thought … maybe I should have been, you know, prepared. It was my husband … his family … his mother that was ill …."

His fault! It was Jerry's fault! She should never have had children with that man! And then she was consumed by guilt. It wasn't as if he'd hidden his crazy mother from her. And would she have denied Amanda's very existence if she knew what she knew now? Of course not! Thank God she hadn't said that aloud. So she added, "But there was my Uncle Joe ... you know, on my side ... he wasn't right."

But who's to say that it was that simple—just bad genes and not bad parenting?

"I was a good mother..." she appealed to the room and then looked to her hands, which were worrying each other, "...or thought so." Her voice grew softer. "I still am, I think...." The mother that didn't want her sick child living at home! And then she couldn't go on.

~

"Honey, are you okay?" Sarah asked as she watched Amanda gingerly set her body down at the kitchen table. Sarah had had student-parent conferences all afternoon, so they were eating later than normal. This was the first time she'd seen Amanda today. Tom set the bowl of peas down that Sarah had just passed him and looked at Amanda. David grabbed a piece of corn and busied himself by carefully smearing it with butter.

"Oh, well ... I had a little fall. You know, in the bedroom." It hurt to breath, so her words came out quick and shallow, mixed with pain. "No biggie." Amanda looked at the food on the table. The chicken looked petrified, but the corn looked good.

"Fall?" Tom asked. "How can you fall in a bedroom and hurt yourself so badly that you sound like you're dying?"

David laughed. "Oh! There are many ways—"

"Hush, David," said Sarah. Tom gave David a warning look and David just laughed.

"Really, Amanda, how did you get hurt?" asked Tom.

She reached for a piece of corn and winced at the movement. "Slipped on the rug last night. Hit the bed. Maybe cracked a rib?"

David had looked at her. She was good. Amanda had refused to let him take her to the ER, had begged him not to tell anyone. She was convinced that her father would lock her back up in the nut house if he found out.

"Broken ribs can be serious…can puncture a lung," said Sarah, with concern.

"Mom, I think if she had a rib in her lung…" David laughed, letting everyone know his mother was absurd. "I mean, really! She'd be dead by now!"

"I'm fine. Really. Just a bruise." Her voice was firm, a little dangerous; she was done with this conversation. It was none of their fucking business, anyway. She felt her anxiety fluttering its eyes open, stretching out its arms. Wake up! Wake up! One more word and she was out of there.

Well, Sarah wasn't so sure. She'd talk to Jerry about this.

Tom considered Amanda for a moment before turning the frown of his face toward David. "You didn't go to class today." It was a statement disguised as a question.

David looked at him. How the fuck did he know that? Was he chalking his tires or something? By the time he got Amanda home and was able to chill—God knows, he needed to—it was six-thirty before he'd fallen asleep. He woke up slightly, sometime late morning, to the sounds of Ryan coming up the stairs, slipping into Amanda's room, and the murmur of their voices, before drifting back to blissful unconsciousness. So he'd slept through his one o'clock class and not bothered with the three o'clock. By the time he'd gotten up, Ryan had left for work and Amanda was apparently back to sleep, only getting up just in time for her four o'clock tutor. He considered lying or making up some elaborate excuse, but instead, he just looked his father in the eye and simply said, "No, I didn't."

Tom set his knife down just a bit too hard. Tom had heard his son and Amanda come in when it wasn't even night anymore, knew that they'd been out doing God-knows-what. He certainly didn't buy this falling in the bedroom crap. "We're not paying for those classes for you to just blow them off. Out screwing around all night on my dollar."

David narrowed his eyes at his father. "I missed one fucking class."

"David!" his mother said in horror. "Do not talk like that at the table!"

Amanda couldn't help it. She laughed. Fuck! It hurt to laugh!

David rolled his eyes, and almost laughed himself, and would have if it wasn't for the fact that his father would freak out. He really needed to get the fuck out of this house. Tomorrow, after class, he was going to put in work applications everywhere. Certainly there was a job out there somewhere that would pay him enough to move out. Then again, maybe Casey and Matt had the right idea. He hadn't felt that he wanted to go away to college after he graduated from high school, but this living at home, working some, and going to school part-time certainly wasn't working anymore. Forget the job. He'd apply to college somewhere full-time. Maybe he could even transfer by spring semester. Yes, that's what he'd do. Tomorrow he'd apply to the university. The University of Fucking Far Away!

~

Vicky Thompson stood in front of a large writing board, a big black marker in her hand. Carol was breaking her second cookie into tiny bites and dipping them into her decaf, which was getting cold. The sweet sensation was just enough to push back the other sensations that threatened to overwhelm her. "Okay," said Margaret. "Let's have a word to describe how your loved one's illness makes you feel?" There was a slight hesitation and then someone called out, "Sad." Vicky wrote this word on the board. "What else?" And then it started and Vicky could barely keep up, writing until the entire board was covered with dark black lines of feelings. "Depressed." "Miserable." "Anxious." "Worried." "Frustrated." "Grief." "Isolated." "Lonely." "Fed up." "Resentful." "Bitter." "Embarrassment." "Shame." "Unfair." "Angry." "Responsible." "Hateful." "Guilty." "Guilty." "Guilty." "Hopeful." Yes, right at the end someone said, "Hopeful," and everyone looked at him. "We can't forget hope."

~

"Did you know, Jerry, that there are more people with serious mental illnesses in prison than there are in all the hospitals and mental health facilities?" Carol called to Jerry as she washed her face in the bathroom.

"Yes, I did," he called back from their bed. He smiled.

"Almost fifty percent of people with serious mental illness are not receiving any sort of treatment. They're living on the streets, in jail... could be contributing to society in a positive way if only they could be reached!" She came out of the bathroom and gave him a hard look. "Do you know the state of psychiatric care in this country is dismal? When over twenty-two percent of adults in the US suffer from some sort of mental disorder!" He nodded slightly. "And do you know one of the reasons why?" He shrugged, keeping his expression neutral. "Stigma! That's right!" she pointed at him. "Lack of insurance coverage, minimal research dollars going toward mental illness, added suffering for the patients, decreased prestige for psychiatric care pro-viders—all this due to stigma! Do you know one survey showed that people rated mental illness as the least acceptable of disability groups? They'd rather have an ex-convict who's an alcoholic living next to them than someone with a mental illness! Do people not realize that this is a biological disease, like diabetes, and is very treatable if only people *were* treated?"

He sighed at her lovingly, no longer able to mask the smile on his face. "No, they don't."

Then she cocked her head at him slightly and matched his smile. "This is why you wanted me to go to this course so badly. You knew it would get me going." His smile widened. Yes. Carol with a cause. Carol pissed off. That was a force he could stand behind. So much better than Carol grieving, Carol despondent.

"Yes, partly," he admitted. "And also, so you'd know that you are not alone."

She joined him on the bed and wrapped her arms around his back. "As long as I have you, I could never be alone." He held her close and enjoyed the tickle of her crazy hair against his neck. Yes, this was a good moment. These were the moments that kept them whole. And there was no reason to shift this moment; there was absolutely no harm in waiting until the morning to tell her about Amanda and her broken ribs.

~

Carol poured the steaming hot water into the teapot and set it aside to steep for a few minutes. "I made some zucchini bread this weekend," she offered. "It's got about two thousand grams of fat, but Jerry likes it." It was Sunday afternoon, and the men were in the den watching the New York Jets lose to Philly. The two women sat at the counter bar of Carol's kitchen, neither one of them giving a hoot about the New York Jets.

Sarah shrugged her shoulders. "Why not?"

As Carol sliced the bread into slivers of dark layers of moisture and fanned them out in a pretty way on a plate, she searched for words—for something to say that didn't sound contrived. She'd known Sarah for over twenty years, spent every holiday with her, special occasions, every significant and every insignificant event that their husbands felt the need to share with one another (and there were many), and yet somehow, she felt she didn't really know this woman. She had not just married Jerry, but married all three of them, and to be honest with—who? Well, just herself—Sarah was not a woman Carol would have chosen for a friend. She envied the relationship between Jerry and Tom—something she would never have with anyone, ever. She turned from the counter and set the plate in front of Sarah. "Thank you, Sarah," she said.

Sarah looked at the lovely offering of sweets placed within her reach, and said, "I love her too, you know."

Carol felt relief and gratitude; the sweet poignancy of the fact that Sarah did not question what she was being thanked for, but just knew. "And she's not always that easy to love!" laughed Carol.

"I'll eat to that!" And Sarah reached for a slice of sweet bread.

16

October eased into November without the implication of winter. There had been many a Halloween in Niskayuna when fairy princesses froze in their pretty dresses, their goody bags swinging as they danced along on their tiny, cold feet through snow-covered sidewalks. But much to Tom's delight, the weather held and he and Jerry were able to christen their new toys. They took advantage of the relatively empty bike paths, getting back that balance that'd seemed so natural when they were boys zipping around the neighborhood on their beautiful Stingrays with the streamers fluttering frantically from the handle bars. Biking was now, in many ways, just as fun as it had been forty years ago—even without the streamers and the attempted wheelies. Yes, there was a certain contentment and freedom, rushing against the air on your own power. Tom had been right about his knee; it was just fine.

Carol went to her class each week looking forward to getting to know these people and their stories just a little better, increasing her knowledge on a subject her husband had spent so many years immersed in. Why had she never shown interest before? Why did it take a personal insult to her life before she was willing to learn about something that so many others were dealing with every day? She began to understand, just a little better, what Amanda was going through, so that when Amanda came strutting into the house unannounced with that defiant, superior attitude—as if nothing had ever happened between them; as if Carol was in the wrong—she no longer felt the need to set her straight. Instead, she offered her dinner, told her there were fresh baked cookies in the tin, and, as slowly as autumn slipped away, Amanda eased back into their home and their lives.

Christy was glad to have her sister back. It was just too weird being there all alone with just her parents, all their attention seemingly on her, watching her every move. (Not that there was much to watch.) James had fallen from her radar, or she from his—in either case, if there had ever been something, it was gone now and there was no one else on the horizon. School was better. Jody Wilson was pregnant and apparently having the baby (no one knew yet who the father was...did Jody?) and Jake Fyles was taken off to a drug rehab place in Georgia. Both, as it turned out, were much more exciting than Christy's crazy sister. It wasn't as if Amanda was going around hacking people up with a hatchet. Overall, she was rather boring. It was rare now that some jerk would come up to her and give her grief about Amanda, which was fine with her. So what if they all forgot her sister ever existed? Except that it kind of made her mad and a little hurt that no one seemed to really care that Amanda was gone and that no one even asked how she was doing.

And how *was* Amanda doing? The answer, perhaps, would depend on who was being asked. After the little rib incident (which Jerry never did quite get to the bottom of), Bill McIntyre added Lamictal to the drug mix. As the Lamictal was slowly increased, the Depakote level was decreased. Amanda, much to her surprise, started feeling better almost right away, but the new drug made her stomach hurt. She hadn't needed to worry about the possibility of weight gain from the drug; she could hardly eat and lost weight that she couldn't afford to lose. And she was so tired—too tired to have much fun.

Amanda looked at her rib cage (most of the bruising gone now) sticking out around her pale skin and her non-existent boobs (they had always been small, but this was ridiculous), and she wondered how much longer she could put this poison into her body. Her father insisted the nausea and stomach pains would improve, but really, why was she doing this to herself? It wasn't like there was that much wrong with her. Sure, she was so tired all the time — it was so hard to get out of bed and get motivated (she probably had cancer or something). Even being with Ryan was dull, almost boring. She didn't feel much like going to the club. It was hard to dance with the *cancer* eating through her; and sex ... well, it was okay ... but she knew it was hard, with her non-existent boobs, for him to even look at her. And it wasn't like she had anything to say that anyone wanted to hear. There really wasn't a lot to do with Ryan, other than watch TV or go out for an occasional dinner or movie. She missed it: the rush ... the way he'd made her feel those first few weeks. Maybe what she needed were some vitamins or something.

Jerry felt encouraged. Was it possible that they had hit upon a good cocktail of meds? Days would go by and Amanda wouldn't lose her temper. It had been over a week since anything had been broken. No walls punched. No profanity — well, just a little. Sure, it wasn't like she was friendly or chatted with them or even smiled for that matter, but at least no walls had been assaulted.

Carol stepped carefully around her house, knowing now not to ask that one-question-too-many and being able to read Amanda's moods. She knew when to back off about homework, and if things seemed especially stressful for her older daughter, she'd simply leave the room, or leave the house if she needed to. It wouldn't take long before Amanda was in some other, and often better, state. She was even able to talk and joke, just a little, with Amanda again. Of course, there were times when she screwed up and read Amanda wrong, causing some eruption, but she knew now to back off, to retreat quickly away from parental reprimand. Would you slap your two-year-old for spilling milk? No. You'd give her a sippy cup. Of course, it just felt wrong giving an eighteen-year-old woman sippy cups of acceptance, but it was as it was.

What Carol found remarkable, as Thanksgiving rushed into their world, was that there would be extra plates for her to remove from the cabinet, extra wine glasses to wash away the dust of idleness from, and extra silver to polish. As was the custom, her brother, his family, and her mother were all going to be there. Both Matt and Casey were coming home, of course. Amazingly, Matt was bringing home a girl—Matt who must have had a hundred (who knows, maybe more) girls, but *never* a girlfriend. But what was *most* amazing was that Ryan would be there, hanging around like a loyal dog. Carol, as Amanda's mother, didn't really have a choice—she was forced, to some extent, to bear Amanda's kicks of abuse. But Ryan *chose* to stay, apparently enjoying Amanda's company. Surely Amanda must treat him better than she treated the rest of her world.

This would be the first time her family had seen Amanda since she became ill. Would they see a different girl? The hair, thank God, was no longer red—Amanda, not impressed with the dark strip growing in at the top of her head, had surprised them all, once again, by transforming her locks from bright red to the darkest of black, which over the red was more of a purple violet. Still, it was so much better than the red; she almost looked *normal*. Carol had been there the first time Ryan had seen it and was relieved to overhear him say, as his fingers played in the transformed tresses, that he loved the color. She was hopeful that there would be no more tinting traumas to endure. Otherwise, did her daughter look crazy? Was the set of her mouth, the shine to her eyes, the tilt of her head . . . just a little off?

~

David waited until everyone had filled their plates; waited through Jerry's annual, obligatory, and often long, mushy, and boring toast (this year: lingering on the importance of family, love, and all that shit—it seemed even longer and mushier than normal). Jesus! Even his mother was wiping tears from her eyes, and his aunt was practically blubbering. Once David had everyone's attention, he picked up his wine and swirled it solemnly, enjoying drawing out the suspense—hoping his father was concocting all sorts of horrible possibilities in his head. What has David done now? Had he gotten some girl pregnant? Kicked out of school? Joined the army? Is he moving to Alaska to work on an oil rig? (Hey… that wasn't a half-bad idea….) Finally, when even he couldn't stand it anymore, he looked up and said, "I've been accepted at the University of Buffalo for spring semester. Almost all my credits transferred. I'll be leaving January tenth."

Carol, who was still mopping tears from her face, turned to him and smiled. "Oh, David, that's wonderful!"

David met Tom's gaze and smiled at the stunned expression on his father's face. "You trying to figure out how your dimwit son managed to apply to a college all by himself?" he asked. He'd actually applied to several schools, staying within the SUNY system, knowing his father would flip out at private or out-of-state tuition. He'd been accepted to all of them, but UB was 260 miles (that's 419 km) away, clear across the state. It was a big school with plenty of girls, lots of parties, Division I in sports, and located in a major city. Yes, this was going to be good.

"You can't leave me," said Amanda, before Tom had a chance to respond.

"Us," added Christy. "You can't leave us."

"You two will come to visit. We'll party 'til the cows come home," he said, reaching for his fork and stabbing at a piece of turkey. David looked back up at his father and watched a smile sneak across Tom's face as he looked at his mother. Yes, it was time. He would have to save the fact that he'd changed his major from English to pre-law for some other time … maybe Christmas.

17

The first significant snowfall was three weeks after Thanksgiving. Even though seven inches fell, this by no means guaranteed a white Christmas. It did, however, guarantee a rash of fender benders, spinning trips off the road, and the not-so-subtle reminders of keeping your feet off the brake when sliding. It was not unusual for the temperatures to behave erratically, and it wasn't, after all, officially winter until December twenty-first, so the snow was a dirty, slushy, melting mess as Carol and her two daughters made their way from the parking lot for some final Christmas shopping.

Carol could tell that Amanda was not having a great day. She was edgier than normal and was not even bothering to step around the cold puddles of melting snow; she walked with stubborn purpose, sending splashes of cold slush onto her jeans as she stomped her way ahead of them to the mall entrance. Carol had considered turning around, abandoning this outing, but the whole thing had been Amanda's idea, and it was rare—no, nonexistent—that Amanda ever wanted to do anything with any of them. So here they were, trying to keep up with her as she disappeared into the mall and down the corridor.

"Amanda! We will not buy anything if you don't slow down and wait for us!" Carol called as they entered the mall. Amanda must have heard her because she slowed, just a little, and with a bit of an effort on Carol's part, they caught up to her. As it turned out, Amanda's main stress was not having a clue what to get Ryan. Everything Carol suggested was just *plain stupid* and Christy's ideas were not much better.

They wandered around the mall with minimal success, picking up a few gifts here and there. They stopped at the makeup counter at Macy's, and the older woman behind the counter was pleased to help as Amanda tried on various shades of eye shadow. There was a particular shade of red that Amanda thought looked especially nice with her eyes and her skin tone, but when the woman nicely suggested that perhaps red made her look a little tired, Amanda's eyes flickered to fire, and she said, with astonishing arrogance, "Really, if I wanted *your* opinion I would have asked." Then Amanda was gone, strutting away from them. The woman looked at Carol with condemnation. (Yes, it was always the mother's fault.) Carol looked back, mortified. "I'm sorry …."

"Mom! Come on!" Amanda yelled, causing people to pause and look her way. Carol glanced at Christy who gave her a helpless look, and they stood conflicted. "Mom!" Amanda yelled again. She was still moving and almost out of the store. Carol repeated her apology as she and Christy turned from the counter.

Before they caught up with Amanda, Carol turned to Christy and said, "I need a sign or a card or something that says, *Please forgive her. She's crazy.*"

"Maybe we could get her to wear a t-shirt," suggested Christy.

"Or a shirt for us … *I'm with a lunatic* … with a little arrow."

Christy laughed. "That's so politically incorrect."

Yes … that was true. Margaret, from her *how-to-deal-with-crazy-people* class might not approve. "Okay. How about, *I'm with someone with a neurobiological brain disease* … but still with the little arrow."

The laughter felt good, so much better than tears.

Finally, Carol and Christy convinced Amanda to get Ryan something that he might use as an architect, and they stopped at a large art and drafting supply store on their way home. Amanda picked out a beautiful drafting pen. She left it to be engraved with a message, which she did not share with her mother, and the ride home was almost pleasant.

~

Christmas was always Jerry's favorite time of year. It had been an incredibly difficult couple of months. He was feeling hopeful as he watched his brother talk to the pretty woman behind the counter. There was no doubt that the Lamictal was working better than the Depakote. Finding the right drug was the biggest hurdle to jump, and they had done so quickly and successfully; he felt perhaps the worst was behind them. She'd been diagnosed and treated quickly. Most people go ten years with symptoms before they are diagnosed—ten long years of irreparable damage to the brain, loss of jobs, broken relationships, opportunities lost—but she appeared to be stabilizing. Yes, he was looking forward to Christmas.

"What d'you think, Jer? Would Sarah like these?" Tom was holding up a pair of diamond earrings. The three diamonds on each earring swung smoothly from three delicate gold chains. He placed them in front of his ears so that Jerry could further appreciate them.

"Oh, they're just lovely!" beamed the woman behind the jewelry counter.

Tom smiled at her. She was a beautiful woman, probably in her mid-thirties, and she was flirting ever so gently with him. Was he still truly desirable, or was he simply hoping to make the sale? Could he, if he wanted to, sleep with this woman? Hmmm … he wasn't about to find out. He had no desire to go down that wonderfully incredible yet horribly slippery slope again.

"Well, of course you'd say that," he told her, giving her his most charming grin. "And I'm sure they look especially good on me, but will they look good on my wife?"

He turned back to Jerry. "What do you think?"

Jerry smiled. "Well … they're just lovely! And they are bound to look even better on Sarah. They say that jewelry is always a safe bet," he said encouragingly. Truth was, Jerry was tired of shopping. He was looking forward to that beer Tom had promised him when he'd been forced to accompany his brother on this little shopping trip. Jerry had been done with his shopping for a week now. He'd managed to procure a rare, original copy of *The Gleaner* by Judith Sargent Murray that he knew Carol would love. He'd also grabbed a nice cashmere sweater, thinking that the shade of teal might look good with her hair; and two beautiful orchids he'd hidden at Tom's—a start in replacing those that Amanda had destroyed. The girls, Sarah, and his nephews were always Carol's responsibility, which was fine with him. As for Tom, well, he'd gone ahead and purchased a gift certificate at the local ski shop, even though he'd been adamant with Tom that he wouldn't consider taking up cross-country skiing. Ever since biking was no longer possible, his brother had been yapping endlessly about the wonders of cross-country skiing; and really, neither of them were loving racquetball, and Tom *had* been right about the biking.

Tom turned back toward the saleswoman. He caught her eye and said with a grin that edged on wickedness, "Let's do it." He noted the slight flush on her face as he handed her back the earrings. Yes. He still had it. "Can you wrap those in a nice little package for me?"

Jerry shook his head slightly at his brother. There're some things that just never changed. As the woman rang up the sale and wrapped the gift, Tom said, "Well, that should about do it." And Jerry could already taste the bitter pleasure of the nice cold ale he was going to order.

~

Carol slipped her finger from the bow as she pulled the ribbon tight. She fanned out the ribbon and was satisfied. That was it! The last present wrapped. She placed it beneath the tree. And to think a few weeks ago she was dreading Christmas, never believing that they'd get to the point that Amanda was actually . . . well, human again. Yes, you could almost have a conversation with her—almost. And she looked so much better; it wasn't just the color of her hair, but her face, the brightness of her eyes, the flush of her skin, the softer set to her lips ... and she had gained a little weight back.

Carol knew that Christy was also happier—so pleased to have her sister back, still young enough to be excited about Christmas, and who was this boy she seemed to be talking to on her cell all the time? Yes, Carol had checked her phone log when Christy had casually left it in the kitchen yesterday. Chris was the name that kept coming up. Chris could, of course, be a girl, but Carol didn't think so. Chris and Christy—how cute was that? Carol's surreptitious attempts to get Christy to admit that there was indeed a boy were not so subtly rejected, so Carol was forced to turn to her other source for information. But when she asked Amanda if she knew who this Chris might be, the only boy Amanda could come up with was Chris Becker, a senior and a known drug dealer. Well, Carol wasn't going to entertain that possibility. No, she would relish the relative calm and keep looking forward to Christmas.

The more Amanda thought about the fancy drafting pen she'd bought for Ryan, the better she felt about it. It didn't matter that she'd spent most of her birthday money on it, as she was sure Grandma Harper would give her more for Christmas. She loved the engraved words she'd chosen, even though they were tiny, forced to fit along the shiny shaft. She imagined them pressed against his fingers as he sat in front of his drafting board creating some incredible structure, or as he penned a poem or words of love just for her. Yes, she felt good, looking forward to Christmas. Yes, she was flying with energy she hadn't felt for weeks now—that awesome frenzy of pleasure. Yes, everything was perfect. Everything was under perfect control. And she—yes, *she*—was the center of that perfection of control. How had everyone put up with her when she was a grumpy, drugged-up bitch? Especially Ryan. Thank God he still loved her! Yes! She was back! With every breath she could taste the joy of life. Oh, the amazing things she was going to be able to accomplish now that she was well! Tonight she would get on her computer and apply to all the Ivy League schools. Maybe she'd throw in a few SUNY schools just for balance. She didn't, after all, want to appear too haughty.

~

"Amanda's in an extraordinarily good mood," Carol told Jerry as he changed from his stuffy doctor attire to something a bit more comfortable. He caught the concern in her voice and looked up—with mild alarm—from the shirt he was buttoning.

"How good?"

"As I said, extraordinarily good."

"Maybe it's Christmas," he offered weakly. He'd just been singing "I'm Dreaming of a White Christmas" in his head. It was the eve before Christmas Eve, and the weather had turned sharply colder. The forecast called for snow, so hopes were high and dreams were being dreamed. "Where is she?"

"Out with Ryan somewhere." Carol frowned at him. "Did you pick up a new prescription recently for her Lamictal?"

Jerry felt the sliver of fear go through him. "No. Why?"

Carol looked at him, pleading for understanding, for forgiveness. She knew how he felt about respecting the girls' privacy. "Jerry, I've been counting her pills. Not every day, but often, when she's not around. I sneak into her room and pour them in my hands." She had to look away from him. Those pills in her hands, like precious gems … but hoping they were gone instead of still being there … one, two, three, four … yes! … three less than the last time she'd counted them—that wonderful sense of relief was well worth the risk of getting caught.

Oh, Jesus, thought Jerry.

"Jerry, I don't think she's taking them anymore."

~

They were playing one of her favorite songs, the beat pulsating through her, mingling with her blood, the music beating to the rhythm of her heart. Dance slower and the music would slow to the movement of her heart. Dance faster and the tempo would soar. How wonderful to have her heart control the very room—what everyone else was feeling; what everyone was hearing. Christmas lights swirled around the room, flickering off earrings and shimmering dresses.

Everyone decked in Christmas splendor: Santa hats, reindeer antlers, elf ears, cute little red and white dresses, some guy dressed up like Christ, fake blood dripping from his thorny crown. (It was fake, wasn't it?) Amanda knew she looked best of all with her shiny black boots, sparkly stockings, painted-on slinky red dress, gleaming silver eye shadow, jingle bells singing from her ears, and the cutest little puffy white cap setting off her luscious black curls.

Ryan swung in close and kissed her, his hands playing along her back as he laughed — as they laughed. David smiled at her from across the dance floor, dancing with some girl, giving her the thumbs up as she caught his eye. Would he like her to slow the music down so that he could hold this girl close? She would do that for him. Then there was the overwhelming need to be with Ryan, to have him to herself, to give herself over to him. Yes, the music would be okay without her. Her hand in his, she pulled him to the door, opening it to the cold night air. Tiny flakes of snow fell like fairies in the street lights and melted on her cheeks. They followed along like Tinker Bell during the short walk to Ryan's apartment as the glow of the tiny blunt passed between them, and wisps of sweet weed disappeared into the night. The stairs to his apartment were hardly an obstacle — fairy wings were helping her along to this magical place where his body was the universe and she was the Milky Way — wet, warm, swirling with sensation. It was almost too much to bear, but he kept her safe in his universe, keeping her atoms from splitting apart and shattering throughout the room.

Suddenly, she had the overwhelming urge to get up from the bed and bounce around the room. She could feel his negativity, catching the words, "Are you okay, babe?" No, she would not answer to negativity. Somewhere on her third bounce around the room, her eyes stopped, coming to rest on his desk and seeing *the* pen, the very pen she'd bought and had yet to give him. She picked it up and turned to him. Her eyes must have held a question, because there was a smile and words came out of his mouth, "My mother ... a present ... last Christmas ... will need it soon."

And then his face changed as he watched her drop the pen in agony and bang her hands against her skull. "Mandy?" He watched with confusion as she slipped her tiny feet into her boots. "What are you doing?" She grabbed her purse and then her coat, not even getting it totally over her naked body before opening the door to the apartment and fleeing down the stairs.

"Mandy!" Fuck! He couldn't get his pants on fast enough, and didn't even bother with his shirt. He shoved his feet into his shoes and grabbed his coat. "Mandy!"

But, by the time he made it down the stairs and out the front door of his apartment building, she was gone and nowhere in sight.

~

"She's not answering her cell. Should I try Ryan?" Carol asked.

"Oh, I don't know." Jerry looked up from the book he was reading and glanced at the clock. It was quarter after ten.

"Mom, Amanda's fine," interjected Christy as she made her way through the kitchen to the fridge for a late evening snack. "I mean, what do you want? You freak out when she's pissed off. You freak out when she's sad. Now she's happy and you're freaking out!"

"Hey!" Carol snapped. "If she's not taking her meds, I have a right to freak out!"

"We don't know if she's stopped," Jerry reminded her calmly.

"What do you think?! The pills are reproducing?" quipped Carol angrily.

Jerry set down his book and sighed toward his wife. "You might have miscounted. She might have had an old bottle you didn't know about. I've brought home a lot of samples..." he said quietly. "I think it's best not to jump to conclusions... let our imagination run away with us."

Carol wanted to scream. If she wanted to freak out, then damn it, she'd freak out! Jerry hadn't seen her. He didn't know.

"Mom," Christy said as she turned from the fridge, taking a large bite from a cold, sagging slice of pizza—not even noting the glob of sauce that dropped with a soft plop onto the floor. "You seriously need to chill."

And then Carol screamed. It was just a tiny one, but a scream nonetheless, and then she saw the absurdity of how she was acting and left the room in angry disgrace.

~

Ryan scanned the swarming, pulsating room. Amanda was nowhere in sight. He pushed through the crowd, not hearing or seeing the complaints from those he shoved aside. He finally located David, way in the back against the far wall, leaning in toward a pretty girl who was smiling up at him. "David!" he called. His voice was lost in the music. He made his way to the back and placed his hand on David's shoulder. David turned and Ryan drew close so he could be heard over the unreasonable noise of the place. "Have you seen Mandy?"

David wasn't quite drunk yet so he acknowledged the urgency of Ryan's question. He shook his head and told Ryan with a light touch against his arm to hold on. David turned back to the girl and said something into her ear, his lips brushing her cheek as he withdrew. Her hand fell against his arm as he turned away, so he gave her a soft smile of promise and then was gone, heading to the door with Ryan.

Once out of the chaos and into the quiet of the snow-covered street, David, feeling the trepidation that had crept into his head, asked, "What happened?" After Ryan was done with his quick synopsis, David asked, "Cell phone?"

"She's not picking up."

"Let me try. Maybe she'll pick up for me." But he tried twice and she would not answer. "Shit!" He ran his fingers through his already wet, cold hair. "Where would she go?" They looked up and down the snowy street. Where to even start?

~

Carol flipped open her cell phone at the very first hint of a ring. "Amanda!"

"Mom…." With that word, filled with so much more than one syllable, all Carol's worries were substantiated. "What am I going to do?" She was sobbing almost uncontrollably, her words just barely discernable from her sorrow.

"What happened? Where are you?" Carol made her way from her office and back into the living room where Jerry sat in stupid, ignorant bliss. "Amanda, tell me what happened," she repeated. Was she wrong to feel some sort of satisfaction and superiority for being right? Jerry looked up at her approach, at her question into the phone.

"His mother!" she was sobbing. "The same exact fucking pen! He's going to fucking hate me!"

"What?"

"I have nothing to give him. I just want to die," her voice was lost to her tears.

"I'm sorry, honey." Carol shook her head in confusion. "What about the pen?"

"And I don't see why all the fairies are so angry, you know, it's not like they really even know me."

Carol raised her eyebrows at Jerry. "Fairies?" She listened to Amanda cry a moment before asking, "Amanda, where are you? Where is Ryan?"

"I don't know! They brought me here!"

A new sort of fear went through Carol as she asked, "Who? Who brought you there?"

"The fairies. I think they want to kill me."

Carol looked at Jerry. Her daughter did not just say that! Oh my God! "Honey, look, talk to your dad a moment, okay? I think he can help you." She handed the phone to Jerry as she whispered, "She thinks fairies are trying to kill her." He took the phone and brought it to his ear as Carol said, "I'm going to try to call Ryan and find out what the hell's going on."

"Amanda?" she heard Jerry say into the phone as she went to the kitchen and pulled Jerry's cell from the charger. She scrolled down to the Rs.

~

They'd checked both their cars, which was rather dumb as they were both locked. Ryan had rechecked his apartment while David searched the stairways and halls of the apartment house. They were back on the street searching the alleyways, trying to ignore the fact that the snow was flying in earnest now. Ryan was fucking cold without a shirt under his coat and no socks; he didn't even want to think about how cold Mandy must be if she were out here somewhere. He brushed the snow from his hair in frustration, his eyes searching the street as he walked. Was that his cell phone? He reached for it, not taking the time to check the screen. "Mandy!"

"Ryan. This is Carol. What's going on? Where's Amanda?"

"I don't know! I've lost her!" he said into the wind. *I've lost your fucking daughter!*

David came out from around a building, and when he saw Ryan on his cell he called, "Is that Amanda?" David saw Ryan shake his head *no* and then drop his head into his hand and sink a little toward the sidewalk as he talked into the phone.

~

"Amanda," Jerry said as calmly as he could. He was pacing now in front of the couch. "You need to try to tell me where you are. Are you outside? Is it snowing where you are?" He paused, waiting for some sort of answer. He pulled the phone quickly away from his ear and checked the screen. Yes, they were still connected. "Amanda?" Nothing. "Amanda, please say something." Nothing....

"Daddy?"

He stopped his pacing and stood motionless. "Yes, honey, I'm here."

"It's really cold where I am," and the connection was lost.

~

It was the police who finally found her—not because they stumbled upon her on that snowy night, and not because Jerry had called them and requested they search for a psychotic young girl. No. She was found because of the nice drunk who had indeed stumbled upon her, who saw her wandering around talking nonsense and swatting at the snow. He took the time out of his night of drinking and of trying to stay warm on the cold, unfriendly streets of Albany to find a policeman and tell him what he'd found.

By the time Carol and Jerry negotiated the slippery roads and reached the hospital, Amanda had already been admitted into the psych ward. Ryan and David were in the waiting room, frustrated because they had not been allowed to see her and no one would tell them anything other than that she was there and that she was fine.

The resident on call was some idiot that Jerry remembered teaching all too well. He assured Jerry that he'd talked to Dr. McIntyre and that he would be in first thing in the morning to evaluate her. Amanda was in good hands for the night. He would keep an eye on her and call Dr. McIntyre if there were any problems. They stood outside her door. Carol slipped in to see her daughter while Jerry continued to talk to the resident. Jerry grumpily reviewed the chart and couldn't find anything to truly criticize, but he still frowned at the young man. "You've given her enough Loxapine to take down a small elephant."

The young man swallowed nervously. "I checked with Dr. McIntyre before anything was done."

"I should certainly hope so!" said Jerry as he turned from the resident and entered Amanda's room. She was already closing her eyes, sinking into sleep. They had her in a private room, of course, directly across from the nurses station. There was really nothing he could find fault with.

Jerry made his way back to the waiting room. Ryan jumped up from the chair he had fallen into and almost cried with relief as Jerry motioned for him to come. "David, you stay here," Jerry told his nephew gently. Ryan noticed that Jerry had to use his ID card to open the door and took further notice as the door shut behind them—he was locked in here now, escape only possible with that magic plastic card. Ryan looked around as they made their way down the hall. It really wasn't all that different from any other hospital patient ward.

Jerry stopped by the desk and told Toni that Ryan should be allowed to see Amanda anytime and could stay as late as he wanted.

Toni started to remind him that Amanda and Dr. McIntyre had to make that decision, that there were strict visiting hours…but then she took one look at Dr. Benson's face and closed her mouth.

As Jerry opened the door, Carol stood up from the chair she'd pulled close to Amanda's bed. "Amanda," Carol placed her hand on her daughter's arm and watched her eyes flutter open. "Ryan's here to see you."

"Hey, babe," he said as he made his way to her bed, sitting down next to her, taking her hand into his.

"Ryan?" she slurred with heavy sedation. "Oh man, they have me so fucked up with so much shit…."

And that's how Carol and Jerry left her; there was nothing more to be done.

~

Jerry was in the psych ward before seven, catching the poor young resident before he could escape. There'd been an unusually large number of admissions last night and the boy looked haggard and sleep deprived. Yes, Jerry remembered those days. But any empathy he might have entertained was quickly discarded as he reviewed Amanda's chart. He looked up from the chart with disbelief. "You gave her more Loxapine?"

"Every five hours…that's what Dr. McIntyre ordered," he said weakly.

Jerry sighed. How had be missed that order last night? He looked back at the chart. Yes, it was there. "Don't you think it's going to be impossible for her to be evaluated if she's a drugged-up zombie?"

"Well, sure…." Now the resident was getting a little pissed. It wasn't like this was his first year or something; he was a third-year after all. "We need to break the psychosis."

Jerry thought about saying something else, something sarcastic and unnecessary. But, really, why was he taking all his frustrations out on this young man? Especially when he was basically correct. So Jerry just sighed, too stubborn to totally back down and apologize, but definitely ready to give it up. "Have you seen Bill yet? Has he seen

Amanda?"

"I'm sorry, Dr. Benson. No."

"Okay…" said Jerry tapping Amanda's chart with his pen. "Go home and get some sleep." Jerry started to turn around and head into Amanda's room, but then turned and said, "Oh…and thank you…for being here for her last night."

Amanda was fast asleep so Jerry checked in on his own patients, students, and other residents. He found himself writing orders for increases in sedatives for his unstable and difficult patients, hating the fact that he was doing it, but doing it nonetheless. It was Christmas Eve, after all. He really would like to make it through the next two days with minimal emergency calls and trips to the hospital. And really, wasn't that the problem and why he felt so strongly that Amanda should be taken off the Loxapine? He wanted her properly evaluated so he could get her the hell out of here and back home where she belonged.

At ten, Bill McIntyre had still not shown up to see Amanda. Jerry had no scheduled patient appointments today and he was pretty much done with his hospital duties. He was back in her room. She was just waking up and although disoriented and mildly delusional, she wanted to go home. He checked his watch again. It was almost time for Amanda to get another injection of Loxapine. Well, he wasn't going to let that happen. He was considering having Bill paged when the door swung open.

Bill smiled at him in a serious doctor sort of way. "Morning, Jerry. Sorry. You know…just crazy stuff." He stepped up to the bed and gave Amanda's foot a little squeeze. "How you doing, peanut?"

Peanut? Did he call all his patients that? Amanda did not answer, but she gave her doctor a little smile.

"Let's talk," he gave her foot another squeeze as he sat on the edge of the bed. He glanced at Jerry and then back at Amanda. "Just you and me, okay, kid?" Amanda gave him a small nod and Jerry had no choice but to get up and leave.

Jerry stepped out of the room and Sonya, the day nurse, looked up from her paperwork. Jerry shrugged, "He kicked me out." She lifted up a platter of Christmas cookies and pushed it toward him. He picked a pretty blue cutout snowflake and hung out at the nurses station, munching. When there was nothing left but crumbs on his shirt, he walked up and down the hall with feigned purpose. He chatted amiably with some of the inpatients, but these were conversations that did not keep you enthralled. Finally, he returned to the nurses station and smiled weakly at Sonya.

"Have another cookie, Doc … a chocolate one. By the time you're done with it, I'll bet he'll be finished." Jerry was considering her advice when Bill stepped out of Amanda's room.

Jerry came from around the desk and searched him with his eyes. He didn't like what he saw. He stepped in close to Bill and was surprised as he realized that Bill was taller than he was, and so Jerry was forced to look up to meet his eye, to look up to this man who was younger, taller, and a slightly better build—but by no means a better doctor—realizing that this man wasn't going to let his daughter go home.

"Bill, I don't want her here."

"Yes, Jerry. I know you don't."

"I want to take her home," he insisted. There was really no room for discussion in his words. "It's Christmas Eve. I want her home."

Bill McIntyre sighed. "Jerry, let's, just for a moment, pretend that she's not your daughter."

"No! No," he repeated more calmly. "I won't pretend that … because I know what you are going to say. And you know damn well what I would do if she weren't my daughter, but I don't give a damn." He was keeping his voice low, trying to keep it calm. "She *is* my daughter and I'm much better equipped, much more qualified to deal with her," he lowered his voice even further, "than these idiots here in this hospital."

Bill gave him a hard look. "You're being unreasonable," he said calmly.

"Perhaps!" Jerry nodded his head roughly. "Perhaps! But I have the right to be unreasonable!"

Bill shook his head sadly. "No ... really you don't." He paused a moment, considering. "I'm sorry, Jerry. Really, I am, but she is an adult. She is my patient and, I don't mean to be an ass, but I have to think about what's best for her. You cannot watch her twenty-four-seven. She could have easily died last night. Your best intentions cannot keep her safe." Jerry was shaking his head in disagreement, but Bill continued, and said exactly what Jerry was afraid he was going to say. "I will keep her here every minute of the seventy-two-hour hold and longer if I feel she's still a danger to herself, or if I can talk her into it. Now I really need to go home to my family. I suggest that you do likewise."

Jerry watched him turn and walk away, saw the sympathetic look Sonya gave him. Jerry closed his eyes in frustration. How? Just how, and when, had he lost control? Perhaps the better question was why, exactly, did he believe he'd ever had it?

When he returned to Amanda's room, the nurse was injecting the third dose of Loxapine into his daughter's body. She looked so small and alone, peering out of the small window at the light fluttering of snow, but when he sat on the bed and she turned to the movement, her eyes were not that of a lost child, but of something dark, something to be feared. "Well, you've got me now, don't you, Daddy?"

~

Jerry drove slowly and carefully on the snow-covered roads, finally pulling into his garage a little after noon. He turned off the engine of the old Volvo and sat and listened as the garage door shut from behind and the old engine sighed as it cooled. He let his eyes drift to the Porsche, covered with its winter blanket, warm and safe until spring.

Yes, his entire life had been wrought and painted and formed by mental illness. It had marred him as a child, fed him as an adult—the Porsche, the house: all paid for with other people's sorrows. Did he have the right to drive on sorrow? Had he ever really made a difference? He could not (had never been able to) help the ones he loved the most—his mother ... his daughter .... And as his vision blurred from tears, he looked away from the Porsche and into his hands. This is where he stayed on that Christmas Eve afternoon until the winter chill forced him out of the garage and into his home to join what was left of his family.

~

Needless to say, Christmas at the Benson house was subdued at best. It was decided to wait until Amanda came home to open presents. Carol just wasn't up to making her annual Christmas dinner. Sarah came over to get the roast and overcook it in her own house. Even though Jerry, Carol, and Christy had promised to come to dinner, they never made it. Visiting Amanda and watching her cry helplessly and inconsolably all afternoon took everything out of them. When Amanda slipped into a sedated sleep, Ryan joined Jerry, Carol, and Christy for Christmas dinner at the hospital cafeteria, which really wasn't half bad—probably better than whatever Sarah had done to Carol's beautiful roast. At nine that night, Tom, who just simply couldn't make it through his first Christmas ever without his brother, showed up at the house with a beautiful bottle of a fifteen-year-old Laphroaig that one of his clients had given him. Although even the best of scotches was not something Jerry ever embraced, he did embrace his brother, and as a result, stayed up way too late. In spite of his morning fogginess, he felt he'd lifted to a better place.

18

Amanda stayed in the hospital the week between Christmas and New Year's Eve. No one sent flowers, which was really okay because Amanda couldn't have them in her room anyway—inpatients were never allowed flowers, balloons, or other deadly objects, which raises the question: had anyone ever succeeded in killing herself with a daisy? But Carol thought cards or calls from friends might have been nice, or maybe a casserole to make her life easier? Fruit basket to the house? So yes, Carol was a little bitter. Sarah and her mother were there for her, and their company was welcome, but it was Margaret from her class that really got her through those days after Christmas; Margaret who called late in the evening when Jerry was on call and still at the hospital; Margaret who called her every few days, just to check in.

Even though Amanda's depression was still severe, Bill McIntyre finally felt, as the new year dawned, that she was well enough to go home. Jerry sat in her hospital room New Year's morning and asked what he'd been wanting to ask, finally feeling that she was well enough to talk about it.

"Why, exactly, did you stop taking the Lamictal?" he asked her gently as she packed her meager belongings for the trip home.

"It made my stomach hurt," she said simply.

"But why didn't you tell me or Dr. McIntyre how bad it was?"

"I did." She looked at him with sad eyes. "You just didn't believe me."

And at first, Jerry wanted to deny this. Yes, of course she'd mentioned the stomach problems; they'd talked about how to make it better by eating with the medication, but she never said it was intolerable. What Jerry realized before he opened his mouth to argue his point was that she was right—both he and Bill had made an all-too-common error: they had chosen to ignore her words because she was doing so well … because the drug was working. So what if it made her stomach hurt—she was sane, and wasn't it better to be sane with a stomachache than a healthy psychotic?

Amanda looked up at him from the sweater she was folding and said, "I also … you know … missed the edge."

Jerry sighed. Yes, there was always that. "But the edge," he said, "is a very dangerous place."

"But don't you see? That's what makes it such a rush."

Jerry felt the dread from her words and knew that it would always be a balancing act, one that he'd have to watch from the bleachers. Bill had changed her mood stabilizer to Tegretol in hopes that it could be better tolerated, and he added the antidepressant Abilify, kept her on the Seroquel at night, and gave her a new supply of Klonopin to be used on an as-needed basis. But all the medications in the world wouldn't do any good if they took away too much; if they took away her very essence. And, ultimately, it was Amanda, and only Amanda, who could find that balance.

~

Margaret tilted her head slightly at the group. She sat back and rested her hands on her funky wool sweater, which covered her substantial chest. "Did we all survive the holidays? It can be an especially difficult time—for anyone, but especially when dealing with an ill family member. Expectations too high … all the family members together … it's a lot of stress." She swiped away an unruly strand of hair from her face. "My son was home. Just for the day." She shrugged slightly and smiled. "Hey, it was okay. But I'm glad they're over—the holidays. Anyways, before we get started, I just thought it might be nice, just to talk a bit, if anyone has anything to share." She sat up and scanned the faces in the room. Her eyes fell and then stayed on Carol's. She smiled her compassionate smile they'd all grown to love. "Carol, how's Amanda?" Carol smiled sadly back. "You don't care if I tell the group?" Carol shook her head. "Amanda stopped her meds, spent Christmas week in the hospital." There was the collective murmur of sympathy. "Oh, it's so common, as you remember when we were learning about medication. That's one of the hardest things—keeping our loved ones on the meds. They all have side effects. Lack of illness awareness. It's so hard. So how is she?"

Carol swallowed. "Well, she came home a few days ago. She's so sad... depressed, miserable to be around, and irritable, of course."

"Yes," said Margaret. "The crash that follows the mania... all those drugs to bring her down... the depression in bipolar, as you all remember we talked about, so hard to treat. And you? How are you?"

Carol sighed. "Well, I guess I'm depressed too. She was so much better, you know. I was so hopeful." She stopped for a moment, looking away to a neutral spot across the room before returning to the now familiar faces in the room. "You know, we have these kids, these babies, and we're filled with all these dreams and hopes. Their cute little baby bodies." She held her hands in front of her, holding this imaginary being. "The possibilities endless..." Carol's eyes did not stray from the cradle of her hands, "and then to be so totally disappointed." She closed her eyes and sighed. "Oh, I know it's not her fault...." She opened her eyes and brought her hands to the safety of her lap. "Not mine either, or at least I think I almost believe that...." She laughed and revealed a smile that was met and returned by the group. "I'm just so tired, you know? I want it to end. It's just so hard... the constant worry... that she might kill herself or something... or that I will spend the rest of my life caring for this miserable child...." She met the faces full-on as she said, "There have been so many times I've hated her... when she's been so hateful... wanted her to just go away … to die—" She looked away. There was a beat of silence. Was she alone? Was she the only one who could wish the death of her own child?

"It's so hard," Margaret said, "to go through that grieving process over and over and over again. Every time our loved ones get better, we feel this hope and then there's another round of illness, another crisis and then the shock, the denial, the anger, the grief and finally, if we are lucky, the acceptance. And we've lost them, the dream of them, just as surely as if they are dead, and yet they aren't …." She looked at Carol with admiration. "And to be able to come here and say what I'm sure all of us have felt … well, that's something."

There was general agreement in the room, and Margaret continued. "But it does get easier. You go through the process faster and with less anger, more acceptance … and let's not forget, there is rehabilitation and recovery. We'll be talking about that tonight."

"You know," Randy spoke from the other side of the room. All eyes turned his way. Randy's son was especially difficult. His diagnosis was unclear, schizoaffective disorder being the most recent, coupled with drug and alcohol addiction. He'd been in and out of jail, hospitals, and rehab for years now. Randy sat back and smiled ironically as he said, "I felt a hell of a lot better once I gave up on hope." The sad tension that had built up in the room exploded into laughter and then something else: silence, as each person digested these words.

Carol grabbed at the words. Yes! That was it! To give up on hope! But how sad was that? Wasn't hope what you needed? But maybe … maybe *hope* was just a four letter word for non-acceptance. Maybe that's why giving up on hope sounded so right. Acceptance. Yes. That's what she must strive for.

19

Winter blew in sharp and bitter after the holidays. Everybody hunkered down for the long wait for spring—really not much to do this time of year other than be miserable and embrace winter like an annoying old friend. David went off to Buffalo without much fanfare. Ryan started his last semester at Albany, taking a full class load and still working, but down to thirty hours a week. Christy turned sixteen. Christy, not willing to risk Amanda's response to a party with her friends, chose to have a small family gathering, which was still pretty much a disaster. David, still in Buffalo, was sorely missed by all. Amanda, unable to tolerate the festivities, retreated to her room with Ryan, leaving Christy with her parents and her Aunt and Uncle. Not exactly a sixteen-year-old's dream.

Amanda, struggling now in school, had dropped physics and now was forced to drop calculus. She was, of course, no longer in the honors and AP classes—but really...did it matter? Her tutor still came faithfully three times a week, bringing her work, giving her exams, shuffling what little homework she accomplished back and forth from the school. Whenever possible, Carol risked Amanda's anger, and came home early to quietly observe the sessions with the tutor. Was anything getting done? Was she failing everything? Wringing her hands slightly as she walked the tutor to his car, she wondered if Amanda was going to be okay. Was she going to graduate? She had plenty of credits. She'd still get a Regent's Diploma, but it was mandatory that she pass English and government, write a few papers to pass phys ed. As far as colleges … well, who knows what was going to happen, but Carol needn't have worried about Amanda applying to schools — they had received their credit card statement and, although it took both she and Jerry to figure out what all those charges were, it quickly became clear that Amanda had spent her last manic days before her hospitalization applying to colleges: twenty-five in all; over twelve hundred dollars in college application fees. Well, they'd had a good painful laugh over that, and what was even more ironically sad was that she'd more than likely get into most of them. She'd been, after all, at the very top of her class — she and Jason Radcliff vied for valedictorian — before she'd gotten sick. She'd done remarkably well on the SATs, and now she could barely get out of bed.

Carol graduated from her Family-to-Family Education Class. It was nice not to have the weekly commitment, but she missed it. She missed the people, she missed the commiseration, she missed Margaret. She would, of course, continue to go to the monthly support group, and she now had people she could call who understood, who knew.

Tom and Jerry made a noble effort to embrace winter. Tom had also purchased a gift certificate for Jerry as a Christmas present from the same ski shop (although, for not quite as much money) so that they bought those cross country skis that Jerry had so strongly resisted. They pushed their aging bodies at least once a week along the soft white landscape, puffing the smoke of exhalation into the cold air of Central New York. Unlike biking, if truth be told, Jerry hated every minute of it. He hated the way his ears got cold, no matter what sort of hat he wore, and how his body, no matter what sort of coat he wore, became hot and uncomfortable. He hated having to pull off his gloves with his teeth and pull a tissue from his pocket to blow his nose or wipe the fog from his glasses — all the while trying to keep moving so as not to get too far behind his brother, who seemed to have a natural love and ability for this newfound sport. But Jerry did it without complaint. He even listened with enthusiasm as his brother gave a small dissertation on the wonders of nature during each and every trip into the great outdoors. And it was good, even if it sucked, to get out, to be with his brother—to have a diversion.

Christy's friend Katy was still dating Brandon and they seemed to spend an awful lot of time together, which left Christy a little lost as a third wheel. She tightened up her friendship with the group she'd hung with in late fall, so it wasn't too bad, but she missed Katy—and really, why did Katy have a boyfriend and not her? Even miserable Amanda had Ryan. Was she really that undesirable? But...damn it...this whole feeling sorry for herself thing was really getting boring. Who could blame the boys? If she'd learned nothing else from Amanda, she'd learned that hanging with miserable, depressed people was a drag. She just didn't know how Ryan did it. It was really time for her to give up on this whole *poor me, I've got a crazy sister shit*, and move on.

~

"So what do you think, babe? Do you want to go see that new movie?" He felt her shake her head into his chest. Ryan shrugged slightly. Really, it didn't matter to him. It felt good just to be here with her. He was so busy now. If he wasn't working he was in class or studying or sleeping. So hanging with her here on this Friday night was his preference. He just thought she might want to get out of the house, but at least she was out of bed, having ventured all the way downstairs. He stretched his feet out a little farther and snuggled a little deeper into the folds of the couch. "That's cool." He turned his attention back to the TV.

Christy clicked past the den on her way to the kitchen. "Hey, Ryan," she smiled. "What's up?"

Ryan looked up from the TV and took her in. "Whoa, check it out." He felt Mandy's body, a blanket across his chest, shift. Her head came up to take in her sister.

"You look like a fucking whore," Amanda mumbled without much conviction before disappearing back into his chest. Ryan rubbed Mandy's head in gentle reprimand and smiled at Christy.

"Hot date?" he asked.

"School dance. You know, Valentine Dance."

He nodded his head. Deciding to risk Mandy's reaction, he said, "Well, you look awesome." He felt Mandy tense slightly and he kissed the top of her head in apology. Christy grinned in pleasure and turned slowly on one heel so as to give him the full effect—her short skirt flaring gently with her movement. His smile of appreciation grew. And it was true. In the short time he'd known her, she seemed to have gone from an awkward teenager to something hot and desirable.

Christy's cell beeped. "That's my ride." She flashed Ryan one more smile and she was gone. That left them alone ....

~

Tom studied his cards, recounted, and looked up at his wife. "One club," he said tentatively. Jerry took a sip of his beer and tapped the table, indicating his pass.

"Six clubs," Sarah declared and Tom put his head on the table. Carol rolled her eyes and settled back into her chair. So much for bidding her long heart suit. Sarah's good luck in cards had continued obnoxiously for months now. But Carol simply didn't care. It felt so good just to be out doing something, not at work and not at home, but spending an evening out with people who knew what they were going through, who felt it themselves because they loved her too. She picked up her wine, swirling it gently, studying the patterns of the liquid as it clung and slipped slowly down the side of the glass.

"Jesus, it was my better minor," complained Tom. "You didn't want to communicate a bit with your husband? Maybe dance around with a few more bids—a little foreplay before jumping to slam, bam, thank you ma'am?" Carol smiled.

Sarah stuck her tongue out at Tom in a way more suggestive than obnoxious. "Stop complaining," she said. "You need to trust your partner." She set down her hand as soon as Carol had made her lead and watched Tom's eyes grow wide. "A monkey could play this hand," she declared.

Tom blinked at her hand. No one got hands like that—seven clubs, with ace and king high, void in hearts, outside ace … and with him opening. "Well, you see Sarah, my point exactly. If you had chosen to communicate with me, we'd be where we should be," he gave her a hard look to emphasize his words, "which is at *seven* clubs."

Sarah turned her attention away from the cards. Even she was getting bored with her annoyingly incredible hands. "So what are the girls doing tonight?" she asked Carol.

Carol, who was just taking a sip of her wine, placed the glass down as Tom trumped her ace of hearts from the board. "Christy's going to the school dance. Fran's giving her a ride." She turned her eyes to her husband, "Jerry we have to remember to go get them at eleven."

Jerry nodded slightly, mildly irritated by the talk; he was concentrating on the game. Was there any possible way to set his brother?

Carol ignored his irritation, and said, "Amanda and Ryan were at the house when we left. I'm hoping…" she pulled a card from her hand and threw it on the table, "that he talks her into going somewhere. I don't think she's left the house for over a week now except only to see her doctor."

"Is she any better?" Sarah's face was concerned.

"I don't know," said Carol. "I don't think she's sleeping as much." She looked at Jerry. "Do you think she's any better?"

"It's your play, Carol," Tom told her, with mild reproof.

Sarah looked at him in exasperation. "Tom! We're talking here!"

"Jesus! I'm sorry! I thought I was trying to make slam here!"

Sarah let her eyes linger on Tom before saying, "What is it that you don't understand about a monkey playing this hand?"

Tom sighed and laid the hand down.

"So you made seven," said Jerry as he considered the scoring.

"Yes, *seven*, Sarah," Tom looked across the table at his wife and gave her an *I-told-you-so* smile.

"That was your rubber and then some." Jerry looked up from the score sheet. "Carol, you and I better start doing something soon." Then added, "Yes, I think Amanda's a little better."

"I don't think she's crying as much as she was…." Carol reached for the cards and handed them to Sarah to cut. "Still mean as hell."

"But Jerry, it's been weeks," said Sarah as she cut the cards. "Shouldn't she be a lot better by now?"

Jerry shuffled the other deck and sighed. "It takes a while. The depression part of this illness can be really tough."

"Can't you just give her a little more antidepressants or something? Maybe a different medication?"

Carol and Jerry both sighed. "Yes, if only it worked that way," said Jerry. "It would sure make my job a lot easier." He looked at Tom. "Hell, maybe even a monkey could do it … if we only had drugs that really worked for everyone, every time."

~

The band was a local group and not half bad really. The bass player was especially good and cute, with his long, stringy hair and deep, sexy dimples. Yes, Christy was officially in love with the bass player. Every time she drew close to the band as she danced, she caught his eye, and every time, his dimples deepened in appreciation of her. Could he play her as well as he played his guitar? Make her sing with pleasure? Not only give Christie her first real kiss, but so much more?

"Hey, Christy!" Zack screamed at her over the music—his peach fuzz, pimply face suddenly close, touching her arm with a light sweep of his hand. Christy's eyes left her bass player reluctantly. "You look amazing!"

She smiled. How could she not smile? "Thanks." They danced unofficially together for the remainder of the song, Christy trying hard not to spend too much time on Zack's sad, adolescent face. He was a boy—just a sad, struggling-to-grow-up boy. What she needed—her eyes drifted back to her fantasy lover—was a man.

~

"We need to talk," he said as he brought gentle pressure to her head, lifting it slightly from his chest. Ryan hit the mute button on the remote and shifted his body, forcing her to relocate.

"You're breaking up with me," she said. Who could blame him? And really … did it even matter? Why would anyone want to be with her? Even *she* wished she could get away, but that'd take a hell of a lot more energy than she could come up with. It was almost funny: she wouldn't mind dying, would've been ecstatic to kill herself, but that'd involve some sort of action that she just wasn't capable of.

"No," he shook his head.

"No, what?" she asked lazily.

"I'm not breaking up with you."

"Why not?"

He shrugged. "I love you."

"That's a stupid reason."

He laughed. And then he was amazed at the hint of a smile on her face. Yes, she had actually smiled. "What I wanted to talk to you about …" he hesitated. "It's been forever —"

Oh … it was the sex thing …. "We can if you want. I don't care."

He gave her an exasperated smile. Yes, it had been forever for that too, but it wasn't like it was going to kill him — the no-sex … at least he hoped not …. "It's been forever *since Christmas*. I know you haven't felt well enough for me to give you my gift, but really … I really want to give it to you … it can be for Valentine's too. I'd really like you to have it before Easter or something. I'd like to give it to you now."

Amanda felt the pressure of his words. Why would anyone want to give her anything? Better he break up with her. There was nothing he could give her that she deserved to get. No response she could give worthy of the giving. She was just an empty shell of fucked up, worthless nothingness. "Please," she heard him say. "You don't have to give me anything."

Ryan knew. He knew about the drafting pen. Carol had told him, and he still wanted it — because it was from her; because he wanted to see what was engraved on it; because he wanted something solid, something he could hold onto — but he would have to wait.

"Okay?" he all but whispered. She nodded her head just enough for him to jump off the couch and make his way to the mudroom. He rummaged around in the just-too-many pockets of his winter jacket, and finally, after locating the small box, returned to her. She was sitting up fully now, her feet neatly tucked beneath her thighs, the tips of her fuzzy yellow socks peeking out at him, a contrast against the loose green sweats. Her sweatshirt (a different color, yet some sort of purple-blue) hung from her small frame. She sighed at him through her long, uncared-for locks. He came close and brushed the hair away from her face, twisting it in a temporary hold behind her head, before placing the small box in her lap. "Open it." He sat down next to her on the couch. Another sigh, but her hands came up and took the box. She slowly pulled at the ribbon, which was a complicated union of red and green. Finally the ribbon fell away and she had to rest a bit from the effort. The shiny silver wrapper proved to be easier than the ribbon and it wasn't long before she held the naked white box in her hand. She looked at him, uncertain. "Open it," he urged.

"It doesn't matter what it is. It won't make me happy."

"I know. I'm not giving it to you to make you happy. I'm giving it to you because I want you to have it, to make me happy." She shrugged and lifted the lid. She looked at the delicate silver form. "It's an amulet...a talisman," he said as he picked it up by its tiny silver chain and held it out for closer inspection. Amanda looked at the fragile threads of silver that encased the tiny glass vial. The vial was capped with a filigreed silver lid. "You know, you're supposed to put oil or love potion or something in the vial. But I figured you already love me, so I wrote you a little message and stuck it in the vial. You know...message in a bottle...." He smiled. "Read it."

He handed it to her. And sure enough, there was a tiny slip of paper in the vial. She had to bring it close to see the impossibly small letters, written in beautiful calligraphy. She mouthed the words silently as she read: *I believe in you...*

She handed it back to him, and he took it, feeling the slight, sad weight of it as it slid among his fingers. He looked into her eyes and was unsure — even though he'd prepared himself for the sting of rejection, damn, it still hurt. Then her hands came up and back to gather up her hair. She turned her back to him slightly, and then he understood. He brought his hands around to the front of her and carefully laid the chain across the gracefulness of her neck and could not stop himself from bending down and kissing that neck after he had united the ends. She leaned slightly into the kiss and then into him. Feeling her hair fall about him as she dropped it and feeling the weight of her as well brought a surge of need that really was just too much. Perhaps, after all, it would kill him — the no-sex.

~

Jerry had switched to water. He had to drive and had to pick up Christy, but the rest of them were still drinking and he felt the distinct advantage of a clear mind. The cards had finally turned, and he and Carol were making a comeback. He was trying to make a difficult three no-trump which would give them a seven hundred rubber and take over the lead ... not that it mattered, of course; it was just a friendly game. Jerry studied Tom for a moment, but his brother blinked back at him in confused innocence. He narrowed his eyes and thought about the bidding. Tom had passed — it was Sarah that had bid the hearts. He really needed this finesse. Okay, he had already chosen this path; it was too late to back out now. He let his queen of hearts ride, playing the six and leaving the ace on the board. Tom grinned at him as soon as his finger had left the six. "You bastard," said Jerry. Tom slapped the king on Jerry's queen and gathered the trick up with glee.

"You gotta love it ... you just gotta love it!" declared Tom. Jerry shook his head and tried to see where else he might pick up that last trick.

Carol was enjoying her dummy status and, having made a quick trip to the bathroom, was placing the dinner plates in the dishwasher. "Carol, don't do that," called Sarah from the table. "I have all day tomorrow to clean." Carol ignored her and started washing a pot. Her mind kept trying to slip to her children, and she was struggling to keep her worried musings at bay. What was the point of a night out if she couldn't leave? She tried to concentrate on the warm suds that caressed her hands as she rubbed the hard sides of the pan—the sensation of *now*. But somehow, scrubbing a pan was not nearly as entertaining as her worried musings. What if Christy drank again tonight? She didn't need a repeat of last week, when she'd come home red-eyed and staggering. They should have grounded her, refused to let her go tonight to the Valentine's Dance, but she'd been so excited to go, had been looking forward to it for weeks. Was she doing other drugs? Why the need to do anything? The image, clear in her mind—Christy sitting on the floor in a corner, her belly swollen with child, her hair dull and lifeless, her face pock-marked from the meth. They should have made her stay home . . . never let her leave the house again. And Amanda, just one pill away from a straightjacket. They should have played cards at their house. She didn't really need to get out of her own house, did she—away from her children . . . away from the sad, apathetic face of Amanda. What kind of mother was she anyway? *Okay, enough! Back to the now, back to the now.* The pan was clean. *Pay attention to the sensation of the hot . . . ow!* Hot water poured over the pan, over her fingers . . . .

"Damn!" she heard Jerry say. She glanced over to the table. Tom was grinning with the pleasure of a conqueror and her husband was shaking his head in defeat.

~

Christy had managed to shake herself loose from Zack without hurting his feelings too much. At least that's what she told herself. Her feet were killing her and she was almost relieved when she checked the time on her phone and saw that the dance would soon be over. The band was probably on its last song. Should she ease back up to the dance floor? Get a little closer to the bass player? She wondered how old he was—college student? Older? Did it matter? He had talked to her briefly during one of their breaks. He was even cuter up close, when all his attention was just on her. She could almost taste his appreciation for her. It was a rush, this new power she had over men and with just her ... sexuality? As if she could control their very happiness—respond to advances and see his world soar; reject him and watch him shrink back in dejection. It was awesome and it tiptoed on the edge of danger. And wasn't it time to edge into danger ... before it was too late? She made her way through the dancers and eased back up toward the band.

~

Ryan found a parking spot just a few blocks from his apartment. He hit the night air and shoved his hands into his pockets as he made his way toward home. He went about a block before he stopped and reconsidered. It was barely eleven on a Friday night, and what was he going to do? Go home and go to bed? Mandy had fallen asleep shortly after he'd given her the necklace. He had stayed with her sleeping against his chest until the movie he'd been watching was over and he'd helped her to bed. She was not quite coherent in her sleepy fog so she did not quite return his kiss as she lay on the bed. He'd run his fingers slowly through her hair and sighed as he pulled up her blankets, and he watched her sleep for a few minutes before leaving. Now, out on this cold street, he fully felt the loneliness of the night.

Ryan turned away from his home and made his way back up the street. There was a small crowd of people hanging outside the club, the glow of their cigarettes and blunts moving as they talked. As he approached, he heard the words of recognition from his friends and already felt better. He was not alone. And there was no reason why he should be. "Hey! Ryan! Long time no see," the friendly slap on his back. "Where you been, man?" Someone handed him a blunt and the sweet burn on his throat further eased his isolation. He talked and smoked a few minutes before leaving the group and heading inside. The music was, as always, loud, and the place its typical mass of bodies. He made his way to the bar, and even the bartender welcomed him back, remembering his brand of beer without even having to ask. Ryan brought the cool wet tip of the bottle to his lips as he turned his back to the bar and scanned the room. Yes, it felt good to be back, even if it was without Mandy at his side, for it was only temporary;

she *would* be back.

"Hey, Ryan." He turned to his right to find his friend Rebecca. She was near him, smiling up at him with those pretty blue eyes, her freckled face edged with her short red hair. "Where's Mandy?"

"Hey, Rebecca," he smiled. "Mandy's not feeling too well." He had to get close for his words to be heard.

"That's too bad," she almost had to yell back. They watched the movement of people and let the music dominate their senses. Ryan finished his beer, felt a little buzzed and high from the weed, so when Rebecca pulled his hand and indicated the dance floor, it seemed like a reasonable thing to do. And it was fun dancing with his friends. There was nothing wrong with what he was doing, nothing that would upset Mandy if she found out.

It was a couple hours and couple beers later when things got a little dangerous. There was a new girl, small and pretty—someone he'd never seen before—who couldn't seem to leave him alone, and he really didn't want her to leave him alone because it felt so good to be out...and appreciated. Wasn't everything always about Mandy? Hadn't it always been? Had his wants or his needs ever come first? All these months dealing with her illness...in the five months he'd known her, had she ever been well? Would he even like her in wellness? Would he ever get the chance to find out? Oh, he loved her, couldn't imagine not loving her, but the ever-present waiting for her mood to change, for her to improve, for her to love him again .... He closed his eyes and once again was overcome with loneliness. He really needed to get out of here and go home. He made his goodbyes and was out the door without too many regrets.

The cold air felt refreshing and cleared his head as he made his way down the street, and he was almost safe and out of danger. Then he heard the footsteps from behind and the soft call of his name—and he could swear he got a brief whiff of her perfume while she was still quite far away—and he knew, oh he knew, he was in trouble. He stopped and turned and smiled at her approach. "Where you going?" she asked as she drew near, the soft mist of her breath momentarily blurring the beauty of her face.

He tilted his head down and smiled his lopsided smile, his hair tumbling into his eyes. "Back to my place." He watched her smile deepen because he'd added a very small, but definite, question mark.

~

The high school driveway was a madhouse of cars and kids. It took Jerry and Carol forever just to ease up the circular drive to get close enough to park the car. They scanned the throngs of students, but could not locate Christy or Katy. "Try her cell again," said Jerry. He was tired and eager to get home and feel the warm softness of their bed. Carol shook her head at him as the phone rang in her ear. "Katy doesn't answer either?" he asked.

"No. Why do we even pay for these phones? Christy answers half the time and Amanda never answers," Carol complained.

The crowd was beginning to thin, and Jerry peered through the glass of the windshield. There was a group of kids near the building. Over to one side there was a couple wrapped around each other in a hot embrace. "Is that Katy with that Brandon kid?"

Carol looked to where Jerry was pointing and agreed: it was Katy. Poor Fran. Katy was a young fifteen. Jerry sighed heavily. He left the car and made his way to her. As he got close he called her name and the two broke apart from their groping entanglement.

Katy wiped at her wet face and smiled slightly with hardly a trace of embarrassment. "Oh, hi, Dr. Benson."

Jerry turned his eyes to Brandon and got a better response—embarrassment, guilt, apology.... "It's time to go," he told Katy. He indicated the car with a flick of his head. "Where is Christy?" Katy shrugged and looked around. "When did you see her last?" Another shrug. He was really getting annoyed. He sighed. "Go wait in the car with Carol. I'll go look for her." Katy had the audacity to kiss Brandon one more time and then headed for the car. Jerry threw a dirty look Brandon's way before heading off in search of his daughter.

Most everyone was gone by now so the task should have been easy, but it took a few minutes before Jerry saw the two figures standing in the shadows of the building. By the time he saw them, he was already asking himself once again, "Why? Why had they had children?" and it wasn't just a flippant question, but a sincere query. As he got closer, still unsure if this was his daughter, the figures drew near in an unquestionable kiss. If they had to have kids, why not burly boys so that he could feel a surge of, perhaps, pride at this moment instead of the uncomfortable surge of fear? "Christy!" his voice came out into the night and the figures broke apart and his daughter's face turned toward him. He was close now and he scrutinized his daughter's assailant. He didn't like what he saw. "Go to the car!" he said, with quiet authority, and she left without a word. He stepped close to this man. How old was he? Late twenties? Older? The man did not quite look him in the eye. "My daughter's fifteen," Jerry lied. "I could have you arrested from what I just saw."

"Whoa, man!" his hands came up in a defensive manner. "She told me she was seventeen."

Jerry stepped closer yet. "And that would make it all right?"

"Hey, I'm sorry, man! It was just a kiss."

Now Jerry wasn't a violent man, never had been; he'd never hit any living thing with the exception of an occasional insect, and this man, with his stringy, dirty hair that fell over the ridiculous chunks of metal that stuck through his right eyebrow and the obscenely large black rings that gauged his ears, was looking awfully bug-like. Jerry took a deep breath and stepped back. His hand came up, his finger in a severe point. "Do me and mankind a favor! Save your slimy kisses for those who've been on this earth for at least two decades, will you?" And with that, he was gone and heading back to the car.

He closed the door with enough force and turned to Christy with enough of a look that Carol knew all was not well. Why, with all that Amanda was putting them through, did Christy have to suddenly put them through hell too? You'd think that since she knew what Amanda was doing to them all that she would try to behave. Jerry put the car in drive, and they all drove in silence until they reached Katy's house. "See ya," said Katy as she got out. "Thanks for the ride, Drs. Benson!"

A lot of their girls' friends liked to call them that. Carol responded to the gratitude, but Jerry remained silent.

"What's going on?" Carol asked in trepidation as soon as Katy had shut the car door. "What did she do now?"

"I found her," Jerry said tightly, "kissing some thirty-year-old slime bag." He pulled out of Katy's driveway and headed up the street.

"He's not thirty!"

"And who was that guy?" He turned his eyes from the road to send her a look. "Some pervert that lurks around the school yard? The janitor?"

"Dad! He was in the band! The bass player!"

"Oh, well, sorry! That makes it okay then!" Jerry closed his eyes for a moment. Sarcasm was never productive.

Carol let out a long and painful sigh. "Why, Christy? Why do you suddenly feel the need to grow up so fast? A man that age—you know he only wants one thing...."

"Yeah? So!"

"Christy, you are fifteen years old!" Jerry exclaimed.

"Sixteen, Dad! I'm sixteen."

"Just barely," and he was lost and defeated.

"Christy, please," implored Carol. "Trust me; you are too young for sex. You've got the rest of your life. Wait until you're more pre-pared. Concentrate on just growing up. You've got plenty of time for all the rest...when you are older."

"How do you know?" her voice was a bit hysterical. "How do you know I have more time?"

Jerry slowed the car and pulled to a stop along the curb. He looked at Carol as he put the car in park, and she looked back with the fear that he was feeling. He turned to look at his daughter. "Is there some-thing going on? Are you having problems of some sort?" He couldn't make himself say the word symptoms, or anything more specific.

"No. But you see? You believe it too! And once I'm crazy, I won't even know if I like sex or not!"

"Christy, you are not going to get sick." And his words came out firm and believable.

Her eyes narrowed at him. "Can you guarantee that I won't?"

Well, no. Of course he couldn't. "I can't guarantee we'll all survive this night. Especially me, after seeing you kiss that...that slimy little punk." He smiled sadly, and Christy's eyes rolled toward the ceiling in a sigh. "But what I can guarantee you," his smile gone with the significance of his words, "is that your mom and I love you, and that we'll always be there for you as long as we're alive, and that if you choose a self-destructive path now in the fear that you may someday become ill, then anything that ever happens to you, good or bad, will be harder and more tainted. That's what I can guarantee." She looked back at him. "You understand?" he asked softly. She gave him a slightly stubborn nod.

Carol was moved by his words, as always, impressed by his wisdom. These were the sort of words to keep with you, words that Christy would come back to over and over as she struggled through the next few years—as she chose her path.

But Christy had barely heard his words now and would have nodded to anything to get him off her back. She was way too busy remembering the slow, sweet pulse of burning—or was it yearning?—pleasure as he had kissed her, the sensation of his moisture on her lips as it evaporated in the cold night air.

Jerry turned his back to her and pulled the car back onto the street. "And besides, since you are now grounded until you're at least twenty-one, and I'm going to lock you up in your room—open it only to bring you food—none of us have anything to worry about." Christy shook her head in teenage disgust and crossed her arms across her chest.

Carol smiled softly as she turned her eyes away from her daughter and sat back in the seat. She turned toward Jerry. "Can't you still get chastity belts?"

"Funny! Very funny!" said Christy.

"Oh, that's a terrific idea," agreed Jerry. "We'll look on eBay just as soon as we get home."

20

Carol was panicking a little now. She called the school at least once a week, talking to Amanda's academic adviser, her teachers, the principal; and even though they all assured her that they would do all they could to get Amanda through, it was still necessary for Amanda to do *something*. Her tutor was great, still coming faithfully three times a week. And he was always pleasant, even on those rare days when all Amanda seemed capable of doing was to stare despondently into space as he talked about her English assignments or went over her government class notes. But most days, they talked and even laughed. He helped her with some of the work, perhaps more than was acceptable, giving her little tips and encouraging her with a pleasant litany of notes and jokes.

It wasn't like she didn't deserve to graduate. She'd spent nearly thirteen long years in school with almost straight As. It would be so unfair for her to fail—but it was only Amanda who could take the tests, and it was Amanda who must pass the English and government Regents examinations, and then and only then would she get her degree. There were good days when she did the work and got things done, but it was the bad days when Carol looked at the seemingly insurmountable pile of work that went ignored that caused Carol's chest to tighten with anxiety and concern. Carol tried not to nag, she really did. She knew it only made Amanda more stressed and less likely to get anything done, but damn it, sometimes she just couldn't stop herself. It was arduous for all involved. Carol finally wrote the damn papers for physical education herself—she would have done all the work if it were possible…not just to decrease the stress on Amanda, but to lessen her own anxiety, her own stress. And it was kind of fun writing a few small papers on fitness issues—and really, it wasn't cheating because surely physical education should not prevent her daughter from graduating from high school.

More importantly, Amanda was now getting up and out of bed, and although she might not be doing what they wanted her to do, which was her damn school work, at least she was doing—leaving the house, spending time with Ryan, staying out too late; but it was all certainly better than constantly sleeping. And really, wasn't that what really mattered—that she was getting better? With all things considered, was a high school degree really that important?

~

It was a Saturday evening, sometime toward the end of March, when it happened. Carol was dishing out ice cream and Jerry was sitting on the couch, flipping through the channels, looking for the basketball game. Amanda and Ryan came into the kitchen and sat down companionably at the counter. "You know what, Mom?" Amanda said, and Carol looked up, the ice cream scoop freezing in midair.

"Do you want some?" asked Carol, indicating the ice cream with a slight wave of the scoop. Both of them shook their head *no*. "Do I know what?"

"This movie we're going to see, it was filmed near Indian Lake," said Amanda. "Maybe our cabin will be in it."

"Oh, yes," said Carol. "I heard about that. That would be really cool, to see our house in a movie."

"And just think. That means Keanu Reeves was practically at our cabin!"

Carol and Ryan laughed. "If we'd only known, we could've had him over for a barbeque," said Carol.

"Oh my god! To have dinner with Keanu," Amanda said wistfully. Ryan put his hand gently on her shoulder. "Settle down, girl."

Carol laughed again as she put what was left of the ice cream back in the freezer. "How are your classes going, Ryan?" she asked, closing the fridge and stepping toward the drawer where she kept the spoons.

He ran his hand slowly through his hair, subconsciously testing its general state. "Good. I see the faint glow of graduation ..." he brought his hand out theatrically and reached slowly toward the light of his imagination, "way down a long tunnel of projects and examinations." He smiled his lopsided smile at Carol as she laughed. "But there is, no doubt, a light." Carol opened the drawer and dug through the spoons, searching out the ones with the fat handles. (She liked the way they felt in her hand.)

"Ryan's mom is coming up for his graduation. You know, in May," Amanda announced.

Carol turned her eyes from the silverware drawer and back to Ryan. "We'd love to meet your mother. We should have a dinner here." She'd almost said a *family dinner*, but caught herself. Still, she could have said that without too much embarrassment. He'd become a part of the family, one of her favorite members, often more pleasant to be around than some of the lawful ones. "Maybe after the graduation ceremony," she continued.

"That would be really nice," Ryan said. He was thinking about the first dinner he'd had in this house, and the memory amused him.

Amanda bounced a little in her excitement. "Yes! We could have a fancy celebration dinner!" She flashed a smile Ryan's way, then back toward her mother. "Mom! You could make that chicken dish I like so much," Amanda continued. "You know, the one with the rice and that fancy sauce?"

"Chicken Devan? With the broccoli?" asked Carol. She placed a spoon in each one of the bowls.

"That's it!"

"Absolutely. Maybe that flourless chocolate cake for dessert?"

Amanda turned to Ryan. "Have you ever tasted my mom's chocolate cake? Oh my god, it's to die for!"

"Not yet," smiled Ryan.

"I'll make one soon," said Carol. "Give it a test run before May."

And then they'd left for the movie. It had been as simple as that. And Carol was astounded. "Jerry," she called toward the living room. "Did you hear that?"

He was matching her smile. "I did."

She and her daughter had just had a conversation—a regular, everyday conversation. Carol brought the bowls of ice cream across the room. She handed him one of the bowls and sat down next to him. "Wow," she said as she slid her spoon through the soft coldness. "She actually sat down and talked to me." She brought the sweetness to her mouth and closed her eyes in pleasure.

"Yes," agreed Jerry. "Wow." And that was all they were brave enough to say.

~

Carol signed the credit card slip and the privacy notice and then gathered up the rather large bag of prescription medication. As she made her way down the aisle, making a beeline for the door, Maura Radcliff turned into her aisle carrying a bag of large cotton balls and an extra-large chocolate bar. There was no escape. Carol had managed to avoid her (and many of her peripheral friends, for that matter) for months now, but here she was—unavoidable. Maura looked up from her chocolate, "Oh! Hi, Carol!" She glanced at the candy guiltily. "Comfort food."

"Yes," smiled Carol. She might just have to go get herself a big ol' chunk of chocolate. Did that mean Maura needed comforting? Carol tilted her head slightly at Maura. "How are you?" she asked.

Maura's smile widened. "Great! Did you hear about Jason?"

Carol felt the rush of inappropriate disappointment, resentment, and anger—why the comfort food when things were great? Don't call it comfort food, damn it, if it's just something you want! She tried to keep her face pleasant and her voice even. "No... something good, obviously?"

The words burst out of Maura's mouth like excited bubbles, "Jason was accepted at MIT, Yale, and Princeton so far! I just don't know how he's going to decide!"

"I'm so happy for him," she managed to get out and sounded sincere—which, really, she was. The words that wanted to burst out of her mouth—words like *fuck you and your perfect son*—were only rattling around deep in the nasty crevices of her brain—because really, she was happy for him. Really. And then Carol thought about the stack of Amanda's acceptance letters sitting abandoned in the back of the kitchen and she felt an overwhelming sadness, a punch of grief. She would not cry in front of this woman!

Then Maura was grasping her arm and squeezing it gently in comfort. "How is Amanda? I was so sorry to hear about her... what she's going through... and you."

"Yes," Carol managed to get out.

"My nephew, he's in his late twenties now; he's schizophrenic. What my poor sister has gone through. I know how horrible it is. But he's better, you know... finished college, has a job. He's doing okay. He's an amazing young man. So, how is she doing?"

"Better. I think she's doing better." Carol subtly looked to the door—to freedom.

"I'm so glad. I should have called you, you know... I'm sorry. If you ever just want to talk or to just get out of the house, call me. Okay?"

Carol smiled. "Thank you," she said, and she meant it, even though she knew she'd never call Maura. In fact, Maura could quite possibly be the last person she'd call, and yet here she was showing Carol her best side—showing her empathy. Carol watched as Maura made her way to the cash register. Maybe Maura really wasn't so bad; maybe it was *she* who had the problem.

So she walked down the other aisle to where the candy was and picked out the largest dark chocolate bar she could find, and did not panic at all when someone else she knew came into the drug store.

"Hi, Beth," she said. It was a mother of one of David's good friends, someone she hadn't seen for some time. They talked briefly about her son and then about David. When the question came about her own girls, Carol told her that Christy had her driving permit now, and they laughed over how scary that was and then she said, "And you know, don't you, that Amanda's been sick?" It surprised her when Beth said *no*; Carol had assumed that all of Niskayuna knew about her crazy daughter. And there was only the briefest moment of hesitation before Carol said, "Yes. She has manic depressive illness. Was in the hospital for a week or so, but she's better. She's doing okay."

~

"You need to be sure you come to a full stop. Make sure you feel the car roll back a bit," Jerry was saying. "Both Casey and your Uncle Tom failed their driving tests because they did not stop all the way."

Christy wasn't worried. If Amanda could pass the driving test the first time, then she certainly could. But then again…knowing Amanda, she'd probably come on to the driver testing dude and that's how she passed. "Did you pass your first time?" she asked her father.

He smiled. "Of course. Take this next right."

"Wasn't it Matt that failed three times?"

"Don't forget your signal. You'll fail for that too. No. It was Casey. The kid still can't drive." Christy slowed a bit, but Jerry had to tighten his hold on the overhead hand grip to keep from tilting sideways. "Please don't ever get in the car with him. Take your turn a little slower next time. Okay?" he said calmly. It had been Jerry who taught all the kids to drive. Tom had tried with Matt, but it had been a disaster; they were lucky to have walked away alive—and not due to Matt's lack of driving skills, but from their deep, innate desire to kill one another when in close quarters. So Jerry had taken over the duty, and now here he was with the last of them, and it felt sad and nostalgic.

He turned his eyes from the road and watched his daughter as she concentrated on her driving. It didn't seem possible, but she looked competent—certainly not a little girl anymore. Her face thinner now, her childish cheeks gone and replaced with the high cheek bones of his mother. Her mouth—Carol's and beautiful—her eyes that were his. "So how are you doing?" he asked. This was the best part of Jerry's Driving School—holding the teenagers captive and having them oblige.

"I'm fine. Driving doesn't make me nervous at all."

Jerry smiled. Nice try. "I don't mean in driving...I mean in life."

Christy kept her eyes on the road, and would not entertain him with teenage annoyance. No, he wasn't going to get to her. She slowed as she approached a traffic light. Would it turn red? "Isn't driving a lot like life?" she asked. "You have to be prepared for anything. You never really know what might come at you next, but...why freak out about it? When it comes, you have to trust you'll know what to do." She turned to him for a quick look before turning back to the road. "You have to trust that *I'll* know what to do."

Wow. He was impressed. "But in driving, like life, experience is crucial," he said. It just seemed necessary to add, "Sometimes you need to trust someone with more experience to guide you."

Christy's lips went up to imply a smile. "Well...true. But the only way to truly learn how to drive a car is to drive the car."

21

Amanda placed a small crystal vase at the center of the table, filled with an assortment of purple and white violets she'd plucked from the yard. They looked a little small and insignificant. She stood back and surveyed the entire room—yes, they were insignificant, but still a tiny piece of pretty. So she left them among her mother's crystal and china, between the candlesticks, and she tried to calm her anxiety. She'd met his mother briefly at the graduation, but it was rushed and a bit frantic. She couldn't even remember her name or the color of her hair. Mrs. Downing…she'd call her Mrs. Downing—but, no, that wasn't right because she'd remarried. She'd have to text Ryan and ask him again. She heard the door of the kitchen open and she panicked. Why were they even doing this? She took a step toward the stairs—she would hide in her room, feign the intestinal flu.

"So where's the graduate?" She heard her uncle's voice, and she almost collapsed in relief. But it was only a momentary reprieve, so she made her way up the stairs to her bedroom and dug through her bottles of pills. Where were they? She glanced around the floor near her bed, and there peeking out from beneath the skirts of her bed was another pill bottle. She grabbed it and read the label. Thank God. She dry-swallowed the Klonopin, gagging only slightly. Now she just had to wait for it to do its magic, to slowly soften the edge of panic.

~

Mrs. Julie Fisher was not too wild about the length of her son's hair, though it was more the style than the actual length, and she fought the urge to lick her hand and spit-mousse it out of his eyes. "Can you see okay, my darling boy?" she asked in her soft, southern drawl, reaching up and fluffing her own strawberry blonde hair away from her forehead.

Ryan turned his eyes from the road as he drove and tilted his head in a slightly exaggerated way so that he looked at his mother through his bangs, and said, "So, I could be, say forty, and as long as I'm making this up ..." his eyes went back to the road, "let's say I'm an extremely successful architect and you come to visit me at my huge beautiful home. The butler meets you at the door. You come into the house and take in the Stickley furniture and the Persian rugs, the imported black Italian marble staircase. The butler offers you a drink ... a small tray of canapés." He glanced at her again, his eyes a pleasant bit of impiousness. "What's the first thing you criticize?"

Julie smiled delicately. "Well, it's obvious, dear. The fact *you* didn't meet me at the door."

Ryan's faint smile did not fade as he nodded his head slowly. "Yes, of course." He watched with his peripheral vision as his mother slowly ran her finger through the dust on his dash and gently scrunched up her still-young-looking and attractive face as she brushed her hands against each other to free them of his grime. Yes, there was a reason why he hadn't seen her in over two years.

~

The Chicken Devan was divine, and if Julie Fisher thought that it was a bit odd that all these people, who had known her son for just a little over six months, would come together to celebrate, she did not voice it. Of course, Tom and Sarah were there. David was back from Buffalo and would not miss an opportunity to delight and entertain, so there were nine in all that sat around the formal dining room table.

Julie, always at her best in social situations, set her southern eyes on this beautiful young girl with the strange black-purple hair, who seemed to have infiltrated her son's life. She smiled her best social smile as she said, "So tell me, Mandy—or do you prefer Amanda?" Amanda smiled uncomfortably and shrugged. Julie's smile widened. "Amanda then. What are your plans after you graduate from high school?" She emphasized the last words subtly, but not subtly enough to prevent Ryan from looking up from the piece of broccoli he was about to put in his mouth to shoot her an equally subtle look of warning—which his mother chose to ignore. Amanda shrugged again. "College?" Julie persisted gently. There was a silence of forks poised and waiting in the room, eyes turned to Amanda. Her hand came up and she caressed the silver charm that she wore around her neck between her fingers. Ryan shifted in his chair, and David set down his wine glass hard enough to tap against the side of his plate with a sound that went *ting* throughout the room.

Carol was conflicted. She wrestled with the urge to come to her daughter's rescue, and the very real desire to hear an answer. What *was* Amanda going to do after graduation?—assuming, of course, she finished that damn research paper and passed English. It was a subject that was unapproachable; somehow just getting through another day without a crisis was enough for now. She saw Jerry's mouth open to say something, but before Jerry could get a word out, Amanda found her voice. "Well, I've been accepted to Cornell, Brown, and a bunch of other schools, but...." Her hand was still at her neck, rubbing harder now. She looked at Ryan and then back to her plate. "I haven't decided yet."

Julie nodded slightly as she took a petite sip of her wine, and David took advantage of the moment. "Hey! That reminds me," he said. "I met this guy from Brown at a party the other day, and he was going on about how smart he was, how rich he was..." Julie put down her wine glass and turned her full attention to David. "...well, he finds out I'm just a lowly UB student, so he decides to play this riddle game with me, and to make it a bit more interesting, he says, 'You ask me a riddle and if I don't get it, I'll give you twenty dollars. Then I will ask you one, and if you don't get it ....' He stops and looks at my old tattered jeans and my stained UB sweatshirt, and says, with his nose stuck up a bit in the air, 'well, you just need to give me a dollar.'" Christy laughed because she'd heard him tell this story before. "So I think for a moment, and then I ask him, 'What's big and hairy, has six legs, takes over an hour to make it across the road, but takes only thirty seconds to get back across?' Well, this guy from Brown thinks and thinks, and finally he digs in his pocket and hands me the twenty, and then says, 'What is big and hairy, has six legs, takes over an hour to make it across the road, but takes only thirty seconds to get back across?' I blink at him a moment or two, and then I reach into my pocket and hand him a dollar, and say with a shrug, 'I don't know.'"

There was mild laughter around the table, while Christy laughed with glee. Even Amanda smiled. "My son the comedian," Sarah said dryly.

"Well, he's quite funny," Julie said to Sarah, before turning her smile back to Amanda. "Do you have something you're interested in, Amanda? An idea of what you want to do? It might help you to choose a college."

Ryan didn't give Amanda a chance to struggle for an answer before he said, "She likes a lot of things, Mom. She has plenty of time to figure it out."

"I like to write," offered Amanda.

Julie's smile turned a shade patronizing as she said, "My brother's a writer—"

"Look how long it took me to figure out what I wanted to do," Ryan continued. There was a tightness in his voice that was new to the rest of them. Jerry's eyes met Carol's across the table.

"He never had two sticks to rub together," Julie continued.

David saw the wounded look on Amanda's face and was trying hard to remember that joke about the caveman rubbing sticks together. What was the punch line?

"I still don't know what I want to do!" said Tom, with exaggerated flair, and most of the table laughed.

"I just want to make a lot of money!" threw in Christy. "Like my dad!"

"Hey! I don't make that much. Don't forget your mother works also," said Jerry.

Julie turned her green eyes to Jerry and said, "Psychiatry... what an interesting field. However did you choose that particular study of medicine?"

David smiled inwardly. If needed, he had a lot of jokes about psychiatry. But he just watched as his uncle took care of himself.

Jerry sat back a bit and considered his reply. "Of all the organs in our body, the brain is, as you said, interesting, but I'd argue it's the most interesting, and certainly the most important. Really an amazing organ. And when things go wrong...." His eyes drifted casually to Amanda. Ryan was leaning over and whispering something in her ear. She was listening with concentration to whatever he was saying, her hand still clutching the lovely amulet. He felt that familiar mix of gratitude and fear that so often hit him when he watched them together. He turned his eyes back to Julie and shrugged.

"...how wonderful it is to have the knowledge to try to make things a little better," Carol finished his sentence.

"What's that quote, Jerry, about understanding the brain, that you always say?" asked Tom.

"I know!" said Christy. "Emerson Pugh, right? 'If the human brain were so simple that we could understand it, we would be so simple that we couldn't.'"

Jerry smiled as the others laughed gently. "That's right...." And although the tension in the room eased away, there was now a soft sadness that slipped in to take its place. Jerry took a tiny bite of his chicken—it really was very good. Julie, who may not have understood the shift in the mood, was at least astute enough to sense it, and kept her mouth shut except to open it for her own food.

David reached for his wine as he said, "So, I'm at this bar in Buffalo when this psychiatrist and lawyer walk in...."

~

Ryan sat on the old mattress with his back against the wall. HOW R U he punched into his phone and sent it to Mandy. GOOD N U? she texted back. MISSING U he texted back. AWWW ... I MISS U 2 and they went on like this, texting, not bothering to actually call one another, for an unreasonable length of time. It was late now, past two a.m. and his mother had been safely tucked into her hotel for hours. He was beginning to get sleepy and began to wind down the texting. SORRY ABOUT MY MOM he texted. NO BIGGY was the reply. I THINK I'LL SLEEP NOW ... ME TOO ... THANK U FOR MY PEN ... WELCOME LOVE U ... LOVE U 2 ... GNITE ... GNITE ....

Ryan flicked his phone shut and settled down on his bed. He hoped he would hear from Schuler & Adams, the firm he wanted to work for the most, next week. He'd worked there as an intern one summer and felt he had a pretty good chance of getting hired. He reached up to turn off the light, but before his hand reached the switch, he had a sudden urge to look at his new pen one more time. He got up and grimaced as his bare feet hit the cold floor as he crossed the room. He picked up the box from his desk and carefully lifted the pen from its silken cradle. It felt good in his hands, and although he knew most of his work would be on a computer, there was nothing like a good pen in his hand. He sat down at his desk, tucking his feet into a dirty sweatshirt that graced the floor, and quickly penned his favorite caricature—a little old man with a big pipe and a straw hat, something he'd been drawing since high school. He doodled a caricature of himself with a few fast strokes of the pen—crazy dark hair and too big of eyes. He followed that up with his own version of Mandy. Soon the paper was full of little pen figures, and he enjoyed the fine roughness of Mandy's engraved words against his fingers. He smiled as he read the words one more time before he set the pen back in its little box. **You are my Scarecrow...love, Mandy**

He had to read the words twice when Mandy had given him the pen earlier in the day. Scarecrow? He just didn't get it. But then his confusion had cleared the moment he looked up from the pen and into Mandy's worried face, her bottom lip held gently between her teeth, her dark eyes so full of hope. Yes, he had followed her on this marvelously ghastly journey, down that yellow brick road, and they were still skipping ever so gently down that path. He only hoped she wouldn't click her heals three times and leave him here in this Land of Oz.

22

The auditorium was hot with bodies. They'd been there sweating in the stagnant air for hours now. It had been at Tom's insistence, of course, that they arrive so early. He'd done his typical drill sergeant imitation, which everyone pretty much ignored, but even the most stubborn crowd will sway under enough duress. The younger members of the group (Ryan, Amanda, David, Casey, and Christy) had finally piled into Ryan's Jetta, dropping his car debris onto Tom's driveway to make room for everyone, with the promises of picking it up later. They were out of the driveway and down the road before Tom could react, too flabbergasted to even speak, much less yell. That left the rest of the family to drive the short distance to the high school in Carol's Lexus. The good thing about their early arrival was the choice seats, close to the front and all together. But it was hot and Carol was fighting boredom.

Carol sat in the middle of the row, with Jerry to her left and Sarah to her right, and she was uncomfortably hot. As the applause abated, she removed the light blazer she was wearing, deciding not to be concerned that she hadn't bothered to iron the back of the sleeveless, cream-colored shell she was wearing. Jason Radcliff bowed his head in modest acceptance of the applause before he sat back down. It had been a clever and entertaining valedictorian speech, with just the right balance of sentimentality and absurdity—the only bright light in a parade of boring speeches. Carol's eyes shifted a couple of rows in front of her and to the right, finding Maura Radcliff, who was grinning stupidly and still clapping. Carol sighed into a faint smile as she considered her own just-right balance of envy and pride. She felt Jerry take her hand and she leaned into him slightly, but did not linger, as it was just too damn hot. She refused to entertain the image of Amanda at the podium and what she might have said.

Carol was pretty sure she'd located Amanda's head in the sea of mortar boards, and she watched that head as it turned to the person on its right to say something. Yes, it was Amanda, and she was smiling; and whatever she'd said to the boy next to her had made him throw back his head in laughter. Carol's heart swelled, pushing back the envy to make room for the pride. Her hand tightened against Jerry's.

Now someone else was talking at the podium, but Carol was not a lot cooler with her jacket off. She let go of Jerry's hand and wiped it surreptitiously on the rough seat of the auditorium chair. Damn! She had meant to turn the meat she was marinating for the party this afternoon. She'd do it just as soon as they got home; they'd have at least another hour before the meat should be thrown on the grill. She still had to slice the buns and throw the salad together. Did Jerry put the drinks on ice like she'd asked him? She turned to Jerry and whispered, "Did you ice the drinks?" He nodded. Okay, that was good. Her brother and his family, along with Matt and his girlfriend—it was amazing that he was still seeing her—would be coming at about three for the party. Carol was sure they did not mind and they were relieved, in fact, by the limited tickets available for the commencement ceremony. It wasn't like sitting through a high school graduation was something most people would go out of their way to do—hours of watching the same ten kids you don't even know make trip after trip up on the stage to collect their awards.

Please, let the rain hold off until after the party. They should have rented that tent, but Jerry could be so stubborn at times. She shoved him a little with her shoulder. "We should have rented that tent," she whispered to him. He looked at her and shook his head, his eyes rolling up in mild disapproval before turning his attention back to the stage. Carol sunk down a bit in her chair—how could he reproach her? This was boring and the place was just too damn hot. He'd been totally unwilling to pay what he thought was an unreasonable fee for the tent rental. Some things were just worth the money, for peace of mind at least. The cake! She'd forgotten all about it. She thought about whispering to Jerry to remind her to get the cake when this thing was over, but when she glanced at his face, he appeared to be completely focused on the stage. She shoved him with her shoulder again, gently, playfully. This time he shoved her back, and a small smile played across his face. He mouthed the word *behave* toward her and she entertained him with a quick peek at the tip of her tongue.

Finally, they began to call the graduates to the podium, and Carol sat up with alertness. Her eyes shifted to the right and then to the left, taking a quick tally of her family. Was everyone paying attention? Amanda would be early in the procession. Her mother was to the right of Sarah and next to her sat Tom. All three were searching the crowd of caps and gowns as the kids made their way out of their seats. To the left of Jerry sat Ryan and David. Casey was to the left of David, but the seat between them was empty. Where had Christy gone now? She would miss Amanda's walk across the stage. Carol turned around and tried to search the back of the auditorium without greatly disturbing the people behind her. Her eyes located her quickly, there along the back wall, talking to some boy. Carol closed her eyes and shook her head in frustration. She sighed. This was Amanda's moment, and if her sister chose to miss it, so be it.

Carol turned her attention back to the stage. They were already up to the Bs. She clapped her hands gently as she watched Jeremy Benoit saunter across the stage. He stopped to shake the principal's hand, looking more than ready for the world. Two more steps and he reached for his diploma. Mrs. Scott smiled as she waited for Jeremy to leave the stage before announcing into the microphone, "Amanda Erin

Benson," and suddenly she was strutting across the stage in a way that only Amanda could strut, as if she owned the world, as if she could do anything she set her mind to. David put his fingers in his mouth and blew out an obnoxiously loud blast of noise, while Casey bellowed out, "You go, girl!" Sarah ducked her head in embarrassment, while Tom, Ryan, and Jerry laughed and clapped. Carol watched, her own hands slapping together to the point of pain, feeling the smile on her face, as Amanda never broke her stride; only her eyes flickered to the audience at the outburst, a slight shift to the set of her lips. Carol had the brief, uncomfortable image of Amanda refusing to shake the principal's hand, or grabbing the diploma in an undignified manner, but she needn't have worried because her daughter stopped and shook his hand as she smiled and accepted the diploma with grace. And then they were announcing Lauren Bitters and Amanda was gone.

Carol set back and closed her eyes in thanks. They still had the entire rest of the alphabet to go, but it was over. She congratulated herself. Yes, she'd been instrumental in reaching this moment, working so hard behind the scenes with the school, the teachers, the tutor, making this happen. And it seemed like it should be the end—the end of her work and her constant worry...THE GRADUATION...a major passage, a milestone into adulthood. She opened her eyes and watched as Amanda found her way back to her seat, the diploma held casually in her hand. Carol hoped she wouldn't lose it before they even had the chance to hold it for themselves. Amanda sat down and her hat tilted back, her head resting against the back of the chair as if she were taking a little nap. Was she staring at the ceiling? Was she okay? Was it okay that she was staring at the ceiling?

And what now—not *now*, with Amanda staring at the ceiling, but after the party? After the summer? What then? Would she go off to college and do amazingly well? Maybe go on to medical school or into biomedical engineering, develop that artificial seeing eye...it was possible...wasn't it? And then the image of Amanda sitting alone, rocking gently in a corner infiltrated Carol's mind. She saw her in a soft, padded room, her hair short and bright orange, sticking up in scary, little spikes. And that scene was replaced with an image of herself, old and grey, bent over the stove with crippling arthritis—Jerry long dead of a heart attack brought on by some sort of exercise Tom had forced upon him—asking her fifty-year-old daughter, who sat at the grubby kitchen table, "What would you like for dinner, dear?" "Leave me the fuck alone, bitch! I don't want to fucking eat!" would be Amanda's answer. And then a brighter image streamed through Carol's head—Ryan, a successful architect, marrying her daughter, living happily ever after. Ryan working too hard; Amanda writing novels that would never be published, in a pretty room, in a lovely house that Ryan had designed just for her. And there would be no grandchildren that Carol would have to worry about, but there would be dogs...lots of cute little dogs bouncing about the room.

Carol closed her eyes and shook the little dogs out of her mind. She stayed the tears that threatened to escape from her eyes—because, after all, you just never knew.... And not one of her fantasies, good or bad, had yet to become any more than that—a fantasy.

Acknowledgments

I would like to thank, first and foremost, my first draft reader and lovely sister, Sherri, who told me right away, "This is really good. It's publishable. Are you sure you want to keep on writing it?" Thanks to my dear friend and editor, Lorna Lynch. You made it shine. I am very grateful to my publisher, David Michael Gettis (lovingly known as DMG), for answering all of my 531 questions and being such a doll regarding all my pain-in-the-ass sentences. Thank you, Michael Pearson (wherever you are), for believing in this manuscript in the first place. I must thank my husband, Paul. Although his support came like a slow train, once it finally arrived, it was a powerful thing. Thanks to my children, Emily and Sarah, for allowing me to write this from my heart.

Special thanks to Dr. E. Fuller Torrey for actually answering my questions. Thanks also to Dr. Carol Polacek, Sheila Le Gacy, Patricia Hetrick, and Wendy Brooks for your personal and professional input.

And finally—and really, least—I'd like to thank Walter and Henry (you know who you are).